Margaret in
HOLLYWOOD

Books by Darcy O'Brien

Margaret in Hollywood (1991)
Murder in Little Egypt (1989)
Two of a Kind: The Hillside Stranglers (1985)
The Silver Spooner (1981)
A Way of Life, Like Any Other (1978)
Patrick Kavanagh (1975)
W. R. Rodgers (1970)
The Conscience of James Joyce (1968)

Margaret in HOLLYWOOD

Darcy O'Brien

William Morrow and Company, Inc. • *New York*

Recognizing the importance of preserving what has been written, it is the policy of William Morrow and Company, Inc., and its imprints and affiliates to have the books it publishes printed on acid-free paper, and we exert our best efforts to that end.

Library of Congress Cataloging-in-Publication Data

O'Brien, Darcy.
    Margaret in Hollywood / Darcy O'Brien.
      p.   cm.
    ISBN 0-688-09169-5
    I. Title.
    PS3565.B666M37   1990
    813'.54—dc20   90-46875
                                                                          CIP

Printed in the United States of America

First Edition

1 2 3 4 5 6 7 8 9 10

BOOK DESIGN BY LISA STOKES

To
Marguerite Churchill and Molly O'Brien
with love

Author's Note

This being a work of fiction, I have taken a few liberties with early twentieth-century American theatrical, Hollywood, and southern California history. The original Broadway production of *Liliom*, for instance, was in 1921, not 1926, and obviously with a different actress playing Julie. Readers familiar with early Hollywood will recognize that the names and characters of some actors, directors, producers, and studio executives are real, others imaginary. While the events surrounding the Julian Petroleum Corporation and its founder are authentic and did occur on the same scale as indicated here, they did so beginning in 1927, not 1928; reverberations continued into the 1930s.

Readers may also wish to be assured that the State of California did change the age of legal majority from eighteen to twenty-one years in 1927 and that a special statute, known as the Coogan law, was indeed enacted to prevent minors from breaking movie studio contracts, whether entered into by a minor himself or herself, or on a minor's behalf by a parent or guardian.

This note gives me opportunity to thank my editor, Harvey Ginsberg; my agent, Robert Gottlieb; my friend R.M.G.; and my wife, Suzanne, for their help.

—D.O'B.

Act One

1

*B*ack in the days when Shakespeare still meant something to a lot of people, I wanted to be a great dramatic actress. Before I knew it, I was in Hollywood—but that is to get ahead of the story, mine and that of others whose lives touched me years ago.

I can't know for certain what made Mother put me on the stage. I can think of two possibilities, one more plausible than the other. Either I was so adorable that she felt compelled to share me with thousands of other people, or from the beginning I was an insurance policy, indemnity against a failure she sensed was coming. Not that I minded in the least. In no time at all, I knew that if I couldn't perform, I was lost.

I made my stage debut at the age of five, at the Garden Theater at Thirteenth and McGee Streets in Kansas City in 1913, when Harry Valentine, the comedian, lifted me out of an oversized bassinet to end his act. My tiny body was gauze-draped and fairy-winged, a sentimental filip to ten minutes of jokes about marriage. What was I supposed to represent? Hope? Dreams? An unplanned pregnancy? Whatever, Little Meg, as I was quickly billed, was a hit. Murmurs and applause rained on me; I opened up to the audience like a sunflower. Everyone seemed delighted except my father.

"I do not approve," I can still hear him saying to my mother after the Garden emptied that night. We were the last people in the greenroom. I was curled up in a chair with my eyes closed; they thought I was dozing.

"A dubious idea," Father said. "I do not want Margaret on the stage. She is too young."

"Didn't you see the reaction?" Mother asked. "There were grown men with tears streaming down their eyes."

"Precisely," Father said. " 'Caviare to the general,' " and I heard him slap his gloves into his palm.

"What generals? I saw enthusiasm, that's what I saw. You mind your business, and I'll mind my daughter."

Father strode from the room. I could imagine one of his magisterial turns, like those of Louis Calhern in later days. He said no more. I do not recall his uttering another word against my being onstage for several years after that. In marriage, he played the straight man.

And so I grew up with funnymen and dancing girls, songbirds, plate-twirlers, animal acts, as my companions. Rehearsals took up my afternoons and Saturday mornings, but they were more exciting than anything going on at school. My classmates may have been envious; I drifted from them. To me, theirs was a world without color and light; they were stuck with being themselves, or what a schoolteacher required, learning life's boundaries. At a later time I would envy them, but for me to be alive was to be in costume, the more fanciful the better; and I grew accustomed to thinking of everyone as putting on an act.

My father was E. P. Spencer. He had built and nominally owned the Garden Theater, bigger than any other in the city, with seats for nearly three thousand people. In actuality he must have held only a small percentage, his backers the rest. But in Kansas City he was known as quite the impresario, a Barnum with a difference: he believed that people craved beauty more than buncombe—an aesthete born every minute. The Garden was pure E.P., a lavish novelty inspired by Babylon and a trip to California, a journey I was too young to remember but which must have included plenty of vegetation and the idea, foreign to the Midwest and perhaps to human

12

nature, that to be out-of-doors, or at least to have the illusion
that you were out-of doors, was uplifting. Here, people accustomed to ice in the winter and chiggers in the summer could
luxuriate, or so my father's thinking went, in a perpetual Med-
iterranean spring.

The theater had trees growing in its lobby, reflecting pools
within and without, a women's lounge with potted plants,
flowers, a festooned grand piano, a waterfall tumbling through
a millwheel, a stream flowing into a lily pond "where goldfish
and downy ducklings disport themselves," as program notes
advised. (Female patrons must have spent a great deal of time
in the lounge in those days!)

The main interior was finished in brick and stucco, broken
by rooflines and gables and chimney pots. Overhead the arched
ceiling was painted blue to represent the heavens, and when
the houselights dimmed, one could see tiny electric stars twin-
kling among the clouds. Vines clung to columns and beams;
clusters of wisteria and crimson rambler swayed in the air cur-
rents driven by a steam-powered ventilating plant in the basement. In place of proscenium boxes Italianate facades framed
the stage, with windows arched and columned and softly lit
from within, reminiscent of Cyrano and Romeo. What ideas
my father had! Thousands of Kansans and Missourians in those
days were flocking to California. Why not bring their dreams
to them? he must have thought. He divined the dreariness of
their lives, that they could travel in their minds without up-
rooting themselves, and that theater should be out of this world.

The Garden was all the rage in Kansas City, if only for a
while, like everything. People traveled in from Ottawa and
Emporia, from as far away as Springfield and Tulsa to see it:
farm families and small-town merchants, the newly oil-rich
anxious for a kind of culture, folks eager to break the monot-
ony of winter with a smile and a tear.

My father wanted to give them nothing but Shakespeare and
other elevated drama, but vaudeville and light comedies and
sketches filled the seats. I heard him say over and over that
once universal education raised the sensibilities of the audi-

13

ence, Americans would settle for nothing less than the classics.
Until then, merely entering the Garden would give people ideas
of a genteel, earthly paradise and move their minds to higher
things. I have no idea how he formed these notions, perhaps
from reading Andrew Carnegie or John Dewey. In his opti-
mism he was thoroughly American, his strengths lying elsewhere than in prophecy.

Father also operated E. P. Spencer, Inc., "Producers, Crea-
tors and Managers of Theatrical and General Amusement
Enterprises," as his advertisement in *Variety* announced.
"Vaudeville Acts, Sketches, Tabloids and Plays Written, Built,
Staged, Produced." "Spencer's Fraternity Boys and Girls: A
Spectacular Scenic Comedy with 25 Singing and Dancing Col-
legians," "September Morn with Violet Greenwood," and "Kid
Days: A Musical Comedy of Childhood" were among the of-
ferings. If you had an empty theater anywhere in the Midwest, E. P. Spencer could provide a show. A new finish for
your acts? Some new music, a new song, a number, a gag, or
an entire monologue? E. P. Spencer could furnish it.

Or almost. Father must not have had more than twenty-five
or thirty people working for him. Everyone had to be able to
perform many roles and to sing and dance on demand; in
those days actors were able to work, instead of spending most
of their lives waiting for the telephone to ring. Compared to
the Shuberts or Balaban & Katz, E. P. Spencer was small potatoes, but locally he had a grand reputation. When he entered a room with his fine clothes and dark full beard, everyone
deferred to him. If he acted more important than he was, in
show business who can ask for anything more? As for me, I
adored him. When I think of him now, I see myself running
again and again into his arms. To me he played the father's
role well.

So it was a natural, perhaps an inevitable, move for me from
the usual child's playacting to the real thing. What other
children did to amuse themselves and relatives on a porch, I
enacted at the Garden. My mother, Alice, arranged for
tap-dancing and singing lessons; by the age of six or seven I

14

could pick out a few tunes on the piano. If at music and dancing I was competent but no genius, my appeal on the stage then came from the novelty of a small creature's behaving like an adult, similar to the quirky pleasure people derive from seeing a nun ice-skate or hearing a bird talk. One of the other acts at the Garden consisted entirely in displaying a pair of poodles in various costumes—tiny raincoats, pajamas, dinner jackets, baseball uniforms, sailor suits. At the time I wondered whether the poodles realized how funny they were, or resented being laughed at, or felt as I did, swelled by laughter and applause. They were given bits of meat when they performed properly, and spanked or yanked with slip-collars when they did not. In my case all that was necessary was for my mother to tell me that hard work was the key to success and that lazy people ended up in the gutter. The applause took care of the rest of my motivation. I must have been born a ham; I was very much a trained dog.

Alice and her mother, Nell, stitched all my costumes—milkmaid, goose girl, street urchin, Little Miss Muffet; as I matured I became a miniature Minnehaha and Evangeline. By the time I was seven, I looked ten, and my appearance as a water nymph, addressed by a kneeling tenor who extolled my clean, pale limbs and tumbling auburn tresses, was a minor sensation.

When I gaze now at a photograph of myself in this role, I see a girl undeniably pretty, slim and graceful, perhaps beautiful in a Pre-Raphaelite way; and over the bridge of many years there comes to me a fainter version of the rush, the thrill, I felt at the effect I was having on men. Of course I did not understand then precisely what this effect was; that knowledge would come later, and soon enough. But one understood it instinctively, as all girls do whether they are dull or bright. It did not take a Viennese doctor to discover it, only to publicize something that before his time had required no advertisement. Standing center stage with my live hair shining, the tenor praising me, the presence of the audience palpable, I felt my skin glow and my head lighten with—something, a pressure,

15

an energy that quickened my breath. I did not wonder what this power was—I permitted it and heightened it by moving my body slightly or touching the tip of my tongue to the back of my lips.

The young man singing to me on one knee was not supposed to touch me—I was a dream figure—but sometimes he did, brushing my hand or my arm or my thigh—surreptitiously, behind, out of the audience's sight. I can't recall his name, but I enjoyed what he did, more thrilling because the audience couldn't see it. He must have become a wonderful lover—unless he ended up chasing after little girls! I never said a word to him about the game we played, nor he to me; but each time we performed, I hoped he would touch me, and in me there was a fluttering of anticipation.

My pleasure must have floated out to the audience in invisible waves. I could see four or five rows beyond the footlights, far enough to observe that it was the men who rose for a standing ovation, their wives or companions struggling up later if at all. "The apogee of femininity with the dew still on her," the *Kansas City Times* wrote of me, a nice piece of Edwardian lip-smacking. "Margaret Spencer exuded the pinkish breath of girlhood. If beauty lies in the eye of the beholder, there was many a shining, grateful eye in the Garden last night." In another time and place I would have been called an eyeful.

I know that my father was aware of this—what is the word? salacious?—element in my appeal. The idea of his child-daughter slobbered over by potbellied ticket-holders, who were, after all, paying him to look at me, must have seemed like pandering. But if he wanted me to quit the stage, live like an ordinary child, he said nothing about it. To have done so would have been to acknowledge more than he cared to, perhaps, and it would have meant a full-scale confrontation with my mother, which he did not have the stomach for, not then.

Instead he did his best to elevate my sensibilities, rattling off high-flown quotations at me—"Use every man after his desert, and who should 'scape whipping?" was a favorite—and giving me books and poems to read, in general treating me as if I were a creature of a higher order. This flattered and pleased me and made me think of him as sent from some better, nobler world, the one where the idea of the Garden came from; I was his disciple. " 'Full beautiful, a faery's child,' " he would say to me at the breakfast table when Mother was out of hearing. Patiently, calling me his pixie, his imp, his elf, he coached me in Puck's "What fools these mortals be" speech so that I could recite it onstage. I did so one night after an act that included pie-throwing. Alone on an empty stage, I spoke Puck's lines in my small, round voice, lingering over *foools* as Father had taught me and gaining applause somewhere in the range of polite. He must have believed that what he was trying to make of me had triumphed over others' ideas, including Mother's. Maybe he knew something—it is a question that has recurred to me ever since. "Wonderful! Marvelous!" he said afterward, gathering me in his arms and hugging me and twirling me around as if I had achieved stardom or, more to his taste, angelhood. "Your father loves you! The world loves you, and you're not of this world! My Margaret!"

I buried my face in his beard.

Late in 1916 the Garden went bankrupt, and Father with it. It was too large and too expensive to maintain, moving pictures had already begun to siphon off the vaudeville audience, people were becoming preoccupied with our possible entry into the war in Europe—there were any number of reasons. I have the sense that my dear, lovely father, my dreaming, noble, optimistic, foolish father, had been operating at a loss for some time but could not think what to do until it was too late and he went under. I also believe that he could not bear firing the actors and others who depended on him, and so he paid them until he was hopelessly in debt. That at any rate is what my mother accused him of, and I have no reason to doubt her judgment in this. She was a practical woman, like her mother before her; but of them further on.

E.P. was then in his early forties, and vigorous except for frequent colds and a persistent cough. Outwardly he took a

positive view of his failure, cheering us up with quotations—
"A minute's success pays the failure of years," and so on. Determined to make a virtue of necessity, to turn bad luck into good, he made frequent references to Dame Fortune's
wheel.

One afternoon, a few days after the bank announced fore-
closure on our house, with other creditors threatening and my
mother saying that if she did not get some grocery money we
would have to start roasting mice, my father announced that
a fabulous opportunity had come his way and that by God he
was going to seize it. From his agitation, thrusting his fists up
like a victorious prizefighter, bobbing up and down on his heels
and toes, one might have thought he had just inherited a mu-
nitions factory.

"Start packing! We're off to Eldorado!"

As this was the name of a small town in central Kansas, my
mother must have thought she had misunderstood him.

"Chicago?" she asked.

"Much farther than that," he addressed me, sawing the air.
"A storybook land in the realms of gold! Vast cattle ranches
where dark men serenade the moon. Exotic cities alive with
enterprise. Houses full of flowers. Men and women dining on
strange fruits. Caballeros strumming guitars. A place where
dynasties have been created overnight. A place the Spaniards
settled many, many years ago. We'll live by the sea and breathe
the salty air!"

My eyes must have been wide, but I didn't know enough
geography to venture a guess.

"So we're going to California," my mother said brightly. "How
nice. I think that is a fine idea. The Pinneys went out last year
and haven't come back. He's in real estate and doing very well,
I hear."

"Guess again," my father said.

"The Holy Land!" I shouted. I had been studying colored
maps and hearing about milk and honey in Sunday school.
"Are we going there? I want to live in Galilee!"

I took hold of Father's lapel and kissed the rose he always

18

wore there. I must have looked like an engraving called filial devotion.

"Argentina!" he said. "We're going to live in Buenos Aires!"

It sounded fantastical. I had never heard of it. I cheered and jumped up and down.

Mother rattled dishes.

2

My father's South American op-
portunity was not quite golden, but it did enable him to escape
his creditors and to salvage something of E. P. Spencer, Inc.
He was to manage a string of theaters down there, two of them
in Buenos Aires, three in the Argentine provinces, one in
Montevideo. He took with him a handful of his acts and added
to them local gourds and castanets, out-of-work divas, fire-eat-
ers. Of the Americans, singers and dancers had preference:
Buenos Aires was sophisticated and multilingual, a southern
Paris, but acts hoping to conquer the provinces had to be able
to transcend the language barrier. Comedians short on slap-
stick were left behind, along with performers not desperate
enough to risk their careers below the equator. Harry Valentine concocted a routine in which he dressed up as a female
flamenco dancer.

E.P. must have been paid in dollars and handsomely, for he
moved us into a big white house overlooking the harbor. I
remember the dark, polished floors, the thick white walls, heavy
and colorful dinner plates, and a tiled patio with a fountain
where I dipped my toes. In the living room with its tall windows, the breeze off the harbor pushed at the sheer curtains
as my mother sat day after day on the couch, writing letters to
her mother. Letters and letters, without end. In the late afternoons the wind whipped the curtains and rustled her dress

and blew her writing paper around the room—but still she sat and wrote, until it was time to fix dinner. The air, as Father had promised, was fresh, but Alice was rarely out in it except to do the marketing, to take me to school, to the theater, and to the Methodist church on Sundays.

She would begin a letter to Grandmother Nell on a Sunday afternoon, continue with it all through the week, posting it on Saturday. The routine was inviolable. Being curious and a natural sneak, I discovered in her bedroom closet the suitcase in which she secreted Nell's letters to her and the pages of her letter-in-progress to Nell.

My chance to read Nell's letters was Saturday mornings, when Mother left to go to the post office. I would lie abed pretending to be asleep. Father would be off to his office or a theater; Alice would leave after checking on me. With the bang of the front door I was into my parents' room, sitting on the floor reading Nell's reports from Kansas City. Mother's key in the lock sent me scurrying back to bed.

What I read upset me. My stomach knotted as I absorbed the disappointments that Mother enumerated. She called E.P. a hopeless incompetent, irresponsible, a failure, a fool, a blowhard, a man utterly lacking in a sense of reality. He reminded her of her cousin Thomas, the crackpot inventor who had disappeared into the West with his rheumatism machine. E.P.'s attachment to the theater and to ideas of culture had caused us to be stuck in a despicable foreign hole. Buenos Aires was nothing like Kansas City. Hardly anyone spoke English, people were indifferent or downright unfriendly. The place was crawling with dagos—the word was new to me, but I gathered it meant something vile. A scattering of English and Germans came to the theater, but real white folks were few on the ground. Everyone was Catholic: it was depressing and irritating to go into a shop to buy sausages and be confronted with a picture of the pope behind the cash register. About the only positive thing she could say about the place was the scarcity of actual niggers.

She had managed to enroll me, she wrote, in the only respectable school in the city, where British and European and American diplomats sent their children along with a few rich Argentines; but these people never socialized with us because we were of the theater and therefore considered beneath them. The food was abominable. She could find few familiar things in the markets; the beef was tough and improperly butchered—cooking times had to be increased by half in the family recipes. Were it not for the church with its friendly old hymns and prayers, she believed she would go mad.

E.P. was working hard, it was true, managing half a dozen theaters; he would probably make himself sick. As for me, I seemed cheerful as ever, and she envied the ignorance of a child, although I was getting too old to lack a sense of sin. Much of my sunny disposition she attributed to the ways in which E.P. treated me, spoiling me and shielding me from the hard lessons I would sooner or later have to learn about life. He was doing me no favors. I was in for a hard fall someday, and it would not be a pretty thing to witness.

Mother's letters carried frequent references to what she termed "that side of marriage." Whatever this was, I could tell that it was disagreeable. She also wrote often and bitterly of "the agreement," for which she blamed Nell. This had something to do with the early years of Mother's marriage. "If it had not been for you," she told Nell, "I would never have married him."

Nell's letters to Mother were laced with biblical quotations having to do with the endurance of suffering. Job was so frequently mentioned that I read his story, horrified at what that fellow had gone through. His chief effect on me was to make Mother's complaints seem trivial. About the mysterious "agreement" for which Alice blamed her, Nell insisted that she had only done what she had thought wise at the time. She had tried to protect Alice from the mistakes she herself had made in choosing a husband. As Alice knew, Nell had succumbed to the advances of a locomotive engineer and as a result had been forced to marry him. Now she was stuck subsisting on a railroad pension. E.P., with his tailored suits, crisp accent, and proper grammar may not have been gentry, but had seemed a big step up from locomotives. At least Alice was getting to see the world.

I tried to believe that Mother had written so bitterly to Nell only to make Nell feel better about her own disappointments. But what was so bad about Grandfather? He didn't even chew tobacco in the house. He kept rotgut hidden in his toolshed, he had shown it to me, but what else was he supposed to do, since Nell wouldn't allow it within sight?

Imagining him miserable at home with Nell snarling at him, I wrote telling him how much I missed our excursions to the railroad yards, where he boosted me into engines and showed me how to work the controls. I recalled the pleasures of sitting in his lap as he told me stories:

"This fella was pointing a .45 at me and I could see that it was loaded. 'What would you do,' he says, 'if a man was to tell you he was Jesse James and asked you to hand over that strongbox?' 'I'd hand it over real quick,' I says. 'Well, mister,' he says, 'I am Jesse James,' 'Take it,' I says, 'and the best of luck to you.' "

Even today I can remember Grandfather's description of what it was like on the Chicago run at night. A hundred miles or so from the city, he said, rushing toward that great metropolis where men drank beer all night in the saloons and you could find people dancing in the streets at dawn, he would lean out of the window of his cab, and with the wind hitting his face at sixty or eighty miles an hour, he could see Chicago glowing in the heavens. God's magic lantern was reflecting the lights of State Street and Michigan Avenue in the sky! And when he pulled into the station and the boys told him he was on time, he'd just laugh at them and say that he had already arrived, hours ago. "I been here," he told them. "You just didn't see me." How could my grandmother wish she hadn't married this man?

Of all the confidences exchanged between Mother and Nell, only Mother's references to the coldness of my schoolmates rang true to me. I had not fathomed the reason for it, but I had nothing like the rapport I remembered with American children. In Kansas City it had been I who had drawn away from the others because of my passion for the theater: they may have thought me different, but they were curious, even a little awestruck. Here, I had attempted to make friends and had not met with much success. Father tried to explain as gently as possible that my school was filled with the social elite who thought owning cattle or apartment buildings was more respectable than show business. Actors were regarded as low-class, unreliable folk, mainly because their incomes were irregular and because they tried to entertain people instead of cheating on their taxes, bribing public officials, and exploiting the poor. And they showed their emotions.

It was my father I turned to when I had important questions. Mother tended to put me off, saying that she would explain some other time, or when I was older, or referring me to a passage in the Bible. The Alice-Nell correspondence bothered me so much that I lay in wait for the opportunity to quiz Father, however indirectly. Partly I was upset, and partly I was confused. Why would Mother encourage me to go onstage if, as her letters indicated, she was not herself enamored of the theater? Why would she wish me to go to a snobbish school where students looked down on me? What was this "agreement," and what did it have to do with me? I knew I could not ask Father whether he thought Mother loved him, but I had to weasel some answers out of him.

One Sunday afternoon when Mother was in the kitchen and Father was reading, I came up to his chair and asked him if he liked living in Buenos Aires. He said he thought it fascinating, and his theaters were doing well. He would have preferred to stay in America, but sometimes you had to take opportunities as they came along. It was a great adventure, wasn't it?

"Oh, yes. But I don't think Mother likes it here."

"You don't? Why not?"

"Because she thinks there are too many dagos and that the best thing about it is that there are very few niggers."

Father put down his book and called to Mother that he and I were going out for a walk.

A few blocks from our house was a park. We sat on a bench opposite a fountain and admired the beds of flowers. Then Father asked me to repeat what Mother had said.

I was unable to lie to him. I confessed everything, or nearly. I admitted reading the letters and repeated most of their contents, omitting the criticisms of him. I emphasized my curiosity about the "agreement."

Father said that I had done wrong to read the letters. People needed privacy; if you took that away, you could destroy a person. What people said in letters didn't necessarily represent the truth. Sometimes people wrote what they thought the other person wanted to hear. For himself, he would never look at those letters. They were private conversations between Alice and Nell. He hoped I would promise not to pry again, although he understood my curiosity. I promised.

He said that I should understand my mother's anxieties. She had never been far from Kansas City before, except to California. She was not educated and not well-read. We had to forgive her for that. I would have a better chance to appreciate life's infinite variety. And we had to understand that the ups and downs of show business were very hard on her. He wanted to give me advantages Mother had never had, so that I could grow up unafraid of life.

Father made me feel mature, and I became bold. I asked him straight out what this "agreement" had been.

He appeared troubled. He looked at the clouds and wondered if there would be rain. He began by saying that this was a difficult matter to explain, because I was still young. It was like this. Mother had been only fourteen when he had proposed marriage. Maybe he should have waited, but he had been very much in love with her. Nell had not been sure of him, and he understood that. So he had given his word not to make love to Mother for the first ten years of their marriage. A formal agreement had been drawn up, witnessed by a judge. That way, if the marriage had not worked out, it could have

26

been annulled. It would have been as if it had never happened, because they had not actually lived together as man and wife.

Naturally I had to ask what making love was. I was nearly as much in the dark as I had been before his explanation. Father said that making love was when a man and a woman got very close in bed together. It was how they made babies. I was too young to understand it completely, but that was the main reason people got married. To make love and have babies and raise a family.

Suddenly, in my mania for truth, I got the idea. "Is it like what you see dogs doing?" I asked.

Father emitted something between a groan and a laugh. He said it was, sort of, and then he announced that it was time for dinner and that we should keep this conversation between ourselves. Mother was a little skittish about these subjects.

Instead of satisfying my curiosity, Father had ignited it. I could not help but think it odd that people would enter into such an agreement. And what a shame that they had waited all that time to make love and then ended up having only the one baby. Were they still trying, and how exactly did you try? I began administering prolonged anatomical examinations to myself, and discovered the pleasures of doing so. I vaguely decided that whenever I got married, ten years would be far too long to wait to experience whatever making love was. It is too strong to say that I became obsessed with the subject, but it was never far from my mind. I began to experience acute longings of an indefinite kind. I felt like my grandfather, leaning out of his engine, searching for Chicago in the sky. I was speeding toward something, and I wanted to get there.

3

*L*ittle Meg was as admired in Buenos Aires as in Kansas City, perhaps more so, since a pale nymph inspires greater enthusiasm in Latins than among Kansans and Missourians. Whatever I did down there depended primarily on visual appeal. It was my mother's inspiration to include me in several numbers in which I stood out as a child, dressed identically to young women in a chorus line, for instance; I would be singled out by the brawniest male to dance, giving the comical but subliminally titillating effect of Lemuel Gulliver's alleged affair with the wife of the Lord High Treasurer of Lilliput.

Father hired a typical Latin American master of ceremonies, hysterical in delivery, who announced each act at the top cf his voice in a torrent of syllables, explaining what was about to take place. I was learning Spanish in school, and I marveled at his shrieking introductions of me. I was the sensational Margarita Spencer, a thimbleful of romance, a tornado in a teacup, the toast of New York City, coveted by the cinema, adored by the courts of Spain, England, and Belgium. After winning the hearts of the South American continent, I would drive brokenhearted Berliners and Parisians to suicide. That my tender age, my obscurity, and the conditions of the war made all this improbable bothered no one. I have said that Buenos Aires was sophisticated, but it was also Roman Catholic and therefore deeply sentimental. I was welcomed with an enthusiasm that might better have been reserved for an appearance of the real Virgin. Father confined my sub-equatorial performances to the more respectable of his Buenos Aires theaters, the Florida, and did not permit me to perform in the provinces, where I might have caused a riot.

I may have been corrupted by all this attention, which I did nothing to discourage but which Father tried to control, permitting no press interviews and making sure I was whisked home and to bed well before the final curtain each night, thereby frustrating stage-door Juanitos. His protectiveness kept me more or less innocent, except for those moments onstage when I could feel the adoration. Basically I understood my role was to please, to make myself subservient to the crowd's emotions rather than to control them. I was too young to understand that once a woman has learned how to please men, she has in her grasp the means to control them—but then how many women ever learn this, or care to act on it?

Many of my routines were strictly for laughs, others a mixture of the comical and the sentimental. In one skit I played monkey to Harry Valentine's organ grinder, dancing about at the end of a tether holding a tin cup, peeling a banana and handing it to him to eat. I had watched organ grinders and had always seen more sadness than humor in the monkey, but it was easy for me to play one. All I had to do was to imagine myself as a prisoner for life. Harry would tug on my tether and pull me over to give me a peck on my cap. We sang a duet of "Santa Lucia," which, my mother told me happily, drowned laughter with tears. Harry did an "O Sole Mio" encore as I stood with my arms about his middle.

E.P.'s work kept him on the run—to Montevideo, to La Plata and Santa Rosa on the Pampas, where the audiences were mostly drunk males. He returned from these road trips worn out. I remember bringing hot tea with honey and lemon to his bedside for his cough. I implored him to take me with him to the provinces, but he refused, saying that my schoolwork was too important and that it was enough for me to grace the stage of the Florida.

When he could, he read to me from the trunk of books he had brought with him—Byron, Charles Lamb's *Adventures of Ulysses, Gulliver's Travels, Penguin Island.* He told me that the kingdom of the penguins had flourished just off the southern Argentine coast, an exciting half-truth that brought to life for me this satire on the folly of mankind. Over several weeks he read aloud most of *Jane Eyre*—I recall imagining through his baritone the voice of my heroine and picturing her in my mind. I finished the novel on my own. It was my favorite story then, and I think it remains so.

Every so often we would entertain three or four of the troupe at dinner. Father would drink wine with them; Mother was teetotal. At the table they would try to come up with new ideas for acts and tell their stories of great and disastrous performances. Much to Mother's irritation, Father would mix a little wine with the water in my glass, and I would sip at it and feel grown-up.

Eventually the actors would get around to talking of their ambitions and, soon enough, of their homesickness and other afflictions—a broken love affair, a parent's death, a husband or a wife who had run off. I took it all in and even then I sensed that the conditions of their work, the long absences and the demands of daily performance, invited troubles. Father acted as spiritual counsellor to these lost ones—parent and priest and psychiatrist to whom in a later day they would have been handing over a big chunk of their salaries. Usually he cited some Shakespearean analogy to their predicaments, believing as he did that the Bard had anticipated every form of human behavior.

One young dancer, whose golden hair and turquoise eyes I envied, confessed one night that she was in despair. She was weary of the same old routines, her work had alienated her from her disapproving family, her boyfriend had cheated on her. Worst of all she had come to accept that she had no real talent and would end up with no name, no money, and no future. Harry Valentine tried to joke her out of her mood, saying that he would be glad to trade places with her but looked silly in revealing costumes. She kept on. She hated show business. It was a fraud, a deception, nothing but a form of prostitution. She had never met a happy actor. Look at the people around the table. How many of them could honestly say they were happy?

In the silence I mulled over what this exquisite young woman had been saying. I could feel my father's eyes on me, and when the actress began talking about killing herself and tried to start a discussion about the relative merits of poison, a pistol, or throwing oneself out a window, E.P. gently reminded her of my presence. She rested her head on the table.

"I have the glooms," she mumbled. "Oh, how I have the glooms. Everything is plain rotten."

I'm glad my father didn't send me from the room, as Mother would have had she not been fussing in the kitchen—or had she already gone to bed? Instead he launched into a speech in praise of the actress, whose name, at least for the stage, was Louise DeWitt, recalling the success she had had when still in her teens. Why, hadn't the New York critics raved about her when, in *The Great Divide,* she had personified the freedom of the West? Someone had written that her hair could inspire men to the madness of the Gold Rush, or so he recalled from her clippings. She should enjoy this brief South American holiday. Her career was undergoing a mere hiatus—it happened to everyone. Persistence was the thing! She should try to save a few dollars and then try her luck again in New York. If her boyfriend had two-timed her, well then, he was no good and she could get another. Or, here was another thought, perhaps she should think about getting married. It might lend some stability to her life.

"Who am I going to marry," she asked, her cheek resting on the table, her hand curled around her glass, "some rich slob of a producer? I'm too old for that. They go for teenagers."

Father, trying to roll over her with rhetoric, launched into a speech in praise of life's wonders and opportunities. He said that she should try to avoid misinterpreting things, as Othello and Ophelia had.

Harry Valentine was usually invited to these dinners. I loved him. When Father was away, Harry paid special attention to me, making sure rehearsals didn't tire me, asking about my schoolwork, hugging and kissing me and saying that his fondest wish was one day to have a daughter like me. For an actor he was unusually generous, less wrapped up in himself than most, and very talented. He was as funny in his own crazy way as Oliver Hardy: both graceful big men, delicate, airborne—for all his bulk, Harry could walk a tightrope. He could transform himself into anything from a trolley conductor to a hillbilly guzzling moonshine. His versatility may have cost him; show business rewards types.

When Father was away, I badgered Mother to invite Harry Valentine to Sunday dinner. She resisted; she was too tired, not up to his antics; I should wash my hair. She did not approve of him, but often she gave in.

Harry must have weighed three hundred pounds—no bigger than a young female polar bear, he liked to say. He had a huge round head, thin brown hair slicked straight back above his child's small-featured face, with the beady black eyes of his Cherokee grandmother, who, he claimed, had scalped her first husband. His hands were huge, powerful as a blacksmith's, but his feet were scarcely bigger than my own. He had been thrown together out of a mismatched set of body parts, he liked to say, and could have made a living in a freak show. He used to try to squeeze his foot into my shoe, and was nearly able. He claimed to have a collection of little shoes back home.

"Why *do* you have such tiny feet, Harry?" I would ask.

"Because I like little shoes," he would say, "don't you?"

Harry professed to adore Alice's cooking—that it was produced in large midwestern quantity was probably the point. He kept me limp with laughter and occasionally even managed to amuse my mother, babbling in nonsense talk that sounded like Spanish or German or Italian or whatever he chose. He could render a song from *Babes in Toyland* in what seemed like twelve different languages. He crawled around our living room on all fours barking, did his macho-gaucho routine with a bath towel as his sash and a length of twine as his bullwhip. Mother was fairly tolerant of all this, except when Harry would grab me, pull me into his lap, and become the villain about to ravish the maiden in a melodrama. He'd let me go when she said sternly that that sort of thing was all right on the stage, but not in her home.

There was no wine allowed when E.P. was away. Behind Mother's back Harry whipped out his flask and nipped, putting a finger to his lips and raising his eyebrows to swear me to secrecy, a game I happily played because the more Harry nipped, the crazier he became. He would dab whipped cream all over his face and say he was Rip Van Winkle or, often, ask me if I had been window-peeking lately. It was a routine between us, one too peculiar for the stage. I would say that I had never been window-peeking. And Harry would begin:

"That's because you're a girl. Little girls don't go window-peeking, but little boys do. That's what I did when I was your age. I'd go window-peeking all over the neighborhood. You'd be surprised what I saw!"

"What did you see, Harry?"

"I saw old Mr. Winterbotham naked in his kitchen pouring himself a whiskey!"

"You did?" And I would start to giggle.

"And I saw Mr. Winterbotham naked in his kitchen washing his dog naked in the sink!"

"And then what did you see?"

"I saw Mrs. Winterbotham come naked down the stairs!"

"And then?"

"I saw Mr. Winterbotham naked and Mrs. Winterbotham naked washing that naked dog in the sink!"

Harry would be shouting by then, and Mother would order him to go home.

But I was always anxious for him to linger. He would take out his harmonica and blow a few bars before singing the words of a song in a warm tenor. I hummed along, sitting cross-legged at his feet. Always before he left, I asked him to sing the strange verses he knew of "Home on the Range":

> How often at night
> When the heavens are bright
> With the light from the glittering stars,
> Have I stood here amazed
> And asked as I gazed
> If their glory exceeds that of ours.

Here his voice swelled and soared:

> O give me a land
> Where the bright diamond sand
> Flows leisurely down the stream;
> Where the graceful white swan
> Goes gliding along,
> Like a maid in a heavenly dream!
>
> Then I would not exchange
> My home on the range,
> Where the deer and the antelope play . . .

There were tears in our eyes, Mother's, too.

"You're the swan," Harry said to me, "gliding along. You're the maid in my heavenly dream, my darling."

"It's so beautiful," I said, "why don't you sing it on the stage? No funny business. We could have a backdrop of a stream and a green meadow, and I could dress like a swan and glide along."

"No, no," Harry said. "If I try to be a serious singer, I'll end up as Victor Herbert's houseboy."

"But the organ grinder isn't all funny. People love it when you sing in that."

Harry put his big fist up to his lips and made a rude noise.

"I think it's time," said Mother, clearing the plates.

"Harry, how old are you?" I asked.

35

"Eight," Harry said in a child's voice.

"No, you're not! Are you thirty years old?"

"I'm twenty-eight," Harry said, "but I'm younger than you are, and a whole lot sillier."

I thought of Harry as somebody who had figured out how not to grow up. He was my younger brother who needed me, or something like that.

We had been in Buenos Aires for several months when one evening I was wandering through the labyrinth of corridors beneath the stage at the Florida. Here were the storage and dressing rooms, the places most theatergoers never see, where actors assume and drop their masks. I dressed in my father's office off the mezzanine, but when I could escape Mother's eye, I explored this underworld, catching glimpses of the actors horsing around, quarreling, embracing, screeching like peacocks, stealing kisses. It was a cauldron of half-naked acrobats, dancers in feathers and sequins and wild makeup, an underground zoo, hot, heavy with perfumes and powders mixed with sweat.

On that particular evening I was checking out the subterranean warrens before the first interval. I was already in costume as a Pilgrim. The passages were deserted; a big production number was taking place above. I peered into empty dressing rooms and was anticipating the rush of bodies down spiral iron stairs when I noticed a door through which I had never passed before. It was at the end of a long hall. A swing door. A rat poked its head out of a corner. I was no longer bothered by the rats and mice and bugs; they were all part of the scene.

I approached the door and slowly pushed on it, finding the corridor beyond dark, letting in light to see.

The rest happened quickly. The second the light hit the end of the corridor, not thirty feet distant, I saw a large figure crouched on one knee. It was Harry Valentine with his eye to a keyhole!

In an instant he was aware of the light and jerked his head around.

36

I let the door go, turned, and ran like a hare, hoping that he hadn't recognized me. Maybe the light had blinded him. I was quickly around corners and into the throng of actors hurrying to their dressing rooms.

I did not know whether Harry tried to follow me; half an hour later we were onstage together.

What was his secret? I had had some experience of keyholes. When my parents were in an argument, which was seldom, I would peer into their bedroom. Keyholes were big in those days. I never saw anything worth bothering about.

I had to know what was interesting enough to send Harry down a dark, disused corridor to peep. The next evening I escaped from Mother and hurried to the mysterious spot. I pushed the door slowly as before, ready to run. This time the corridor was empty. I made my way to where Harry had knelt and peeked through the keyhole. Whatever lay beyond was concealed in darkness. I could not bear to leave without finding out what I could.

I opened the door. The light sent cockroaches and waterbugs scurrying to safety across the floor.

A pile of blankets lay in one corner. The place stank of mildew, more like a cavern than a room. Propped against a wall was an old painted flat depicting a pair of lions.

Obviously whatever Harry had found was no longer there. But it was earlier in the evening than before. I resolved to return to check things out during the production number. What if Harry showed up again? I would take my chances, but I would wait till the next evening, just to make sure that I really wanted to go through with this.

For the next twenty-four hours I could think of nothing else. I entertained all kinds of possibilities: Harry had seen a dead body. An animal? Maybe there were actors playing dice back there; Father frowned on that, I knew.

The next evening, I checked Harry's dressing room just as the production number began. Since he wasn't there, I assumed he must be at the keyhole again. I decided that I would confront him and make him share his secret with me.

I pushed open the door to the corridor; it was deserted. Light, however, shone from beneath the door at the end. Maybe Harry was inside. Doing what? I had to find out. I let the swing door close behind me and crept along.

Now, I heard grunts and cries; a woman's voice, a man's. She groaned; he uttered what sounded like Spanish curses. If Harry hadn't been there before me, I would have turned tail. Was this a torture chamber?

I bent to apply my eye to the keyhole. The first thing I noticed was a hurricane lantern burning brightly on the floor. Its orangy glow illuminated the painted lions showing their teeth. Just to the right on the pile of blankets was Louise DeWitt without a stitch on her. She was astride a dark man I recognized as an Argentine dancer famous for his leaps. He was on his back, facing her, running his hands over her belly. She rode him up and down like a carousel pony on its pole.

It took me a moment to absorb what was going on. I concluded that whatever it was they were doing, they were willing to risk great inconvenience to accomplish it.

I was mesmerized. It did not occur to me to shield my eyes and run. Most of all, Louise's violent beauty held me. Her wild yellow hair, her teeth chewing at her mouth, her eyes wide and staring into the man's face, her hands digging into his sides and flashing up to press at her breasts—I could feel myself redden in the dark. Her thighs flexed as she rose and fell. She impaled herself again and again, fierce, groaning, grunting, spitting out hard words—possessed! Was she killing herself or him? She was a marvel.

As was he. I did not know enough to identify an erection, and could not help wondering how he fit that thing into the tight trousers I had seen him wearing. Was this some subequatorial product of heat and barbecued meat?

At last Louise, after a a burst of shouts and tearing at her hair and pressing the heels of her hands to her temples, began to roll off. At that instant I felt myself hit by a shaft of light and turned to see Harry's bulk framed in the doorway. He was a shadow; then I made out his features. He gestured frantically at me to get up and follow him.

When I reached him, he grabbed my hand and led me to his dressing room and shut the door.

"You crazy kid! What were you doing down there? What was going on? What were you looking at? What was all that noise?"

"You can't fool me, Harry, I know you saw what I saw. I caught you, too. Now, you tell me. What *was* going on?"

"Shh! Don't you know? You don't, do you?"

"Maybe I do. Let me guess. Were they making love?"

"You could call it that," Harry said. "Are you in shock?"

I said I was fine. I hadn't had time to think about it. If I'd been seen by anyone but Harry, I would have been mortified.

"Is that what people do?" I asked.

"What were they doing?"

"You know. She was, you know, never mind."

"Tell me."

Harry sweated as I described the scene. All at once I was embarrassed and stopped. I wanted to leave, and I started giggling.

Harry grabbed a fedora from a rack and did a little dance. I wondered how we were going to get through our routine tonight.

"This will be our secret," Harry said, "okay? Just you and me. You're not going to tell your parents, are you?"

"Of course not!"

The performers were returning. I hurried out.

I floated through my act that night. I was especially graceful, according to Mother. When I watched Louise and her partner, the man from the basement, perform a new dance called the tango, I undressed them in my mind. I decided that I preferred them with clothes on, but I may have been jealous.

4

*I*f this was the sort of experience that is supposed to turn a child neurotic, so be it. In my view that is so much hokum. Harry and I had our private jokes and surreptitious glances from then on. I don't mind saying that I could not get the Louise DeWitt sideshow out of my mind. I was convinced that I had discovered something important and that, somehow, it told me about why I had been placed on this earth. The more I thought about it, the less frightening I found it, and the more I wanted to become old enough to try it and related exercises. Harry let me know that there were alternate configurations. He even drew me some pictures, which I traced over and over, until in an outburst of prudence I burned them. Drawing was another of Harry's talents. I thought that he and Louise and her lover had made me suddenly grown-up; I was sure I knew more than any of my classmates. To hell with their snottiness.

I became more curious about my parents' private life, pressing my ear to their bedroom wall at odd hours. I never heard a thing worthwhile or saw anything through their keyhole. Had they signed another agreement? Harry said that everybody made love one way or another, or tried to. I had the sense that I was made to try it sooner rather than later. I knew one thing: I was not going to wait until I was twenty-four.

*   *   *

Meanwhile I grew closer to my father. I came to know his appetite for luxury and spectacle as he escorted me on walks through elegant quarters of the city, commenting on baroque buildings and ladies and gentlemen in their finery. He hired a motorcar to drive us down the widest street in the world, explaining that it had been constructed to prevent rebellious citizens from taking command. In a broad street the authorities could crush rebels like ants, whereas a handful of people could take over a cul-de-sac or a tiny passageway and live there according to their own rules. I understood exactly what he meant.

It was just the two of us together on these excursions. Father took me to visit monuments and museums and to *Madame Butterfly* at the Colón Theater and other events, giving me nights off from my own performances. He invited Mother, but she always declined with one excuse or another. I remember his telling her that we ought to have servants and that we could easily afford them—even in Kansas City we had had a live-in maid—but Mother did not want some foreigner poking about.

On school holidays Father and I lunched together at one of the grand hotels or at a smart café in the Calle Florida near the theater, where the waiters fussed over me and said that one day I would be known as the great beauty of the North: "The señorita makes my heart to sing," that sort of nonsense, which naturally I encouraged. They treated my father with deference. In his English suits and shoes and with his patrician manner, they must have taken him for that rare creature, an American millionaire with taste. I was so proud of him.

I think he wanted me to know that one could enjoy many of the pleasures of great wealth without actually having it. One afternoon he asked me whether I would care to accompany him to purchase some clothes. We rode the trolley to the center of town. On the way he told me that the actual destination of this outing should remain a secret between us. So many secrets in my heart! But I was eager to share yet another one with my father.

We alighted at an unfamiliar stop and walked past what my

father explained was the city morgue. Next door was a shop crowded with men's and women's clothing of every description. I had no idea of money, but Father was delighted with the prices. He picked out a Chesterfield coat, smoothing his hand over its flawless black velvet collar, and a pair of boots. He told me that under normal circumstances these things would have sold for five or six times as much, and he gleefully peeled off colorful bills from the big roll he carried.

Outside, I asked why everything had been so cheap. The shop, he explained, belonged to the morgue. As a man of the theater, he had long ago discovered such places, where clothing from the newly dead could be had for next to nothing, a way to save on costumes and on his own wardrobe. In America he frequented thrift shops operated by Episcopalians, who had the most money and the best clothes. He removed the boots from their wrapping and showed me the unworn soles. He said that you could always find good shoes at the morgue or at shops run by hospitals, because the dying are light on their feet.

I was impressed by Father's practicality because it refuted Mother's view of him as expressed in her letters to Nell. At the same time I didn't care for the idea of his walking around in dead men's clothing. It was courting bad luck, and I wanted his clothes to belong to him as absolutely as I did—or something like that. I looked forward to the day when his fortunes would improve and he could buy himself—and me!—whatever he wanted.

If Mother knew he wore secondhand clothes, she would probably think it further proof of his phoniness. She had her own slant on things, and he his. I seemed to be somewhere between them. I shared my mother's enthusiasm for my fledgling theatrical career and appreciated her care for my costumes and talents, but it was Father's company I craved.

Often he took my hand and strolled with me down to the waterfront to watch ships arrive and depart. I was fascinated by the vast cargoes piled neatly on the docks to be hoisted item by item, box by box into a ship—such arduous, patient work.

Father explained how everything had to be arranged in perfect order in the hold, so the load wouldn't shift in heavy seas. We would see a cargo one day, and by the next afternoon it would be half-loaded, by the third day gone with the ship. It was like everything else in life, Father said, bits and pieces gathered painstakingly together to make a cargo or a play, a book, or a family or a person's life. Some people, like the stevedores, did what they were told; others, like the captain, had to have a vision of the whole and of the end. Some people let their lives collapse in a heap of disconnected incidents. With the kind of cornball idealism that touches a child most deeply, he told me that he wanted me to be a captain in my life, knowing where I was going and what had to be done to get there.

"You're a captain," I said.

"Maybe someday I will be."

Surveying the harbor, he liked to read out the names of home ports painted on the sterns—Marseilles, Liverpool, Barcelona, the words unreeling from his lips. " 'Your mind is tossing on the ocean,' " he said, hugging me to him, and " 'O well for the sailor boy, that he sings in his boat on the bay!' " He made Naples sound full of dark grapes and Gypsies. The light in Athens was as bright and clear as Athene's eyes. In Lisboa the women sang in the streets of their lovers at sea.

If a ship carried the name of an American port, we talked of home. I said I missed the snow, Halloween, and Grandfather. We'd be going back before too long, Father replied. In a rare reference to the war, he told me that when it was over, he would like to own a theater again. Everyone was talking about the motion pictures. I had yet to see one, and he promised to take me to *The Vicar of Wakefield,* which had opened in Buenos Aires along with a musical revue.

He in his dark suit and Homburg hat, I in my long cotton dress with parasol—we watched the ships for hours. One afternoon high, smooth clouds covered the sky, the water reflecting grayness to the horizon. "Isn't it wonderful," my father said. "It's like living inside a pearl!"

*   *   *

Our exile lasted nearly three years. Few of E. P. Spencer, Inc.'s original troupers endured that long. Father was always cabling talent agencies for replacements. Louise DeWitt lit out for Hollywood—without her underground lover. My father said that she was very talented and he was sorry to lose her, and I said that I was sorry, too. Harry Valentine sailed for home when his girlfriend wrote him that she was about to marry someone else, but soon he was back, alone and afraid that if he stayed in the United States he would be conscripted into the war, the fattest soldier in France and the biggest target.

"I don't want to end up as *Kartoffelsalat* for some Heinie general," Harry said.

Several months after the Armistice, a position opened up for my father with the Shubert organization in New York City. He was to manage two Midtown theaters. He accepted.

"Home at last!" he said, lifting me into his arms. My mother said that she did not consider New York home, but that it was bound to be an improvement. E.P. called New York the center of the universe, and he predicted great things for us. I managed to imagine that before long Mother would be telling Nell that she had been wrong about E.P. and that she would never have said such nasty things about him had she known what the future would bring.

5

We sailed on the *Setauket,* an American passenger ship, toward the end of 1919. The voyage was to last a week, and I would celebrate my twelfth birthday, December 14, on board.

Father and I stood on the stern listening to the valedictory cries of sea gulls and watching the revolving beam of a lighthouse grow brighter as dusk gave way to night. Surely great adventures lay ahead, days fresh as the wet breeze.

We made our way to our promenade-deck staterooms—a lounge, a bedroom for my parents, an adjoining bedroom for me. Lo and behold, Mother had ordered hors d'oeuvres and a split of champagne for Father. The gesture was so uncharacteristic that I felt it must be a happy omen. E.P. kissed her on the cheek, and she did not so much as wince when he gave me a sip.

That evening I noticed that I was the only child seated in the first-class dining room, a salon sumptuous with mirrors, crystal chandeliers, polished woods. A small orchestra played quietly on a corner stage bedecked with flowers. At some thirty tables people sat in dinner jackets and long gowns, my father distinct with his rose in his lapel. Had these people all left their children behind?

Father explained that there was a special dining room or "nursery" for children under fifteen. The food was different, and if I were there I could be enjoying myself with the other infants. He had assured the purser that I was thoroughly adult and that I would behave better than some of the grown-ups.

"But where's Harry?" I asked. I knew that he was going home on the same ship. Harry was below in tourist class, Father said, saving his money for New York, where he was going to appear at one of the new theaters. If I liked, I could visit him tomorrow. First-class passengers had the run of the ship.

"May I invite Harry to dinner with us?" I asked.

"It's not done," Mother said, "though they might let him eat in the nursery!"

Between the soup and the fish Father led Mother around the little dance floor in a waltz. He danced with me during dessert, the tip of his beard tickling the top of my head.

I found Harry the next morning, lying in his windowless cabin gasping and pouring sweat. The noise and vibration from the engines were terrific.

"This is how they transport prisoners," he said, mopping his face. "They had better chain me to this bunk or I'll throw myself overboard." He apologized for being in his underwear and took a swig from a bottle. "There's nothing else to do down here." From his trousers, hanging on the door, he brought out his watch. "Two hours till lunch."

He had originally booked an outside cabin with a porthole, but when his roommate had complained about his bulk, Harry had agreed to move.

I asked if there was anything I could bring him. A first-class ticket, Harry said. Then his dark beads of eyes brightened. An iced bottle of champagne! Could I manage that? No, no, he was asking too much. Merely my presence from time to time would be enough! He knew no one else on board, and the only place he had to pass the time was a horrible little bar where men jammed themselves together and threw up. The dining room was a cafeteria smelling of old steamed Brussels sprouts.

*　　*　　*

Margaret in Hollywood

A sea voyage can be boring. My father read and my mother wrote incessantly; I felt like doing neither. Thinking about how to sneak champagne for Harry occupied my thoughts.

I was back in first class, standing beside the shuffleboard court on the boat deck. I was wearing a white dress of thin cotton, what was known as ladies' sportwear in those days, that Mother had bought me specially for the trip.

A boy and a man were playing shuffleboard, exhorting one another in French. You could not have mistaken them for anything but father and son. The one was a miniature of the other; the bigger one had hairy arms and the shadow of his beard. The boy, slender and probably a year or two older than I, seemed tall for his age.

The father must have noticed me staring at his son. He took the boy aside and spoke to him with a few energetic gestures in my direction.

The boy came over and introduced himself to me with a slight bow as Philippe Daguenet and, speaking in English, invited me to play a match, his father all the while eyeing us from the other side of the court.

Philippe permitted me to win one of the games we played. His father disappeared. I learned that the senior Daguenet had been the French consul in Montevideo and was being posted to New York. Philippe complained about his sister, who was two and occupied all of Madame Daguenet's hours. I said that I did not have any brothers or sisters, but I did have a friend who was like a big baby brother to me. After I explained Harry's predicament and the challenge of the bottle of champagne, Philippe agreed that surely something could be done.

Philippe, who it turned out was thirteen, had been relegated to eat in the nursery. He had complained bitterly to his parents, but had been unable to persuade them otherwise. A dog, he said, deserved better than this fate.

We stood at the rail on the windward side chatting for about an hour, the spray dousing us and making us shout with pleasure. When I let on that I was something of an actress and

49

had actually been on the stage in America as well as Argentina, Philippe said that this was truly a formidable and romantic circumstance. His large brown eyes made me think of melting chocolates. He showed none of the snobbery of my Buenos Aires classmates toward a girl of the theater, although I did exaggerate my father's importance, saying that he had purchased three theaters in Manhattan and was about to produce a motion picture.

"When shall I see you again?" Philippe might have stolen the line from a play. While I was in the dining salon, he would be in the nursery thinking of me and mulling over the question of Harry's champagne. We agreed to meet after dinner, beside a lifeboat.

I managed to get away from my parents, expressing an urge to observe the heavens. I brought Philippe a pastry, which he devoured with curses against the nursery. Under a half-moon, we marveled at the stars, which seemed to have dropped down for us to touch. In a play the directions would have called for us to kiss. I did my best to be alluring. I wanted so to feel what kissing was like, but we were too shy. All we did was make a date for shuffleboard in the morning.

The ship was a cradle. I slept through breakfast, and when I woke up, puffy and logy, Mother had left a note saying that she and Father had already gone to lunch. I joined them, gulped something down, and raced up to find Philippe, who was tossing a rubber doughnut across a net with his father and two other men. When I caught his eye, he let the doughnut hit his arm, and his father teased him.

We stood watching the wake trail out. Philippe confided that he had solved the dilemma of the champagne. His parents took a nap each afternoon. When they were in their bedroom, he would order a bottle delivered. The steward would think it was for Monsieur and Madame, and it would end up buried on their bill. Philippe would leave the bucket down the passageway.

Later that afternoon he appeared, carrying the bottle concealed in a bathtowel. Without thinking, I stood on my toes and pecked him on the cheek, eliciting a touch of crimson in his tan face.

We raced downstairs, skipping over the chain that divided the classes. The heat and the throbbing of the engines and the smell of cooking grease and fuel oil enveloped us as we neared bottom. It must have been 90 down there.

Harry hadn't shaved since Buenos Aires, and his hair was wet and matted. He was wearing a stained pink chenille bathrobe that must have shrunk.

I introduced Philippe, who produced the champagne with a flourish, and instantly Harry transformed himself into a courtier, or a court jester, babbling in nonsense French and treating Philippe like a nobleman.

"You've heard the one about Louis the Fourteenth and the papal nuncio, haven't you, *mon vieux*?" Harry asked.

"Please, Harry," I said, "not that story." I heard it several times before, and it was vulgar. Harry pressed on. While other children my age were beginning to say risqué things to each other, Harry had initiated me into his own peculiar brand of mild smut, as if we were boys behind a garage. The gist of this story was that Louis the Fourteenth required all the courtiers to attend him when he went to the royal toilet. The papal nuncio drew the line at wiping the royal arse. He would observe, but he would not wipe. So King Louis angrily dismissed him, and the Vatican had to dispatch a fresh nuncio.

"Are you prepared to assist at the royal toilet?" the king inquired of the new man.

"Indeed, Your Majesty," replied the nuncio. "I am eager not only to wipe the royal arse, but afterward to kiss it!"

Philippe was convulsed. I didn't laugh this time. While Harry had been talking, I noticed something odd. I had been missing a pair of pink tights. There they were, one foot and half a leg, sticking out of Harry's suitcase on the floor, shoved partway under the bunk.

The three of us sprawled in the lower berth, myself squashed between the other two. Harry uncorked the bottle, his bathrobe falling open to reveal big, soft, hairy paps. We insisted

51

that he deserved all of the champagne himself. He made it last, gargling and cracking jokes, then said he needed a breath of air. Did we wish to go on deck with him? We could stay here if we promised to misbehave.

Neither of us moved. With his back to us Harry slipped on trousers under the robe, donned a jacket without bothering with a shirt, and was out the door.

We were side by side and alone. Philippe noticed that there were a couple of inches left in the bottle and suggested we finish it. I thought I could feel the stuff going to my head, but there were only two or three swallows. I wondered how long Harry would be gone.

"How shall we amuse ourselves?" Philippe asked.

"I don't know. What do you want to do?"

Our arms touched. I crooked my hand and took his fingers in mine. I had not thought about it; I just did it. I looked down at our joined hands, his brown and mine white. The ship rolled and creaked. It occurred to me that he was about the same color as Louise DeWitt's Argentine and that we were as alone as they had been and that there was no keyhole. A drop of champagne clung to the corner of his mouth. As I felt myself pulled to him, I kissed away the wetness. Then I closed my eyes and offered my lips the way actresses do.

It was a soft, child's kiss, but we clung together. I could smell the sea on his skin and I felt a pressure in my chest. I was with him, and in my mind I was watching us as I had watched Louise and her friend, who kept creeping into my head. I didn't want them there, but they persisted.

"Have you kissed a boy before?"

"No. Have you kissed a girl?"

"Yes. No. Not really."

"Kiss again."

When our tongues met, a current took me. Was Harry going to leave us alone? What if he burst in? I lost my balance and Philippe came down with me and there we were, stretched out beside each other.

"Let me do something," I said, and I got up and threw the bolt on the door.

"What if we got undressed?" Philippe said.

"What? Are you insane?"

"That's what people do, isn't it?"

"We're not people!"

"We're almost people."

"We mustn't," I said, silently approving his boldness. "But we could get just a little bit undressed. I'm too embarrassed, and I'm afraid, aren't you?"

"Turn out the light, then, and come back here with me. We could have a great pleasure. Do you have breasts?"

"Shh! You can touch what I have, if you like. I give you permission."

"This is the happiest day of my life!"

I forgot about the light, and there was no more talk. Being in that strange room in the middle of the ocean made us brave. Embarrassment melted away. Feelings took over, and heightening wonder, until I heard Harry at the door and for an instant feared that we had been caught. By that time, we were clinging, touching here and there, exploring with pure and tender awe. We weren't supposed to be doing this, and I wanted to go on covering him with kisses and touches. His mouth and his bony, soft-skinned body were everything. He touched my buds of breasts so lightly, as if he worried that he might damage them; and when he pushed himself at my thigh, I wondered how it felt to him, all squashed down there, this sweet boy who was making my heart race. He took big breaths of me and slid his hand over my bottom, and I was thinking, could anything be more wonderful?—and then the sound of Harry's key in the lock stopped everything.

I sprang up, dizzy, and brushed down my skirt, buttoned my blouse. Philippe tried to squirm his way back to decency on the bunk.

"Are you kids still in there?"

I got the door open and started yapping about having pushed the bolt by mistake and not being able to unstick it.

"It's hard to unstick them when they're stuck," he said making his eyes whirl like pinwheels. "You little devils didn't go all kissy-poo while Uncle Harry was away, did you?"

"Come along, Philippe," I said. "Where were you, Harry? You were gone so long."

"I was thinking about jumping overboard," Harry said, "just to test the water. I saw porpoises. What did you see? Philippe, *mon Dieu*! What's the matter with your hair? Are you in pain, son?"

As we made our way back upstairs, Philippe said that he thought Harry was very bizarre and droll. He would not tell our parents that we had been alone, would he?

"Harry would never tell. Harry is my best friend in the world."

We made a pact to meet again after dinner.

When Father wished me happy birthday, I found myself saying that I thought it would be a fine idea if we could invite poor Philippe Daguenet to celebrate with us in the dining room. He was such a nice boy, and so clever. He was going to teach me some French. Wasn't that lucky? It was a shame that he had to eat with babies, a smart young gentleman like that.

Mother did not care for the idea, but Father must have been amused at my having a crush—I am sure I was transparent. He said that he would speak to the Daguenets.

It was a grand party. Philippe looked debonair in his dinner jacket. I wore my favorite dress, raspberry pongee silk with a dropped waist and a lace collar, and white silk hose. When I blew out my candles, I wished that Philippe and I could know each other a long, long time.

Mother was cold to him. It didn't matter. On the dance floor he whispered that his mother was strict, too. He told me that as a dancer I was superior and marvelous and that being with me was an experience of the most romantic kind. He was sure that I would become an actress famous the world over. I was the loveliest creature he had ever seen, and he wished he could undress me and dance naked with me across the floor and let everyone see how beautiful I was. My breasts were like the first berries of the spring showing through snow.

When the ship tipped over a wave, we took advantage, holding each other. Philippe told me that he was intoxicated by the smell of me that clung to his hands and that he would lie awake with his hands to his face, summoning me.

We visited Harry again, but he was seasick, lying there heaving and puffing like a trapped elephant seal. We contented ourselves with kissing and groping behind lifeboats and around corners until the wind in the northern latitudes grew bitter.

When I was not with Philippe, I kept mostly to my bed, thinking of him and enjoying the way the ship rode the swell and shuddered on the crest of waves. I wished it would take us round the world.

6

A few days after our arrival in New York, Philippe presented himself at our apartment, bearing flowers. The blooms, whatever they were, matched the color of the dress I had worn on my birthday. Philippe had brought them when I was out registering at school. I was vexed to have missed him.

"A nice gesture," Mother said, "to remember our trip."

I wanted to telephone him immediately. He had left a number, hadn't he?

"No, dear. It is not appropriate for you to contact him."

I sensed that something was wrong, but I restrained myself and asked questions in as sweet a voice as I could manage. Certainly I should respond to his courtesy? What would he think?

Unable to fend me off with it isn't done and it's not proper and you are too young and you'll be busy with school, Mother laid it on the line. I was forbidden to see or to speak to Philippe again. What had been a pleasant diversion on a ship was one thing; now, Philippe had proposed to invite me to his family's apartments at the Consulate. This was altogether something else. I was still a child. What ideas did I have? Obviously my head had been turned by books.

I kept my composure, simpering that Philippe was such a gentleman and that I hoped we could all become friends. It seemed a shame to get to know someone and then part. I would learn French more efficiently. We could all picnic together in the park.

"Your father and I will decide what friends we have," Mother said. "You had best attend to your own responsibilities. I have spoken to Mrs. Daguenet. . . ."

She mispronounced the name. I corrected her. That did it.

"Listen to me, you little hussy! I'll hear no more out of you. Believe you me, your father agrees with me on this, so don't waste your time trying to play up to him! I don't ever want to hear that boy's name spoken in this house again!"

"Philippe!" I shouted. "Philippe! Philippe!"

Mother grabbed my arm and smacked me across the face. With my dramatic sense I screamed that she had broken my nose and disfigured me forever.

Mother had strong hands. She led me to the kitchen sink, turned on the tap, and vigorously applied a bar of soap to my mouth. I tried to keep my teeth clenched, but enough seeped in to make me spit, and she managed to force the bar into my mouth. She stopped when I gagged.

As I was trying to rinse out the vile taste, Mother retrieved Philippe's flowers from the vase, dumped them into the sink in front of my nose, broke the stems, and threw them into the trash, saying that if she had not been foolish enough to have saved them in the first place, I would never have known the difference and none of this would have happened. Oh, no, I thought. I would have known. Somehow I would have known.

Alone in my room, I must have bawled for half an hour. I wished my father would come home, although I sensed that my mother was telling the truth when she said that Father agreed with her. It was the sort of dispute in which he gave way. The ship had been never-never land.

And Philippe had told me enough about his mother for me to believe that Madame Daguenet would conspire in the breakup. Philippe, enterprising little chap that he was, had probably bought the flowers and appeared on his own initia-

tive—possibly with his father's connivance. I had supplied him
with our address, assuming that we would meet again in our
new world. Now, he must be going through the same misery
that I was—or I hoped so!

It did occur to me, much to my frustration, that perhaps,
just perhaps, Mother and Madame were right. We were aw-
fully young. But I did not wish to think about what was or was
not proper. My misery was what mattered. I was a victim of
the hard-heartedness of adults.

That afternoon, through teary eyes and with trembling hand,
I started keeping a diary. The blank volume itself had been a
present Father had bought me one day during our wander-
ings, fine paper bound in soft brown leather, hand-sewn. I
have it still, and the first entry, January 5, 1920, well-stained
with tears, is all about Philippe. The first line is *I hate my mother,*
but it is scratched out and emended to *I don't want to be like my
mother.* The second is *Will I never see him again?*

I must have been aware that in writing about Philippe I was
making more of our liaison than it had been; I began the diary to dramatize myself. I wanted it to be a friend my own age
to whom I could confide and appear as a romantic heroine.
To protect my thought, I devised a code, scrambling the letters of the alphabet, so that *A* became *V*, *B* became *Q*, and so
on. I lay on my bed coding and striking tragic poses.

I gave the diary a name, Jane, or "Xvln," after my favorite
heroine. Soon I was beginning each entry with "Ynvc Xvln,"
or "Dear Jane." At first I wrote out entries normally, then
transliterated according to my code sheet and burned the
original. Soon the new alphabet encoding my life become second nature to me.

After much thought, I found the perfect hiding place for
Jane. From one of his trips to the provinces, Father had brought
back a pair of Argentine dolls, a boy and a girl, dancers that
came in a black lacquered box along with costume changes. I
kept their clothes folded in tissue paper in the cedar-lined
drawers the box provided, and I hid Jane in there.

*   *   *

Father talked to me about Philippe and explained that I was too young for a serious attachment, that my future would be alive with romantic opportunity.

He was so calm and understanding that I could almost agree with him. But the idea that this boy whom I had known more intimately than my parents would ever realize would disappear from my life continued to depress me. Something told me that if it had been up to Harry Valentine, Philippe and I would never have been separated.

My grief and petulance ebbed amid the luxury of our apartment on Riverside Drive, an enviable address then. It was light and large, six big rooms on the tenth floor of the Glanmore Arms, a gray granite building complete with doorman and brass nameplate. I could lie on my canopied four-poster bed, contemplate the mirrored dressing table and the Persian carpet, and gaze through big windows across to the park and the river beyond. Father stocked my bookshelves with volumes meant to inspire me, including a set of the *Britannica,* which I found good medicine for melancholy. I suppose I picked up a lot of useless information, if there is such a thing.

And Mother, thank goodness, seemed pleased with her new life. She occupied her time furnishing and decorating the place. Every week there were new cabinets built to order, rooms repainted. She acquired a full-time maid, Edna, who, being Irish, was in Mother's eyes inferior but racially less than thoroughly repugnant. Mother continued her sewing, but on a new electric Singer machine that was usually whirring when I came home from school, and she wrote to Nell less obsessively than in Argentina. I made no attempt to intercept the letters, preferring to believe the best, and with some reason. My parents were frequently out in the evenings. I would hear them come in, occasionally laughing. I noticed a warmer, more girlish quality in Mother. I recall often telling her that I loved her, and she often responded in kind.

My parents' only big row in that apartment was over me. Father wanted me off the stage, at least for the time being, to concentrate on my studies. He seemed convinced that I was some kind of a genius and alluded to Edith Wharton and Madame Curie, neither of whom meant a thing to Mother, who was not even sure that it was proper that women would soon be granted the right to vote. In our family Father was the suffragette. Here I was not yet in my teens, and he was talking about my going to college some day—a notion, as she termed it, that Mother insisted was not only premature but pointless and possibly dangerous. It could make me unattractive and frightening to men, too smart for my own good, without giving me practical experience, such as the theater, that could lead to a steady income. From her observations most women who went to college ended up spinsters. Did I expect my family to support me for the rest of my life?

As silly as I sensed my mother's arguments were, and as much as I instinctively sided with Father and wished to please him, I was torn about leaving the stage. It was like hearing that suddenly my life was to become all work and no play. Everything boiled over one morning when I blurted out that I missed the theater's excitements and hoped that I could return soon.

"You're better off thinking about school," Father said.

"I don't approve of this one bit," Mother began.

"I am aware of your opinion," Father broke in, "but there's no need for further argument." He rapped the table with his knife. "I have decided." This for him was unusually stern and adamant.

"Since when is that the way things are decided around here?" Mother said.

We got through the meal in silence, but afterward Mother and Father went into their bedroom and closed the door. I listened against the wall.

Mother accused my father of impracticality, not a new charge, with his "crazy academic" ambitions for me. What did he have in mind, turning me into a man? Here everyone thought I was born for the stage, and he was taking away the one thing that might give me some security in life. And besides, wealthy men were always attracted to pretty actresses. It was about the only way a young woman from my background could move up in the world.

I was not pleased at having Mother for an ally. What she was saying had nothing to do with what I loved about the stage.

Father was the calmer of the two. As he explained himself, Mother interrupted, but he ploughed ahead, outlining his position in such an orderly fashion that I could tell he had thought it through carefully. I was getting to an age, he said, when he did not want me hanging around the theater. All kinds of things could happen behind that curtain; Mother knew that and should take it into account. There was a looseness to the lives of theater people, irregularities that he did not want his daughter exposed to.

I knew what he meant. Mother must have, too, because she became silent. My father continued that if, after I reached a certain maturity, I still wanted to return to the stage in a serious way—say, to try my luck at dramatic acting—that would be fine with him. But not now. Mother should face the fact that my appeal from the beginning had been one of novelty, not any particular brilliance or skill. I was a pretty child, which was all the more reason for protecting me. Did Mother understand now? Was he being quite clear?

Furthermore, Father added, Mother did not understand that the world was changing. Privileged women were being educated in all the civilized countries. Her ideas, if he could be permitted to say so, were becoming outdated.

"What do you think you know about the future?" Mother said. Her voice was full of contempt. "The future is one item you've known nothing about your whole life long."

"The matter is closed," Father said.

I would miss the stage, but I was willing to try Father's way. His confidence in his opinions, the serenity with which he expounded his arguments, reminded me of some great actor playing a role of authority. His newfound prosperity must have given him the courage to master the part.

So it was that I came to devote myself full time to my work at St. Catherine's, the Episcopal girls' school Father selected. I threw myself into my studies. If I was precocious, it must have been because of the hours Father had spent with me reading and talking, giving me the sense that I was, improbably, his equal. If he wanted me to be a student, I was anxious not to disappoint him.

I believe I must have been a little horror, the sort of child others resent and despise. I excelled in everything but arithmetic, dazzling my teachers and infuriating my schoolmates with my vocabulary and literary and historical references, and most of all my grown-up airs. Where the other girls blushed and stammered when called on to recite, I performed with the bravado and flourish of the old trouper I was—although this time I was careful to conceal my theatrical connections. The school authorities must have known what Father's profession was, but at least I was not any longer that despicable thing, an actress.

No matter, my schoolmates despised me anyway! With one or two exceptions; exactly the girls I wanted nothing to do with, brains like me. As for the rest, I can still see a slender girl, pretty if overbred, no doubt the daughter of some Yale man, the heiress to a meat-packing fortune, sticking out her tongue at me and telling me how obnoxious I was for showing up the others on a geography quiz.

I recall a birthday party early in the term. I was invited because everyone was, all twenty girls in our class. (A boys' school, St. Dunstan's, was associated with St. Cat's, but there was little interaction at the lower levels.) I agonized over what to bring as a present; against Mother's advice I settled on a small stuffed llama that was one of my souvenirs. I thought its uniqueness would impress the birthday girl. Wrong! The llama stood out among the conventional gifts of silk ribbons and insipid storybooks. The girl held it up at arm's length, suffered my explanation of its exotic origins, put it down on its side, and ignored it and me.

The party took place in a grand five-story house somewhere in the Eighties off Madison that had the atmosphere of a funeral parlor for the rich. In our finery we sat at a table the length of a railroad car through a lunch of tea sandwiches, sherbets, and white cake. A pianist and a violinist played, and afterward to my surprise, girls got up to dance with one another under the direction of a crone identified as a dancing mistress. "Everyone's a member of Miss Whittle's cotillion. You must join." I found fox-trotting with my dishwater-blond partner unromantic. Out of the embarrassment and boredom that compel such things, I managed to commit a major gaffe.

I approached the musicians, with whom I felt an affinity, and asked if they could play a tango. They struck one up, bringing everyone to a standstill, except me. I tried to glide my partner into the rhythm of the thing, gave up, and broke free, striding back and forth across the floor in imitation of what I had loved and admired in Argentina. I must have looked like a tiny female Groucho Marx (wasn't his walk a tango parody?). I stopped when I heard Miss Whittle's grave voice:

"We have not done that dance. We'll return to something more appropriate, shall we?"

When I got home, I told Father that my schoolmates lived in a world I did not understand. He said that he was sure things would work out and suggested that I invite some of the girls to lunch at our apartment.

I did not tell him that near the end of the party, when I was sitting by myself with a soda, the mother of the birthday girl had come over, chatted with me in what I thought was a blessedly friendly fashion for a moment, and then had asked me about my family, where we were originally from, where we lived, and finally what my father did for a living. When, feeling defiant, I said that he managed theaters and actors and even uttered the word vaudeville, she said icily that that was "very interesting," turned her back, and walked off.

Yet I was not entirely unhappy at St. Cat's. During the next week at school a couple of the girls asked about the funny dance I had done and had me show them how to tango. At least they thought I was amusing. The misery of being odd was counterbalanced by my teachers' praise and Father's pride when he learned that my grades were the best in the class.

Nor was my connection to the theater totally cut. Harry Valentine still came to dinner, as did other performers along with various show-business people, writers and directors. Mother tolerated Harry's shenanigans more than before, especially when he played the Continental gentleman, bringing her flowers, praising her table, toasting her, and pretending to be smitten with Edna, who blushed when he invited her to run away with him to the Côte d'Azur, where they could live on his yacht and hobnob with the decadent.

I loved the theater people. They were so loud and funny and full of life, and I vowed that one day I'd return to them.

7

*H*arry came to our first New York Thanksgiving dinner: it was my idea; he had hinted to me that he was dreading being alone. Grandmother Nell and Grandfather Bill arrived from Kansas City, and Father astonished them by putting them up at the Hotel Pierre.

I helped Edna prepare oyster dressing. We sat down to eat late in the afternoon, after the men had drunk some whiskey amid talk of Prohibition. My father condemned the legislation as an assault on personal liberty, but said that if it made actors sober, it would have one benefit. Harry replied cheerfully that he already had a bootlegger and would be happy to supply Father with the name. At the table Grandfather told me that I wrote fine letters and that when I grew up he could get me a job on one of the Kansas City papers. The editor had been a railroader, and there were already a couple of girls working as reporters.

"Margaret's a New Yorker now," Father said.

I wasn't positive about that. What I liked best about New York were the plays and the movies and the view from my room. I watched sunsets from up there, waiting for the boats on the river to switch on their lights.

"Find a nice young man with a bright future and you can live anywhere," Nell said. "Europe. There are many magnificent estates."

"I'm going to stay put," Grandfather said. "People ought to stay where they belong. I see in the paper where the Japs is fixing to take over California." Grandfather had that morning read a *New York Times* editorial warning against the mongrelization of the white race. The Japanese were breeding a colony in the plantations of Hawaii and would soon invade the mainland.

"Who said anything about Japan?" Nell asked. "I am talking about beautiful homes, about getting what a person deserves. There is nothing worse than being stuck in one place with no money. You might as well curl up your toes and die." She dropped a fist on the table. "Opportunity knocks once! You better be ready!"

"Have some mashed potatoes, Nell," my father said. "Care for a pick of the dark meat?"

"I'll pour some wine," Harry said, reaching across to Nell with the bottle.

She shrank as if from arsenic and turned her glass upside down.

"Neither wine nor beer nor spirits have ever passed these lips," she said. "I am sorry to see that the same cannot be said for other people at this table. My husband, I notice, took three, count them, three, drinks before dinner. I am glad he is not driving a train. And you, E.P., giving wine to a child! Do you know that there is nothing more disgraceful than a drunken woman? Do you want to see Margaret ruined?" She pronounced it "ruint."

"Why, Mrs. Hinson," Harry said. "And here I took you for a tippler! Tell us the truth, my darlingness, what were you doing down by the cooking sherry? I saw you, Mrs. Slyboots!" He cast her a wink and poured freely into Grandfather's glass.

At this Mother burst out laughing. Her merriment was so unexpected that she surprised herself, covering her mouth with her napkin. Father gazed at her with affection. Mother bowed her head as if to pray and pressed the foot-buzzer that summoned Edna.

* * *

Just after Christmas, E.P. fell ill. It had been a fine holiday, with a big party at our apartment for theater people, everyone singing carols and Harry playing Santa. Christmas Day we spent quietly together opening presents, Mother wearing her new fox coat around the house. Father's cough was worse than usual, however, and by late afternoon he was in bed.

He did not get up the next morning. Mother summoned the doctor, who diagnosed a mild case of influenza. A day later, when Father began coughing up blood, the doctor revised his diagnosis.

A tubercular infection, inactive for years, had returned. E.P. was to have complete bedrest. The doctor cautioned us not to go near Father when he was coughing and to wear surgical masks whenever we approached him. There was talk of sending him to a sanitarium, but he insisted that he would be all right if permitted to rest for a couple of weeks. He told us that he had endured a similar attack in his youth. He had been working as a handyman, constructing sets, cleaning up, trimming lights, being in general a hauler and drawer for a theater in Montreal. Meanwhile he had been sleeping in the unheated storeroom at the rear of his uncle's grocery shop. When he could not sleep from the cold, he said, he would stay awake most of the night reading books from the library, which was how he had educated himself. To try to keep warm, he would act out plays or scenes from novels, hopping about in the storeroom, wrapped in sacks he pretended were costumes. But he had paid a price. Had the owner of the theater not taken care of the bill for rest and recuperation, who knew what would have happened to him?

Father maintained that what he was undergoing now was nothing but a minor recurrence. When he was well, he would make one concession to his illness. He would curtail his practice of walking the thirty or so blocks home from his theaters in the wintry air.

I looked up tuberculosis in my *Britannica* and was frightened. I developed a dull, sympathetic pain that crept upward from my chest to my throat and started coughing all the time until Mother told me to stop if I didn't wish to see the doctor. *Jane,* I wrote, *I know that Father is not going to die, but it is terrible to see him weak and suffering. He is the best father in the world.* I tried my hand at verse:

> Whenever you're around me,
> My father sweet and dear,
> The angels of heaven surround me
> And I have nothing to fear.
>
> God I know will make you well,
> And send tuberculosis down to hell.

I knew I was as worried for myself as for him. I tried not to think of what might happen if he died, but I could not help wondering, selfish as my speculations were.

Mother moved across the hall into the spare room. Wanting to show my love for him, I decided that I could do for him what he had always done for me. In the evenings I stationed myself in a chair by his door and read aloud to him across the room, mostly Shakespeare and Kipling's poems. Mother would go in to change the damp towels to try to cool him off; he was running a high fever. He had his beloved Peruvian vicuna blanket tucked up under his beard; and he was surrounded by other objects precious to him—on one wall a pair of Argentine silver spurs given to him by the mayor of Buenos Aires; a sombrero from his trip to California; on another wall a photograph of the Garden Theater with a big crowd outside and "E. P. Spencer Presents" on the marquee. I'd read to him for an hour and tell him that he would be better in the morning. His coughing woke me in the night.

Mother blamed his condition on the excitements of our new life—too many parties and too much drinking. When I asked her to tell me more of what she knew about Father's youth, she said that I was like the little boy who had dug so deep that he discovered a buried treasure. He was a poor child and had never owned a pair of shoes. He went to town to buy a pair of beautiful red boots, and he was arrested and thrown in jail for twenty years for having stolen the gold. Did I know that story? I should remember it and think about it. Common sense taught us that we should leave well enough alone and accept what God gave us rather than dig where we did not belong.

Father had been in bed for about ten days when, one morning as I was off to school, he summoned me to his bedside. In a raspy voice, short of breath, he told me that he had had a wonderful dream. He had been in the audience for a performance of *The Tempest,* but he had also been onstage. I was playing Miranda to his Prospero. The set was not a set, it was real, an island with white beaches and a clear green sea. The notes of a flute floated through the warm air. When he came upon me playing chess with Ferdinand, he blessed us and was overcome with happiness.

I had neither seen nor read the play, but this sounded like a pleasant dream. Who was Ferdinand, I asked him, and was he handsome?

"A prince," Father answered, trying to catch his breath. "The king of Naples' son. He was handsome and kind."

"Did we get married?"

"You did. Then you sailed to Naples in a barque and lived in the palace. You were happy and made everyone else happy. Everyone loved you. Your subjects brought you baskets of fruit and flowers on your birthday, and you sang to them from a balcony."

I told Jane my father's dream. Now I wonder whether he made it up—it sounds too tidy—but who knows? It was a different version of what he imagined for me from his usual one of the self-reliant woman of the world, hunting microbes or writing novels or whatever. That was the way he was, desiring everything for me, wildly impractical—or perhaps in his way he did know what was best, dreaming contradictory things, the moon and stars and a house and garden, independence and a rich husband. That day he began hemorrhaging. I arrived home from St. Cat's to find the doctor in his room with the door shut. A nurse arrived to tend to him. When the doctor emerged, he shut the bedroom door again, leaving the nurse inside and advising Mother and me to stay out.

I took up my post in the hallway and would not be budged. I sat on the floor, scrunching myself up against the wall. The nurse carried towels in and out. Mother remained in her room except to come out and insist that I get to bed.

I resumed my vigil after Mother was asleep. Edna found me in the night and sat down beside me and put her arms around me while I cried. We said prayers together until she coaxed me to bed.

The sound of the doctor's voice awoke me early in the morning. I found him in the living room, filling out papers.

Edna, holding my hand, took me in for a last look at Father. We agreed that he had gone straight to heaven.

A hundred or more mourners joined us in the church. I sat between Mother and Nell in a front pew. Nell had come East for the funeral, but Grandfather had stayed behind in Kansas City, probably because there wasn't enough money for both of them to make the trip. The minister's eulogy was a pastiche of comments about Father solicited from those who had known him and worked with him. A good man. A man of vision. An understanding employer to whom others could turn in need. If E. P. Spencer had had a fault, it was generosity. Several of the actors who had worked for him had spoken of his loaning them money and never asking for repayment.

Mother and Nell shifted in their seats.

He was a man devoted to the theater who delighted everyone with his fondness for quoting Shakespeare, a family man with a selfless love obvious to all. The minister concluded with, " 'We are such stuff as dreams are made on, and our little life is rounded with a sleep.' "

It was a bright cold day. As we followed the hearse to Woodlawn, I wished that someone would tell me what to do or say. I felt I had no part to play.

At the gravesite Harry Valentine stood behind me holding me by the shoulders and pressing me into his soft tummy.

Margaret in Hollywood

As they lowered the coffin into the ground, I stepped forward on an impulse, knelt, and retrieved a pebble, slipping it into my pocket.

Everyone dropped by afterward in the customary way. Edna had set out a feast. I could not imagine eating, and I went to my room after kissing Harry good-bye. I felt an anger that I did not like and could not understand. I threw open my window, stuck my head into the cold air, and screamed, half-hoping that someone would hear me.

I heard the visitors departing. When Mother looked in, I pretended to be asleep.

8

I returned to school the next day, but sat through my classes hearing little. My teachers were understanding, and the girls were decent enough to tell me that they were sorry to hear about my father; but in limbo would be the only term for how I felt.

That afternoon when I came home, I looked for Edna, but she was out, shopping, I presumed. When I sat down to dinner with Mother and Nell, Edna was still gone. I asked after her.

"I have sent her away, Mother said.

"She'll be back tomorrow?"

"No, she has been dismissed. Eat your soup, I don't wish to discuss it."

Back in my room I was too worn out to cry over Edna. I ran my hand over books Father had given me and heard voices from the living room, Mother's rising and falling, Nell's in response. I had to find out what they were talking about.

I had a listening post for the living room. In the kitchen was a closet that passed through; sitting on the floor in the dark under the shelves, I could hear everything, even the clicking of Nell's knitting needles.

"You work and slave," Mother was saying, "and for what?"

They were discussing Father's will, which was evidently a source of disappointment. He had left everything to his "beloved wife, Alice." Mother was dwelling on the phrase.

" 'Beloved wife' is not at all grateful, thank you very much. He was always good with words."

"Never trust a fancy tongue," Nell said.

Mother must have had the will in her hands. She read out "all my worldly goods" and said bitterly that these amounted to six hundred dollars in the bank account and our furniture. There were no savings, no investments, no pension. And no life insurance.

She had asked about insurance, more than once, and he had told her not to worry. His contract with the Shuberts would take care of everything. What lies! "And you, Mother, you ought to have protected me. You should have known he'd been consumptive as a young man."

Nell defended herself. What was she to have done? Should she have hired a Pinkerton man? There were limits to a parent's responsibilities. Life was full of suffering. Look at her own, washing, cleaning, cooking, and waiting for pin money. Nell's needles clicked furiously.

"The bastard!" Mother spat.

"Alice!"

"He was one. Making everyone love him. Throwing money around he didn't have. Spoiling the child. He never mentioned his parents, you know. I think he must have been found in some lumberyard. I wouldn't be surprised if his mother was a whore [pronounced *hoor*]. I can tell you one thing, he was no one-hundred-percent American, that much is as plain as the nose on your face."

"That is very strong language," Nell said.

"Stingy Jew bastard, is what he was!"

"Oh! Why would you say such things?"

"How should I know what he was?" Mother said. "He may as well have been one. Didn't he get on so well with all those New York Jews? Of course, they left him penniless."

"You had high times, Alice."

"And what am I supposed to do now? Tell me that!"

"Better than I've known," Nell said. "Your own father doesn't even own a decent set of clothes."

"I'll trade you E.P.'s suits for your pension."

"We have always saved, it's true. I saw to that. Work hard in the summers, for the winters are long and hard." Nell suggested that perhaps Mother should take advantage of her sewing skills. There was always a demand for costumes in New York. She had all the contacts. And she could add to her income by making those silk lampshades that were so popular, the ones with the tiny roses along the borders.

I heard something crash to the floor or against a wall. It must have been a lamp, because Mother shouted, "That's what I think of your lampshades!"

"Alice! Control yourself!"

"I have not come this far to end up in a sweatshop!"

"Shh! What about the neighbors?"

"They won't be my neighbors for long!"

"You'll wake Margaret!"

"It's about time she woke up! She's led a charmed life. It is time to pay the piper. There is going to be a revolution around here."

"Calm yourself, Alice. Have a cup of Ovaltine. We'll think of something."

"I already have," Mother said evenly. "My mind is at last made up."

She spelled out her plan. She would sell off everything of value—the china, silver, crystal, the rugs, frivolities like E.P.'s vicuna. And she would move with me into an inexpensive apartment. That would get us through the first weeks. Then she would put the second part of her plan into effect. It involved me.

She had been searching for answers in the Bible. Her courage to make a decision had come from Matthew 25.

"The parable of the mustard seed," Nell said.

"No," Mother corrected her, "the parable of the talents."

"Of course."

"I did not ask for a child. Oh, no. I did not even ask to marry. But God was watching out for me."

"I am glad you know that."

"Now, he is telling me to make good use of the child who is my talent," Mother continued, "and not to bury it in the earth."

Bury me in the earth? I made a mental note to check the text.

She outlined her divinely inspired program.

"Margaret will earn her keep. I shall guide her. I shall husband her talent and make it prosper, and thank God that He showed me the way years ago without me even knowing it. Who do you think it was that was telling me to put Margaret on the stage? Who do you think it was that was telling me not to listen to my husband?"

"It was the Lord," Nell said.

I did not mind at all the idea of going back on the stage, but the reality of Mother's plan was less glamorous than that. After we saw Nell off one morning a few days later, Mother told me to sit down in the kitchen. I would not be going to school that day.

"Some people would say that you've been a pretty lucky little girl. Some people would say you've lived like a princess. Your closet is full. Your stomach is full. Do you know that there are girls in this city, thousands and thousands of them, who wake up every morning with nothing in their stomachs and an empty cupboard?"

I said that I was grateful for everything that I had been given.

"Let me tell you something, young lady. All that is over and done with. Do you understand me? It is completely and utterly finished."

Mother explained that there were two kinds of people in the world, those who worked for what they had and those who had things handed to them. The ones who had it handed to them were called spoiled rotten, and the ones who worked hard were called God's children. God's children prospered and went to heaven, and spoiled rottens failed, led miserable lives, and went straight to hell. If I kept on the way I was, I would be damned. From now on I would have to work very hard for everything I got.

Did I know what hell was? Hell was eternal torment. Hell

78

was having no home on earth and no rest after death. Hell was freezing and boiling and never any peace.

What worried and frightened me were less the threats of damnation than my mother's intensity. Her voice was as angry as it had been the other night ranting to Nell. She fixed her eyes on me until I had to look away. She kept poking me in the arm with her finger. I told myself that my father's death had unhinged her and that I would have to find a way to cheer her up—but for the moment I could think of nothing to say. I gripped the hard seat of the chair and twisted my legs together to brace against the storm.

Very soon I would be entering a different school, Mother went on, her tone making it clear that this was an accomplished fact. It was called the Professional Children's School, and it was designed so that students could work in the theater and in related fields and still keep up with their studies.

I saw my chance.

"You mean I get to go on the stage again?" I said, trying to sound as if I had been handed an ice cream. "Do I?" I clapped my hands and wondered if I was overdoing it. I was willing to try anything to get Mother down from her pulpit. It didn't work.

"Not so fast, young lady, not so fast." I looked into her face and saw her smile unpleasantly. "So you think everything comes easily in this world, do you? You think you can just snap your fingers and have what you want. You seem to have forgotten that you don't have a father anymore who's deciding who goes on and who doesn't. Let me tell you, you've a few lessons to learn. No, you cannot just go on the stage. You have to earn it. You think because you could shuffle your feet and look cute that every manager in New York is going to be breaking down your door?"

Mother explained what a model was and how she was going to try to get me jobs modeling clothing for department-store advertisements. She would arrange for my auditions. She had already made a few inquiries. I would have a series of photographs taken, and she would send them around. There was no time to waste. Soon enough there would be bills to pay and nothing in the bank. My father had died broke, did I understand that? The great man had left his wife and daughter next to nothing. Let that be a lesson to me, never to trust anyone. Self-reliance, that was what she was going to teach me.

Shortly we would be moving to a smaller apartment. Much smaller. There would be no luxuries. I would have to earn whatever I had.

"I promise to be good," I said.

"That's what I want to hear. That's a good girl. I don't want to hear any complaints. I have enough burdens. This isn't going to be easy on me."

It took me quite a while to absorb the changes that took place—I mean not only in our physical circumstances but in Mother. It was as if in a matter of a few days or weeks I went from being her daughter to becoming her employee—but that was an analysis of which I was incapable at the time.

I never did return to St. Cat's. Mother sorted through my clothes and told me to fit everything into two suitcases. I was to take only four or five of the books most precious to me and to leave most of my toys and dolls behind. In the end I kept only my Raggedy Ann and the pair of Argentine dancers in the box that hid Jane.

When I asked Mother where our new place was and what it was like, she told me that I had been born under the sign of Jupiter, and that as a Sagittarius I was cursed with an overabundance of curiosity. I had heard her natter on about astrology before and remembered Father kidding her about it. She added that E.P. had also been a Sagittarius, which explained his impracticality. Sagittarians were dreamers who spent money like water. I would have to watch this element in my character, or I would end up a sorry creature indeed.

"But I thought God gave us free will," I said. "I thought we could be anything we wished. You mean to say the stars tell me what I am?"

"Finish packing and stop asking questions about things you don't understand."

I wanted to look up Sagittarians in my *Britannica,* but it was already in a box, ready to be carted away to the auction. I hoped that the same people who bought it would take my father's things.

At last moving day came. The men from the auction house arrived; I watched them dismantle my bed and carry it out, and I wondered what my new bed would be like—not as grand, I was sure, but perhaps as soft. When the apartment was empty and echoing with our footsteps, I stood at my window looking out at the park and the river. Then I saw a taxi pull up. Mother called that it was time.

The doorman and the driver helped us with our bags. I carried my Argentine box. When the doorman kissed me on the cheek, I started crying. Mother bundled me into the cab, and we were away.

It was a ride of only twenty blocks or so, but to a different world. Our new apartment was on Fifty-fourth Street, just off Seventh Avenue, and the streets were dark and close after the open air of Riverside. As the driver unloaded our things, I searched around the entryway for the elevator. When I told Mother that I couldn't find it, she said that there wasn't one and that I should start up the stairs. Our place was on the sixth floor. The stairwell was heavy with a cabbagy smell. I heard Mother having words with the taximan and agreeing to a bigger tip if he would help us all those flights with our belongings. For the first time, I felt sorry for her and realized that she was having to do things Father had always taken care of. I only wished she could leave her bad temper behind.

I had the silliest fantasy that when I reached our floor, Father would be there and my bed would be waiting for me in my new room. The fantasy evaporated. At first I thought I must have the wrong apartment. One room and a bath. Furnished with a deal dresser and table, a couple of lamps, two straight chairs, a ratty easy chair, and against one wall a sink, a small stove, and an icebox. A strip of lino indicated the kitchen. The one window opened on an air shaft.

In the few moments I had to look around before Mother

81

made it up the stairs, one panicky thought overrode my disappointment in the place: how was I going to write to Jane under these circumstances?

When all the bags were inside, Mother sat down in the easy chair, out of breath and looking grim. I came over to kiss her; she let me but closed her eyes.

"I've torn my coat," she sighed, and showed me where a nail had ripped it. "It's a good thing I sold the fox. I would've ruined it and got nothing for it. See that door? Open it, but be careful, there's a bed in there. Don't let it fall on you. That's all we'd need."

I had never seen a Murphy bed before. I thought it was kind of fun, but I asked where the other bed was. Was this one for her or for me?

"We'll be sharing it," Mother said. "We'll be sharing a great many things now. Don't look so shocked, Miss Princess. There are other people in this building sleeping three and four to a bed. Sheets and blankets are in that bag there. We'll make it up. Come on, let's get organized."

There was already a bedspread on. I drew it back and let out a yelp. An extended family of bugs had already made their home there.

"Oooogh!" I said as I backed away. "What *are* they?"

"You mean you've never seen a bedbug? No, I guess you haven't. Well, introduce yourself. I'll go find something to get rid of them."

She opened the door to leave. I asked if I had to stay there alone.

"Yes, you do. Don't worry. They won't eat you."

I covered them up so I would not have to look at them. I was convinced that the building was alive with vermin and that all its tenants must be bug-ridden and that before the night was over I would be, too. I imagined bugs staring at me. I couldn't stand it. I waited for Mother on the landing.

She returned with a bottle of kerosene. She soaked a rag with it, pulled back the spread, and rubbed at the mattress. The smell was powerful.

"Won't that make the bed stink?" I asked.

"Which would you rather have, bugs or an unpleasant odor for a few days? Don't drop any lighted matches on it, or we'll go up in smoke."

Mother knelt down and applied the stuff along the base-boards and the bottoms of doors. I opened the window and tried to breathe.

"You may have the bottom two drawers and half the closet," Mother said. "I want you to get plenty of sleep so you can look your best. I've arranged an important appointment for you in the morning."

Act Two

9

*F*or Mother, getting me accustomed to my new life must have been like training an animal. She proved equal to the task.

She had my clothes laid out for me the next morning when I emerged groggy from the bath. Our smelly, crowded bed and the sounds of her slumber had kept me awake; and unclear about what was being asked of me, I listened to her pep talk as I was getting dressed. She showed me advertisements to give me an idea of the job ahead of me. I was so ignorant of life that I had had no idea that children were actually paid to put on someone else's clothes and stand there. It seemed quite a few steps down from acting and dancing and singing. She could tell that the idea of having my picture taken for the sole purpose of exciting people to shop did not arouse my enthusiasm.

"I don't care for that expression. Let me see a smile on your face. I want you to think, This is a brand-new morning, and I am going to do something that is going to make Mother proud of me. Are you listening to me, Margaret?"

Concentrating on her nose so I would not have to look into her eyes, I said nothing. She brought her face close to mine and took hold of my upper arm:

"Cheer up, dear, and learn to put on a more becoming

expression." She squeezed at my flesh, short of a pinch, the way you test a peach without bruising it.

We walked to a photographer's studio on Forty-third Street, Mother keeping up a line of chat all the way—how I should think positively and do exactly as the photographer told me.

I must have posed satisfactorily since I was rewarded with soup and a sandwich. When a messenger delivered the photographs the next day, Mother seemed pleased, more or less:

"They're fine. Not every one is as good as it could be. See this one? I call that a frown. That's what happens when a girl isn't thinking sunny thoughts."

"I was getting tired. The lights were so hot. I was thinking about lunch."

"We think about lunch when it's lunchtime. When it's work time, we think about our work. Have a song in your heart. Think a pretty melody and your eyes will dance. No one loves a grouchy girl, dear. Grouchy girls are the last ones to get ice cream and cake. Usually they get nothing at all."

This baby talk was something new. I wanted to ask her to cut it out, but she was in no mood to be challenged.

Mother selected half a dozen photos and in her formal, ornate hand wrote on the back of each:

Margaret Spencer
201 West 54th Street, No. 606
Age ------ 12 years
Weight ------ 95 lbs
Height ------ 5′0″
Eyes ------ dark brown
Hair ------ auburn, natural curls

I studied this list. I had actually just turned thirteen, but Mother thought that twelve would give me greater job flexibility. The rest of it was more or less me, toted up. The weight put me in mind of the time Grandfather had taken me to visit the stockyards. We watched men with sticks prod cows around a ring while an announcer identified breed and weight. Come to think of it, my coloring was purebred Hereford. A half-pound of rump steak, thank you very much.

I did not think the pictures looked particularly like me, and I was bothered by the obvious insincerity of my expressions, but only one embarrassed me. I was posed in profile standing in the gap between slightly parted velvet stage curtains, one hand at the top of my head as though probing for a deep thought, the other waving to the rear. The photographer had told me to think about something *profound,* and I remembered imagining a tall, frosty glass of Coca-Cola. I wore a loose-fitting short shift provided by the photographer, whose studio was crammed with costumes and props.

My legs, bare from two or three inches above the knee, curved delicately enough, but they bothered me. There was too much of them. I asked Mother if it was necessary to include this picture in the portfolio she was assembling. I didn't want my legs on show that way about town.

"It's not something to worry about," Mother said. "You do your job and I'll do mine."

I didn't care for what was going on. I had never felt so powerless: perhaps I always had been, but I had never thought about it as long as Father was around. Couldn't Mother add something a bit more dignified to my statistics, such as "Has brain, can talk?" It was not that I minded being attractive. All my life I have heard beautiful women speak of their appearance as a curse, and I have never believed them. It is true that men equate beauty with stupidity and that women are envious and spiteful toward someone better-looking. A sharp remark, however, disabuses male assumptions, and as women are inherently jealous of one another, one accepts that as a condition of existence. The photographer, who later became a wildly successful Broadway producer, told me that with my thick hair and fair skin and fine-boned features, I looked as if I would be at home in a drawing room or sipping tea on the lawn of an English manor house. I did not resent his praise.

"Don't say you're from Kansas City, darling," he advised me, placing my hair just so over my shoulder. "Say you were born in Shropshire. Shropshire has class. Kansas City's nowhere."

It was Mother's management of me that made me feel uneasy and irritated. I felt attached to her by a rope. I went more or less dutifully along, but inside I was beginning to boil.

One Saturday Mother took me to an exhibition being held underneath the Hippodrome, the largest theater in the country—or was it in the world?—seating something like six thousand. During the Wild West and other bovine and equine extravaganzas, the animals were stabled in a vast maze of stalls and pens and cages beneath the floor of the arena.

The current show, however, featured human beings of a type: midgets, or little people, as the gentler term had it. As Mother pulled me along by the hand, we wandered through a subterranean warren that had been converted into a miniature town named Toyland. Here, midgets and dwarfs—a dwarf is malformed; some of these people certainly were—pretended to go about the tasks of daily life as if they had been born and raised in caverns beneath Broadway, native troglodytes, so to speak. None of the inhabitants of Toyland, as a brochure informed us, was over four feet tall.

Toyland appeared to have been designed and laid out in imitation of a Middle European village, and was meticulously authentic save for the absence of visible squalor: thatched roofs, half-timbered facades, dirt streets, and potted shrubbery. Tiny lamps burned in windows; couples filled doorways adequate for a doghouse. When I noted that there were no midget kids in evidence, Mother explained that little people had ordinary children, who would not fit in down there.

On a stand in a mock-park, tiny lederhosened men emitted oompah-oompahs from little instruments. In his dark shop beside a stable a blacksmith with arms like lumpy summer squashes pounded glowing iron on what was labeled "World's Smallest Anvil"; a horseshoer applied this handiwork to a Shetland pony's hoof.

Mother pointed to a sign in the baker's window informing us that he was busy making shortbread.

"Isn't that adorable," she said. "Have you ever seen anything so clever and cute?"

There was even a jail. On its steps a dwarf with a hideous little shriveled-up face brandished a ring of keys menacingly and sort of growled. He wore a big black overcoat that brushed the ground and came very near to tripping him up as he paced back and forth.

I heard a cracked female voice begin to accompany the band as Mother led me toward the open market where we could buy some dwarf vegetables. She had read in the newspaper that they were delicious and cheap.

"May we leave now?" I asked, trying to slow her brisk and eager pace. "I don't feel very well."

"You know this cost a dollar and a half."

"We have to leave," I insisted. "You don't want me to up-chuck on the burgomaster, do you?"

"I don't appreciate sarcasm," Mother said. "Are you developing a warped sense of humor?"

Meanwhile I became a child model. From instinct and theatrical experience, I knew how to strike a pose and was not self-conscious with people watching me. My portfolio in hand—she added clippings from the Garden days and Buenos Aires to the new photographs—Mother had several agencies after me, and I had no trouble landing jobs.

In group shots, my head tilted just so, my body turned at a barely perceptible but eye-catching angle, I managed to stand out, the other children relegated to supporting roles. The photographers noticed this and encouraged me. Most of the sessions took place at the Underwood & Underwood studio, located in the West Thirties in a forty-story building that was called a skyscraper then and that swayed ominously, or so I thought, in the wind. The sessions lasted anywhere from two to four or five hours under blazing carbon lights. The crude Max Steiner stick makeup and the lights burned my skin, and the shoes they gave me rarely fit. To save time while I was posing—say, for a department-store catalog—the crew would seat me on a stool under the lights and rush up after a shot to change my hat and coat as I sipped on a chocolate milkshake intended, I suppose, as a pacifier. That way I would sit under those lights nonstop for an hour at a stretch. As summer arrived and we photographed the heavy fall lines in those airless, dusty rooms, sometimes I had to beg for a break.

Nowadays one hears of models, even children, receiving a hundred dollars an hour or more, with laws strictly regulating working conditions. In my era it was whatever the child would bear. I do not mean to suggest for a minute that my situation was comparable to that of a child who grew up in the coal mines or a brothel or a factory. Given a choice, I would have chosen modeling over selling newspapers or begging. It was far less onerous than farm work. The contrast with my earlier life made it seem tough.

For my good looks, my obedience, for my endurance and for keeping my mouth shut, I was paid a dollar an hour—as much as twenty-five dollars a day for modeling in the fashion shows put on by wholesalers at the Plaza and other big hotels. I enjoyed working the shows, relatively speaking, because the lights were less brutal and it was more like being onstage, complete with applause. The dollar being worth some ten times as much then as now, I was paid well. Of course I kept none of the money. Mother took care of that end of things.

She did confide after several months that we had accumulated enough for her to open a savings account—for a rainy day, she said, in case I fell ill and couldn't work. Soon we were eating meat two and three times a week. That my labors showed a profit was hardly surprising, because from March well into September of that year I did nothing but work. There would be time enough, Mother said, to start my new school in the fall. I worried that I would find myself behind the other students, but with Mother it was work first, school second, and I was not to get my priorities mixed. Pipe dreams of college were over.

"I knew a man once," Mother said, "who wanted to go to college. But guess what? He found out that college was not on the agenda. There happened to be no such item in his father's budget. So do you know what the man did? He went out and started a bicycle factory. He began by fixing bicycles, and today he is one of the richest men in Missouri. He lives in a mansion with servants. Remember that."

"What? To start a bicycle factory?"

"You are headed for trouble," Mother said.

I became dull in my mind. It was not, as Mother said, that I believed that the world owed me a living, but I thought it owed me a better living than this. I had no energy to read, scarcely enough to write to Jane, little interest in anything. I began to hate what I was becoming.

I made my move one scorching morning in July after the Fourth, when Mother took me down to the docks to watch the celebration. Everyone said the fireworks were spectacular. I had no reaction at all except boredom.

At home I smuggled Jane into the bathroom and wrote one line: *I hate the Fourth of July.* I knew that was perverse, but I couldn't help myself. I was thinking about having to go to work the next day.

I awoke in a foul temper. Mother said that I had tossed all night and asked what was the matter. Nothing except your hot, gross body next to me in the bed, I refrained from saying, and staggered to the bath. I had morning and afternoon sessions scheduled. I looked in the mirror and stuck out my tongue. Maybe if I disfigured myself, I wouldn't have to work.

By noon it was in the 90s outside, and God knew what it must have been under the Underwood & Underwood lights. Here I was dressed in a double-breasted wool overcoat and a wool hat trying to look like Christmas. By the end of the day I had worked myself into a mass of resentment, and it showed. The photographer kept imploring me to sweeten my expression, and inquired if I was ill.

I picked at the salad Mother fixed for dinner, turning my face to the wall and studying stains on the wallpaper. Mother took away my plate and announced that I was going to bed.

The impulse to strike must be inborn. In the morning I refused to get out of bed. Mother's reaction was swift. She ripped off the covers and ordered me to turn over and pull up my nightgown. I refused to do this, holding fast as she took the hairbrush from the set E.P. had given her as an anniversary present and whacked me with it until I begged for mercy. My nightgown protected me, it didn't hurt that much, but she had never beaten me like that before, and Father had never touched me. I could hear her grunt with each blow. She stopped when the cameo adorning the back of the brush fell out.

"I'll have to glue this," she said, panting. "See what happens when you don't do what you're told?"

I refused to cry. I lay there feeling my bottom throb slightly. I think she knew I was too old for this. Then I felt her sit down on the end of the bed and heard her begin to weep.

"I am only doing what I have to do," she said between sobs. "Please try to understand." I looked around. She was holding her face between her hands. Her eyes rolled up toward the ceiling. "I hadn't counted on this. I didn't ask to be left without a penny. You must understand! You've got to! Oh, God, what am I going to do?"

I felt sorry for her and guilty. I looked around the room, so bare, so sparse, and had a sense of having let her down. Wouldn't Father want me to help her?

She continued on about her plight, our plight, running her hands through her hair. She had prayed, oh, how she had prayed. She had heard God's voice telling her what to do, even if it was hard on her, on me. What she really wanted for me was to be happy and successful, but we were being put through a great trial and had to work together.

She was working, too, didn't I see that? There was the cooking and the cleaning and finding me jobs. She was making costumes and double-silk lampshades in every spare moment. Through a new shower of tears she reminded me that it was not I who had been left in middle age with no income and a child to raise. I had my entire life before me. If I didn't want to end up like her, I would get ahead and not have to depend on some man who would run off with a younger woman or drop dead.

I was young and youthful and pretty. I had strength. Perhaps I was even talented, who could say? Someday I might thank her for encouraging me to go on the stage when my father had been against it. I might even thank her for getting me the work I was so resentful about now.

Then, with several heaving sobs, she lay her head down on the bed at my feet.

I inched down to her and took her head in my hands and we had a long sob together.

It felt good to get close to her that way. She stroked me gently where she thought she had hurt me.

Afterward she fixed me a glass of lemonade, and I got dressed and went to work. That night we held each other in the bed.

6

*T*here must have been other, comparable loving scenes with Mother, although none comes to mind. I think that we established a kind of unwritten, unspoken Treaty of Versailles between us, except that she was more successful than the Allies in reducing me to the status of a tenant farmer.

Perhaps I overstate the case. Maybe life did brighten after that expression of mutual sympathies. Certainly I accepted to a greater degree the necessity of my working, although I took no pleasure in it. I observed that the other children spending days under the lights were no happier about it than I; I had an urge to make friends with them, but our schedules allowed only fleeting conversations.

My chief delights came on those free Saturday afternoons when Mother took me to see a play or a movie. I wrote the titles and a comment about each of these in my diary, but I remember most vividly the films of Mary Pickford, Charlie Chaplin, and Buster Keaton: either my taste was the same as any other person's or, like them, I was influenced by the publicity. My favorites that summer included a Buster Keaton short called *Hard Luck* and Chaplin's *The Kid*. In the latter, according to my diary, I identified with Jackie Coogan, who played the abandoned child thrust upon Chaplin. I wrote that I did not know whether to laugh or cry—which is as close as I have ever come to a philosophy.

The comedians always made me think of Harry Valentine. Where was Harry? Couldn't we go to see him perform? In time, my mother always said, not this week. I resolved to get in touch with him one way or another. I missed Harry, and I must have missed the stage.

I may have been thinking of the stage one evening when Mother announced that she was going to teach me to sew. Whether it was an aversion to Mother's situation or the inward conviction that I wanted to be an actress and would settle for nothing less, the idea of becoming a seamstress repelled me. I told her not to bother; whatever my talents, they did not include sewing.

"That is nonsense," Mother said. She held up a lampshade. "We can do it if we try."

I pretended to listen to her instructions. I plunged ahead and made as much of a botch of it as I was able without being obvious. She stood over me clucking her tongue.

"You're not paying attention. Let me show you again."

After an hour of my sabotage, she began to lose patience.

"Can't you sew a straight seam?"

"What difference does it make?" I was tiring of the game.

"What do you mean, what difference does it make? A thing not done well is not worth doing at all."

"In that case let's forget it."

"Do not take that tone with me."

"All I mean is, if I can't do it well, wouldn't it be better to stop?"

"Don't you see that I'm trying to teach you something important? What man would want a wife who couldn't sew and cook a meal and sweep a floor? He'd throw you out in the street, believe you me."

I found her inconsistency maddening. My voice began to rise. I couldn't help it.

"I thought you told me not to depend on men. Now, you're telling me to sew so I can please my husband." I could feel the pulse in my temple. I don't know why I chose to draw the line there; something was telling me to take a stand.

"Why don't we make an agreement," I said. "I'll do the modeling, and you do the sewing."

"I'll decide what agreements are made around here. You'll finish that edge before you go to bed."

"I'm not going to bed."

"Just what do you mean by that?"

"I'm not going, because the bugs are back." This was untrue. At the first hint of bedbugs Mother always placed the bed's legs in empty soup tins half-filled with kerosene. It was a foul but effective preventive. "I've decided not to sleep with *vermin*."

Mother strode over to the sink and picked up the soap. I was not about to let that happen again. I dropped my handiwork, rushed to the bathroom, and locked the door. I lay down on the floor and threw what could fairly be called a tantrum, banging my feet against the door as hard as I could. I set up a terrific racket and kept it up for some minutes.

When I emerged, Mother was sewing on the shade I had discarded. I climbed into bed, and nothing more was said.

The next Sunday, Mother was at me again as if my protest had counted for nothing. I was determined not to let her wear me down. I deliberately pricked my finger and bled on the material, sending her into a fury over the waste and expense. She did not ask me to sew again.

We had other skirmishes. I do not mean to say that we quarreled constantly—I did not have the energy for that—but the peace I had felt on the night we had held each other never returned. The next time I tried my foot-banging routine, I emerged from the bathroom to find Mother gone. She returned within the hour, gripping what she described as a present for me from Central Park. It was something between a limb and a twig, which she applied to my calves, a remedy her own mother had taught her, she said. I had to beg her to stop. From then on she left the switch in a corner as a visible deterrent. A gesture toward it was enough to have me mumbling apologies.

A boy my age might have threatened physical retaliation,

but that did not seem to be an option for me. Instead I tried a form of passive resistance. But if I was a forerunner of Gandhi and Martin Luther King, my approach proved less successful.

In a ploy calculated to avoid going to work, I tried to become sick by refusing to have a bowel movement. I believed that if I held it in long enough, I would burst and make my point in the strongest possible way. After two or three days Mother remarked that my color was bad. I was green. I assumed a pitiable expression.

I kept this up, or rather in, for nearly a week, until the photographers and others at Underwood & Underwood told Mother to take me to a doctor. It was the same man who had tended Father. His powers of diagnosis and cure were greater this time. He prescribed castor oil, and that was that.

I was pretty well tamed, resigned to my new way of life until, as I never gave up believing, it would one day change for the better. In October the new school term began. It saved my life or, not to exaggerate, at least my soul.

The Professional Children's School had been started in 1913, when Deaconess Jane Hall of the Episcopal Church of the Transfiguration came upon some child actors rehearsing a play. She was distressed to discover that most of them were illiterate and that none had had any education whatsoever. With admirable zeal she soon organized the first classes of the school, with herself and other idealists in charge.

Of course, there have been virtually illiterate actors who have made a success; nor has ignorance ever been a barrier to triumph in show business—it is arguably an advantage. It's when show business no longer wants you, that's the thing to worry about. An out-of-work, uneducated actor is no better equipped to face life than . . . my mother was.

As PCS flourished, it moved to several different locations around New York. By 1920 it was established in a large private house at Seventy-second Street and Riverside Drive. When Mother informed me that I would be attending the school, I

100

knew nothing about it. I may well have assumed that it had something to do with teaching one how to become a professional child in the literal sense, as in a professional acrobat or mechanic—classes in table manners, keeping silent, curtsying, with maybe some ballroom dancing thrown in. When I read about its origins some years after I had left the place, I was moved to think what might have happened to me without it.

Mother accompanied me on the first day. I had to keep my emotions in check at the sight of the neighborhood; I wondered if Mother felt the same. I strained to see our old building up the street, and from the outside the school itself looked something like the Glanmore Arms.

We went to see the principal, Mrs. Nesbitt, in her office, a room bright with theatrical posters. A kindly sort of older woman, she told us that admission was restricted to children "engaged in some sort of theatrical work." She understood that I was modeling, that I had formerly been on the stage, and that I might be looking for stage work. She referred to a letter Mother had sent her.

"We like to think that, once you're on the stage," Mrs. Nesbitt said with a smile, "you never leave it, or it you. We think that you're engaged in theatrical work for the rest of your life, even when you're idle." She addressed me, not Mother. "Do you wish to become an actress, Margaret?"

"Oh, yes!" I burst out. "I do! I want to become a very great actress, if I can."

It was my voice, but it was as if some bold creature within me had spoken. I was not conscious of having already formulated so definite an ambition in my mind, but I must have, sitting in a darkened cinematograph (to use the quaint old term) or theater, imagining myself as this or that character.

"Sometimes our reach exceeds our grasp," Mother put in.

"There is nothing wrong with ambition," Mrs. Nesbitt said. "We tell all our children that no one ever achieves anything without ambition. Of course, there are disappointments. Unless you have disappointments, you haven't tried for much of anything. In that case you probably have no business in the theater, or in much of anything else in life."

I could have kissed her. She made me feel as if the sun had burst through. I knew then where my heart was.

Mrs. Nesbitt explained how the school operated. There were about 250 children enrolled. Of these, about half were engaged in work that made it impossible for them to attend classes regularly. The weekly lessons were sent out each Monday, to be completed at home and returned by the following Monday, corrected and annotated by the teachers within one or two days. Failure to keep up resulted in dismissal from the school and the withdrawal of the child's work permit. Mrs. Nesbitt wanted to know what sort of work schedule I had planned for the next two weeks. I turned to Mother.

"She has steady modeling work," Mother said. "I have been able to secure that for her."

Mrs. Nesbitt said that it would be better if I could attend regular classes for at least the first two weeks. That way the teachers would be able to evaluate me, I could see what would be required of me and get what help I needed, and I could get to know some of the students.

"But under normal circumstances, Margaret will be free to miss classes?" Mother asked. "In order to pursue professional opportunities?"

They had a lenient policy, Mrs. Nesbitt said. I could miss classes to look for work and I could attend auditions, just so I kept up with my studies by correspondence and attended class when I could. One of the goals of PCS was to have the children grow up as normally as possible, to know other children and to participate in school activities. They had a drama program. She was sure I'd be interested in that.

"I am very much a believer in what is normal," Mother said.

"Then Margaret will be attending classes for the first two weeks?"

"If you think it's advisable," Mother said.

That evening Mother complained that she would have to dip into her savings to get us through the two weeks without a paycheck. With a sigh she acknowledged that she would be able to manage and launched into one of her litanies about the dire consequences should I have been motherless.

Having a mother seemed to me more the rule than the exception. I thought having my own bed ought not to lie beyond my grasp, either. Throw in art, drama, beauty, and a fair amount of money, and you would hear no complaints from me. I didn't see why I should be an American for nothing.

PCS ran from kindergarten through high school. I suffered from the usual jitters entering a new school, but I could tell at once that these children were kindred spirits. I saw the difference at once, a show of self-confidence, a touch of flamboyance about them that marked them as performers all. On my first day in class, however, I made a blunder.

The French teacher, Madame Roussan, called on me to read out some simple phrase. She corrected my pronunciation, I repeated after her, and she complimented me on my improvement.

"Thank you, Mother," I blurted. Most of the class guffawed. I lowered my eyes and studied the initials carved on my desktop.

"You are fools to laugh at her," Madame Roussan said. "You are all my children for a few hours each day, it pleases me to believe. I am sure that Mademoiselle Spencer loves her mother very much. One should never laugh at a mistake that comes from the heart."

I was gratified by this defense, made all the more eloquent by the liquid syllables of Madame's accent. I knew why I had made the error. Mother and I had been together twenty-four hours a day for months. I had scarcely spoken to another soul. For all the balm of Madame Roussan's words, I still felt like crawling under my desk, however, and I wondered if the other children would despise me for being protected by the teacher that way.

Imagine my relief, then, when the girl seated across the aisle slipped me a note saying, *Don't feel bad! I've done ten times worse! See you after class!* I looked over and she was smiling at me, a bright, toothy smile in a dark face.

Her name was Rhoda Meyer. We had a chance to introduce

ourselves between classes. We were about the same size, but in every other respect we were physical opposites, she as dark as I was fair. Her skin was caramel.

"Are you a singer or a dancer?" she asked me.

"I think I want to be an actress."

"Wonderful! So do I! Maybe we can be friends." She wrote out her telephone number on a piece of paper torn from her notebook and asked for mine. I said we didn't have our own phone. There was one at the bottom of the stairs.

"Well," Rhoda said, "if it rings, you'll know it's me."

I explained that it rang all the time and that only the tenants on the lower floors answered it. But we would probably be getting a telephone soon.

"You'll have to call *me,* then," Rhoda said. "Call me tonight. Promise!"

"Promise," I said.

When I got home that afternoon, Mother asked me how the day had gone. I didn't tell her about my mistake in French class. I said that it had been a wonderful day and that I thought I had made a friend.

"A girl, I presume," Mother said.

"Yes, Mother. Don't worry. She seems to be a very nice girl."

"What is her name?"

"Rhoda Meyer."

Mother pondered that for a moment. Then she asked how Rhoda spelled her name.

"R-O-D-A, I guess. I don't know."

"Not her first name," Mother said, "her last name. How do you spell that?"

I sounded it out. I said I had no idea how to spell it. Why did she want to know?

"Is this little girl a Jewess?"

"Jewish?" I said. "How would I know that?"

"It would be a shame if you made friends with a Jewish person on your very first day in school. I'm sure there are some perfectly nice Christians."

"I don't see what difference it makes."

"I'm sure you don't," Mother said. "You're very young, dear. Take my advice and find some other friends."

"But you don't even know if she's Jewish."

I spent the next hour pretending to do my lessons and thinking of how, under the circumstances, I was going to keep my promise to Rhoda. The task would have to be performed secretly. When Mother began preparing dinner, I noticed two tiny potatoes ready for the pot. I requested an extra potato with my chop, citing the excitements of the school day. If she would give me a few cents, I'd run down to the grocery store. She fetched her purse and dropped the coins into my hand.

I raced downstairs. When Rhoda came to the phone, I told her that we had company for dinner and that I couldn't talk. We agreed to meet for lunch at school, and I ran happily to the store and back.

I had not given much thought to the Jews since my days at Sunday school, where they had been the focus of considerable discussion and portrayed as a mixed lot but superior to the Egyptians and, well at the rear of the pack, the Babylonians. The phrase "Jesus Christ, King of the Jews" rang a bell. There was some debate, if memory served, about whether Jews were inexorably destined for perdition, but heaven seemed an eternity's distance from me. Why had Mother told Nell that Father was a Jew, or might be one? Did it make any difference? I was a Protestant, I was sure of that. What was Harry Valentine? A comedian, was all I knew.

For the moment I understood only that Rhoda had been friendly and kind and did not seem to care one way or another what I was. I liked that a lot.

*R*hoda and I had lunch together every day during those first two weeks. On my last Friday of steady attendance, my first menstrual period came on as we were sharing a piece of cake together. It was hardly a trickle, that first time, but I could feel something going on, and I immediately described the sensation to Rhoda. Something about her made me confide in her without hesitation. She rushed me to the girls' lavatory.

Mother had never said a word to me on the subject of my body, nor had she so much as seen me naked since babyhood. I had not discussed at all with her the changes that were taking place. I wasn't alarmed, but I would have preferred some detailed knowledge of what was happening.

Rhoda took charge. She was having a period herself that day, and she provided me with everything necessary to keep things under control. She enlightened me with details of eggs and cycles during the few minutes we spent making me leak-proof. Rhoda was a fast talker, the words clicking out like a tickertape, and by the time we emerged, I knew that I had become a woman.

At home I had to tell Mother what had happened. She was perfunctory and grave. It was obvious that she did not wish to hear any more about it than necessary. She provided me with what she referred to as "sanitary equipment" and managed to convey the sense that all this came under the category of a necessary evil.

Probably to irk her, I asked her if it was true that I was now capable of having a baby.

"Who told you *that*?" she asked. Rhoda had, but I said only that it was a matter of Sagittarian curiosity.

This was indeed the case, Mother said grimly. I was far too young, however, to be thinking of such things.

"There is an old saying," she droned. " 'The doctor's wife, she has a dirty mind, too.' Think about that."

I did, and I could make no sense of it. I still can't.

If it is possible for words to have an odor, everything my mother said to me that day gave off the smell of old, unopened rooms. She added that I should be careful not to touch milk during my period. Women in my condition could turn milk sour if they came into contact with it. For the same reason I should avoid holding fresh flowers during those days. They would shrivel up and die. These were among the many reasons menstruation was called a curse. It was a mark or sign that set women apart. It was a woman's burden.

I was drawn more toward Rhoda's lighthearted approach. But I found it difficult to shut down my brain that night in bed as I lay puzzling over the doctor's wife's dirty mind and other mysteries. It was remarkable that I had known my mother all these years and had slept in the same bed with her for many months without once becoming aware of this phenomenon. Evidently boys did not experience anything similar, or did they? A monthly erection that wouldn't quit for days? At least I now had someone to ask.

I woke up the next morning resolved to put Mother's warnings to the test. She was still asleep with muffled grunts. Quietly I opened the icebox and took out the milk bottle. I stuck my finger down the neck and tipped back a good swig. It tasted all right to me. I forced two fingers in, wiggled them around, and tried another swallow.

Later Mother poured some over oatmeal and ate without complaint. I would have to consult Rhoda. Maybe I was different from other women.

* * *

Finally I received a note from Harry Valentine asking me out for an ice cream. He mentioned having written to me weeks before, but said he understood that I had probably been too busy to answer. I had never seen this earlier letter, and despite my suspicions about what may have happened, Mother professed ignorance.

"Are you sure seeing Harry just now is such a good idea?" she asked. "You're a very busy young lady."

I telephoned Harry to make our date.

We reminisced about Buenos Aires, which had taken on a magical aura for me, but Harry was in a serious mood. He worried about me, he said, and about himself. He had just gone through another unsuccessful love affair; his girlfriend had run off with a stockbroker. He was still in vaudeville, but was thinking of going to Hollywood to make his fortune. When I told him that I had decided to become an actress, he said that I was crazy. A girl like me should go to college.

"I quit school in the sixth grade. That's why I'm not a brain surgeon. Actually if I'd tried to go to college, they'd have locked me up in a lunatic asylum. Someone like you, it's different."

"I don't think going to college is in the budget anymore," I said.

He asked about my mother. Where was she working? I explained.

"Poor E.P.," Harry said. "He sure checked out too early."

We agreed to see each other once a month, and Harry said to keep him posted on my acting career. He was sure I'd be the next Bernhardt.

"I haven't even tried out for a school play!"

"Don't think like that. Think big. Think about all the money you can make to support me in my old age. Is that a deal?"

It was as if my brain had suddenly reawakened. I applied myself to my PCS studies with a passion. I always took a book with me, and I daydreamed about my reading during modeling sessions. During a typical week I might spend Monday morning at Underwood & Underwood, Tuesday afternoon posing at Grand Central Station, have all day Wednesday free for school, miss Thursday for a fashion show, work Friday. My modeling varied seasonally, with a surge in the fall and spring that kept me out of school nearly every day; but some weeks I was almost like a regular American kid.

At home, Mother sat listening to the radio she had purchased for my fourteenth birthday, while I would be at the table outlining the rise and fall of the Athenian and Roman empires. I wondered about things the books didn't tell me, what people ate and what Egyptian perfume must have smelled like and was there shampoo? The story of Vercingetorix the Gaul moved me to write a story about Mrs. Vercingetorix, as I called her, resplendent in skins, hiding her children in caves and among the reeds from Roman soldiers.

I reveled in Arthurian romance. I concocted a tale in which Lancelot and Guinevere marry after Arthur's death and have a child they name Marie, who is the most beautiful princess in Europe. An evil witch imprisons Marie in a tower for three years, where she lived on bugs and rainwater and waits to see the sun each day through a chink in the stone. Finally an angel rescues Marie and whisks her away to live in a crystal palace where she dines on ambrosia, bathes in rosewater, and combs out her raven locks until they shine for her prince.

I spent hours designing a heraldic emblem for my heroine, a burning castle from which an arm, holding a sword wrapped in Marie's heart's-purple scarf, protrudes in undaunted defiance. Mother asked what the drawing had to do with my schoolwork. I told her that it was an assignment. PCS believes in educating the whole child, I said with what I hoped was a touch of condescension.

That whole-child business was true enough. One of my classes involved sewing costumes for school productions. I was careful not to tell Mother about this, and I made a point of being absolutely the most inept student with a needle. My work always had to be redone by someone else. But in all my other classes, except mathematics, I excelled. My teachers, God bless them, suggested extra reading for me and loaned me books from their own libraries. What selfless, wonderful people those teachers were. I wrote little sketches of them and tributes to them in my diary: "Mrs. Cornwall has a big nose and a bigger heart. Madame Roussan wears purple lipstick and purple nail polish and writes in purple ink because she wants us to know that the French are a passionate race."

That spring we received a telegram from Grandmother Nell saying that Grandfather had died. I was saddened, but I did not grieve as deeply as I thought I should. Perhaps I had spent my emotions on Father, who was still never far from my mind. The pebble I had taken from his grave remained in my dolls' box, where I touched it every time I took out Jane. When Mother said that she did not see how we could attend Grandfather's funeral, what with my work and school and the expense, I was silently relieved. I rather hoped, as only a child can, that I had seen the last of funerals. Grandfather had already faded from my life. For ages my only communication with him had been a few lines appended to Mother's regular letters to Nell. I had not even known he was ill.

Then a plan formed in my mind—or a plot. Rhoda had repeatedly asked me over to her house. Reluctant to do battle with Mother, I had always made some excuse. Without being specific, I had let Rhoda know that my mother was very strict and rarely let me out of her sight. But I had been waiting for an opportunity, and here it was.

I told Mother that it seemed a shame, wrong even, that she should not be able to attend her own father's funeral—and only because of her devotion to me. Two round-trip tickets to Kansas City would be expensive, but surely she could manage one. I had a solution. My friend Rhoda had often invited me to spend the night. I was sure that the Meyers would be glad to put me up for a few days. Rhoda and I could go to school together, and I could get down to Underwood & Underwood on my own—I had already done so several times.

The Meyers were fine people, I added, attempting to anesthetize the ethnic issue. Mr. Meyer was a lawyer, and very prosperous. Some of his clients were theater people. The Meyers lived in the East Sixties. From what Rhoda had said, it was a grand house. There would be plenty of room for me.

I had anticipated quite a bit of wrangling. When Mother hesitated, I reiterated Mr. Meyer's connections to the theater. I understood that they attended all the important opening nights, which was why Rhoda had been inspired to enroll at PCS. She didn't have to work for a living; she was in love with the theater.

I waited for Mother to bring up the Jewish question. Of course the Meyers were Jewish, I was prepared to say, but they did not seem to make much of a fuss about it. Rhoda and I had discussed all this. Hadn't they invited me to their house? Wasn't it rude of me to refuse? Wasn't Mother always drilling me on the importance of good manners?

As it turned out, I did not have to raise these issues. Mother abruptly agreed that mine was a fine idea and that it was thoughtful of me to consider it. Was I sure that I would be all right for a few days without her?

Rigid though she was, Mother could shunt principle aside at the prospect of some advantage. Mr. Meyer's business and theatrical prominence rendered his Jewishness only a minor drawback.

Having my own bed again for a few precious days was heaven. The house was a five-story brownstone on Sixty-third between Park and Lexington. Rhoda's older brother was away at college, and the cook departed after dinner. Every floor was an adventure, every bathroom a fantasy of marble and chrome. How Father would have appreciated it, I kept thinking. There had been good times ahead for him, but he hadn't lived to see them. I had the peculiar idea that I was carrying on his legacy, that this luxury was meant for me.

There were paintings everywhere. The living room, hung with heavy damask curtains, rose silk covering the walls, with a rug luxuriant with dominant reds and blues, held my favorite picture. In a filigreed golden frame above the mantelpiece, it showed a Parisian café, lamps glowing warmly in the background. Pretty women wore jackets and jaunty hats trimmed with fur. They danced bunched together with bearded men in top hats and cutaways. I was fascinated by the bright red lips of the women, brilliant in pink and olive faces. At a table in the lower-left foreground a brunette whispered into a red-head's ear; a third beauty, all in black except for a sky-blue ribbon on her rakish hat, leaned on an elbow and cast a co-quettish eye across the scene. The light caught her white teeth and the empty carafe and glasses on the table.

I didn't have the wit to examine the signature or to ask who the artist was. It was just a wonderful picture that I stared at every day. I saw myself in it, I was the one in black, looking over the scene and knowing that many men would ask me to dance.

I lived at the Meyers' for a week, eager to settle back into those surroundings when I was through each day with school or modeling. Getting to PCS in the mornings was simpler than usual; a driver whisked Rhoda and me across town in a big black car. Nothing disturbed my serenity and ease except Mrs. Meyer's irascibility. She spent most of the time in her room, complaining of headaches and dyspepsia. "This aggravation I don't need," she moaned over and over when we went in to visit her and bring her a cold cloth. It seemed that the maid had committed an act of treachery Mrs. Meyer was finding it difficult to forgive.

On a chair beside the bed a Pekingese, called Mrs. Wong, kept watch over her mistress and growled when I approached. Rhoda said that Mrs. Wong had bitten everyone in the house except Mrs. Meyer.

What had disturbed Mrs. Meyer was that her maid had in-formed another woman's maid that Mrs. Wong had peed and pooped on the living-room carpet. This was not only a gross exaggeration, but a serious breach of confidentiality. The story had got back to Mrs. Meyer because the other maid had re-peated it to *her* employer, who in turn had reported it to Mrs. Meyer in the insulting terms, "I hear your Mrs. Wong ruined your Oriental rug. My Buttons would never do such a thing."

Rhoda and I got little sleep. We talked for hours after we

were in our beds in her top-floor room. I told her what life had been like in Buenos Aires and about our fall in fortune. She said that she never would have guessed that I was poor, because I had such pretty clothes and didn't smell and spoke so well. She told me I was beautiful, and I returned the compliment, saying that I could imagine her as a sultan's favorite concubine—this required some backpedaling on my part; I had meant it as a tribute to a kind of beauty I associated with silken pillows and spicy unguents, in a word Scheherazade, but it struck the wrong note. We exchanged ideas of what we thought to be romantic and found some differences between us. I was all for being spirited across the sands of the Sahara on a foaming steed; her dreams ran more to domestic grandeur and tranquility.

By the second or third night I found myself confessing to her about Philippe and how I had written about him in my diary and never had thought that I would reveal my secrets anywhere else. She had never kissed a boy or carried on the way I had. She thought me bold and said she envied me; I suspected that she also thought me a little crazy and possibly loose.

There was a boy at school to whom she had written a poem, since torn up. She would strongly consider surrendering her virginity to him—no, she took that back. Of course she would save herself for her husband. But then again, under the right circumstances . . . As for me, she could see that I was becoming a great beauty and would have many, many lovers.

On my last night with the Meyers, we went to the opening of a play. In evening dress the gentlemen smoked cigars, ladies did their best to look beyond price in jewels and beaded gowns. Beside me a woman made kissing noises at her pet marmoset and coaxed it up her coat sleeve; I caught sight of a doll's rubber underpants beneath its frilly skirt. Marmosets were all the rage that year, Rhoda said. She had asked for one, but her parents said monkeys carried disease.

Mrs. Meyer had permitted us to paint our lips, and Rhoda

insisted that I borrow her brocaded, fur-trimmed jacket. I imagined that we were like the women in the Parisian painting.

Any number of important people were milling around outside the Cort Theatre that night; I tried to find out who was who. Rhoda pointed out George Kaufman, who waved and raised bushy eyebrows at Mr. and Mrs. Meyer. He was one of Mr. Meyer's clients. There was Ethel Barrymore, who, Rhoda said, had just flopped as Juliet, and Mr. and Mrs. Frederic de Belleville and Leo Ditrichstein and Zelda Sears standing next to Francine Larrimore. Viola Allen was that woman smoking and flourishing a gold-headed stick.

We were awaiting the arrival of the producer, George Tyler, also a Meyer client. When he drew up in a limousine five minutes before curtain time, Mr. Meyer introduced me as if I belonged there, Mr. Tyler kissed Mr. Meyer on both cheeks, and we made our way down to third-row-center seats. Rhoda pointed out the critic for the *Times,* the producer Sam Harris, Neville Fleeson the lyricist, and I don't know how many others.

The play was *Merton of the Movies,* by Kaufman and Marc Connelly. We were hoping for a hit, since Mr. Meyer was one of *Merton*'s biggest backers. Rhoda said that if the play was a success, her father would be rich.

Richer, surely you mean, I thought to myself.

I had not seen a great deal of Mr. Meyer that week. A small, fast-talking fellow with a habit of twirling his watch chain at a great rate, he led a strenuous social life. On the few occasions I encountered him rushing to his office or to some engagement, he peppered me with questions about my favorite books and whether I was serious about becoming an actress. He was delighted that Rhoda and I had become friends, and he told me that my father had been highly regarded in theatrical circles. I doubted that he knew who E. P. Spencer had been, but I appreciated the sentiment.

There is nothing like seeing a play that wins over the audience from the first scene. I laughed along with the house as poor Merton, the hick who longs to go to Hollywood and become a star, saves his fifteen-dollar-a-week wages from his job as a clerk in a general store, and heads for the Coast with his head full of nonsense out of movie magazines and his suitcase stuffed with costumes and photographs of himself with a horse, in pirate's getup, as a doughboy, in bathing costume—his life consecrated to a great career.

On the studio lot, Merton swoons at the sight of his favorite stars, Beulah Baxter and Harold Parmelee. Merton is rebuffed by them and a collection of supercilious, pretentious, ignorant, egomaniacal, dumbbell producers and directors. Broke and in despair, unable to land even an extra's role, he is rescued by the tough but tenderhearted Montague girl, who makes her living doubling for Beulah Baxter. She tricks gullible Merton into trying out for the lead in a comedy, telling him that it's a serious, arty picture.

Merton becomes a star. He gets fabulous offers from all the studios. But when he discovers that he is admired for being a perfect dope, he is crushed. The Montague girl talks gutsy sense to him, he agrees and signs a big contract, and we leave him as he airily grants an interview to a fan magazine. He is the greatest success in Hollywood because he is even more idiotic than everyone else.

We stood and cheered at the final curtain. Mr. Meyer beamed, and Mr. Tyler embraced him. Rich, I thought, very rich. And why not? The play was terrific.

I hoped we would go backstage. I especially wanted to meet Florence Nash, who had played the Montague girl with a combination of brassy savvy and sweetness I thought great. But Mr. and Mrs. Meyer were hosting the party afterward, so we hurried home.

In the car we went over favorite scenes and lines and I wondered aloud whether Hollywood was really as silly and outrageous as in the play. Looking back, it seems a naive question from someone who had grown up in show business.

"It's a comedy," Mr. Meyer said. I didn't know whether he meant the play or Hollywood or both. And then he said, "People are making a lot of money in pictures." I found this an enigmatic answer to my question, but before I could pursue the matter, the driver opened the door.

Margaret in Hollywood

There must have been thirty actors in the cast. They trooped into the Meyers' with their companions and husbands and wives. Kaufman and Connelly came, George Tyler, and Hugh Ford, the director, everyone mad with triumph, shouting and hugging and kissing. It was nothing like one of those scenes in a movie where everyone waits breathlessly for tomorrow's notices. They knew they had a hit.

Waiters, who, Rhoda told me, were out-of-work actors themselves, dispensed glasses of champagne from trays, and you could get hard liquor at the bar. I heard people say that they hadn't had an honest drink in days. You didn't get poisoned at Joe Meyer's. This was the real thing, straight off the boat.

I couldn't get near Florence Nash, who was thronged by admirers, but I was able to listen to her talk. She seemed just as tough and funny as the Montague girl. As I was standing there, I felt something on my rump. I jumped and turned around to see a man I recognized as the actor who had played the casting director.

"Don't be frightened, my dear," he said, drawing on a cigarette through a holder. I looked into his rheumy, red-rimmed eyes. His teeth were unnaturally even and bright, incongruous with cracked lips and wrinkled skin to which orangy smudges of makeup clung. It was like confronting the work of an incompetent mortician.

He must have been on the bad side of forty. For someone who had had about four lines to speak, he had quite the grand air.

"I have to see my friend," I said.

"Dump him, sweetheart. Where's your drink?"

He must be drunk, I thought, not to see how young I am. I slipped away and found Rhoda in the kitchen. When I told her that this creep had tried to feel my bottom, she thought it hilarious.

"I know who he is," she said. "I think he prefers boys anyway. He must be trying to branch out."

We managed to sneak a half-empty bottle of champagne upstairs, and we sat on our beds talking. From below we heard

117

the piano, a few random chords, a glissando. Then a smooth contralto—

> At twilight's white star,
> Come to me, come to me . . .

"What a wonderful song," I said. "What a wonderful night."

"Who are you thinking of?" Rhoda reached across to give me a pinch on the back of my hand and shook out her dark hair. "Come on, confess!"

I wasn't thinking of anyone. It was the whole experience. I told Rhoda how this evening with the play and the people and all the glamour and excitement had made me remember how much I missed the theater and how much I wanted to be an actress. I also was thinking of how much I would like to be able to go to the theater and return to a house like this or to a beautiful apartment with my own bedroom. I also didn't tell her that I was a little jealous of her.

Rhoda asked me what roles I would like to play if I became an actress. I said Juliet, more than anything. We had read the play at St. Cat's, and I had been rehearsing it in my mind ever since.

"Me, too," she said. "Juliet is what I want to play. I was just thinking, I'm going to have my father talk to them and get them to put it on."

"Get who? Who is going to put that on?"

"PCS, silly. My father's a big benefactor, you know. If he says they should do *Romeo and Juliet,* they'll do it."

You're not right for the part, I thought, not right at all. I am. You could play a different part. You let me play Juliet, and you can have everything else.

118

12

*T*he idea of becoming an actress and
playing Juliet obsessed me. For more than a year I thought
about it constantly. It came into my mind on the subway and
during modeling sessions and while buying an apple or walking through Central Park. Why this role? Why any other? I
have to think. For a young girl, who else is there but Juliet?
She is youth and, by the way, she's far more interesting than
Romeo, and more eloquent! I had the idea that if I could play
Juliet, nothing else in the world could affect me. The thought
drew me on and made it easy to accept unpleasant circumstances.

It was hard to imagine Rhoda's claiming the same ambition.
She was not Julietesque; Junoesque was more like it. I had
little doubt that I would win any fair competition against her,
but would her father dangle a check, demanding that his
daughter get the part? Meanwhile my acting career consisted
of mimicking, rather well, I think, actresses, after seeing a movie
or a play and performing in PCS workshops with fellow
dreamers.

I wrote to Harry Valentine about my ambitions. He had gone
to Hollywood and was landing parts in Harold Lloyd pictures
and working for Hal Roach with Will Rogers. It sounded marvelous to me, but he didn't seem happy. He always signed off
with the same line: The girls in Hollywood were beautiful, but

nothing to compare to his Margaret, and so dumb they couldn't even understand *his* jokes, which were aimed at morons. If only he were young and not just mentally an infant, he would marry me. When he wasn't working, he was alone. He had begun to paint and hoped to have a second career as an artist. He sent me drawings—chaste ones!—and a watercolor of a Christmas tree with a face on it that looked like his, with branches for arms and gnarly hands holding lollipops and presents strewn at its feet all labeled "To Margaret."

Finally good things began to happen to me again. My essay "The Vamp" won the English Composition Prize at PCS for the year 1922–23. I was asked to read my sketch at the June exercises before an audience of students, faculty, parents, and benefactors. It was a festival of the arts, featuring chamber music, aspiring opera singers, dancers, actors—oh, we were all prodigies and delighted at being little geniuses together.

At the same time a production of *Romeo and Juliet* was announced for the following fall. Rhoda denied that her father had had anything to do with it, but she was going to try out for Juliet, too. I wondered if our friendship would survive this. We made a pact to be loyal to one another no matter what happened. Auditions began in May. Whoever won the principal roles would rehearse throughout the summer.

Instead of merely reading my essay, I decided to memorize it. If I could hold that audience spellbound, it might help me win Juliet.

I approached the occasion as if it were a Broadway audition. I convinced myself that my life depended on it and on playing Juliet. Otherwise I saw myself modeling forever or marrying someone just to get away. Being around so many other ambitious children whose lives were dedicated to showing off must have given me impetus, even as being part of Father's company had instilled bravado in me years before. I had this conviction that I was born lucky, no matter what.

The question for the essay competition had been, "Imagine yourself in the role of an actor or actress. Describe the scene, identify with the character, and create an atmosphere and a personality fully realized before a packed house."

A packed house! This was made to order for me. The words flowed as I sat scribbling at our table, shutting out the Yale Glee Club, to which Mother was listening on the radio. When told that I had won the prize, ten dollars and a pair of tickets to the play of my choice, I felt as if my life had taken a turn.

On the great day I dressed demurely in skirt and blouse, my hair pulled back in a bun. I had my lines by heart, and once I commit something to memory, I do not forget it—a talent of sorts. I stood behind the lectern before an audience of about a thousand, hoping that the contrast between the prim appearance I affected and the words I was about to utter would create an energy. My knees were weak, but I vowed not to falter.

" 'The Vamp'," I began.

"As she paced restlessly back and forth on the floor of her boudoir . . ." I made my voice low but clearly audible, my enunciation precise and emphatic in the dramatic style of those days. The notion of a *natural* delivery was unthinkable. People then believed that art and nature were distinct from one another. Mumbling was no virtue, a slovenly deportment still unadmired. Life was something the artist was supposed to alter, improve upon, transcend. You went to the theater to discover something other than what you could pick up on a street corner. How long ago it seems! Try to imagine a time when audiences were sophisticated enough to judge by appearances, and only superficial bores worried about deep meanings and uplifting messages. Performance was the thing, and illusion.

Immediately I sensed that I had my audience. Through my voice, through slight movements of my hands, through a haughty toss of my head, I transformed myself. I was not quite become the creature of my imagination, but I was the medium through which my audience could see her, the way a religious emblem or image suggests not itself but the thing beyond itself. All this was instinctive to me.

"She reminded one of some beautiful wild animal. . . ." I reached back and loosened my hair, which cascaded to my waist and swirled about my face like a mantle the color of embers. My words painted other tints:

"She had jet-black hair which was cut as short as a boy's and dark, angry eyes. They were narrowed down to long slits now, and you could see her lids, which were dark, naturally dark as if they had been touched by a sooty finger. She wore a tea-gown of black satin with long, flowing diaphanous sleeves.

"The only color on her gown was a girdle of dark gold [here I paused], a long gold tassel hanging at her side. She wore sheer black stockings and tiny gold mules. Her skin was dark and she wore no rouge but had painted her lips a vivid ver-million. Her throat was long and graceful [I showed the audience my throat] and her arms were slender, her hands slender with long, tapering fingers that fondled nervously her tassel.

"As she glanced quickly from side to side, unspeaking but radiating her restless, nervous, ceaseless passion, she was a ti-gress!"

The composition ended with three slow raps on the boudoir door.

At the first applause my mother rushed up to the stage. It must have looked as if she were congratulating me. She did keep a smile on her face as she hissed into my ear that this had been a scandal, thoroughly inappropriate for a school as-sembly. Perhaps she thought that she would rescue me from an angry mob, but as the applause continued and the audi-ence stood, she had to back off and let me take my bows.

My teachers and friends came up to grasp my hand, Rhoda at the head of the pack, beaming, with tears in her eyes. We embraced. "My dear," said Mrs. Cornwall, "you have earned our heartfelt admiration," this in a grandiose delivery; she was ever onstage. Mrs. Nesbitt said to me, "I greet you at the be-ginning of a great career." Madame Roussan's French was too rapid for me, but I gathered that she thought my essay very French, for her the supreme compliment.

Was my essay really that spectacular? Obviously not. It may have been better than any of the others submitted, but I doubt even that, for there were several truly brilliant students at PCS then, including a boy who went on to become an important playwright, and Milton Berle, who probably suffered from the prejudice against comedy by judges who are inclined to take themselves too seriously when evaluating school essays, Pulitzer Prizes, or Academy Awards. But my performance carried the day; I had made something worth watching out of mediocre material.

Nothing pleased me as much as when Frank Hern, who was competing for the role of Romeo, came up to thrust a bunch of flowers at me. They were unwrapped and unevenly cut; I guessed that he had stolen them from the park. I already had a crush on him. Frank was tall and lean, pale like me but with black hair and a devilish cast to his blue eyes. We had broken up laughing several times delivering love speeches to each other, which I hoped would cost neither of us a part. He bowed as he handed me the flowers, and I leaned to place a quick kiss on his cheek, I hoped with appropriate nonchalance.

Rhoda teased me. Where had I come up with that regal gesture? Did she think, I said, that I'd been on the stage all my life for nothing? She wanted to know how I really felt about Frank Hern. Was I in love with him?

At home Mother asked about the young man with flowers as I placed his bouquet in a milk bottle. They seemed to transform that dingy room. We should always have flowers, I announced grandly, hoping to fend off further inquiries.

"Who is that boy?" she persisted.

I considered saying that Frank Hern was a lunatic tolerated by the school who was always presenting flowers to everyone and had been arrested several times for stealing them. But I told her that Frank was trying to become Romeo. None of us was sure why the cast had not yet been announced. Rhoda and I were finding it difficult to talk about. I had the suspicion and the fear that Mr. Occhipinti, the drama teacher, and Mrs. Cornwall had chosen me or someone else other than Rhoda for Juliet and that Joseph Meyer was making a fuss behind the scenes. Mother said that I should not count on anything and ought to concentrate on my modeling. She had the idea that if you wished too hard for something, you were bound to be disappointed; I was of the opposite conviction.

Mother repeated her displeasures with my composition. She thought it had sounded "foreign." Had I been reading other than assigned texts? It wasn't a good idea for young people to read indiscriminately. That was what schools were for, to tell children what to read and to keep their minds healthily occupied.

"Only Oscar Wilde," I said.

"And what sort of books does he write?"

"He's dead. He wrote one about a man who falls in with bad company and loses his soul. It was most instructive."

She pressed on. Didn't I think my composition was rather advanced in certain respects?

I bent like a ballerina at the waist to smell my flowers and ignored the question, thanking her for coming to hear me.

I did not tell her that my composition was a hodge-podge of movie vamps and Wilde's *Salomé,* a copy of which, with the Aubrey Beardsley drawings, I had examined in Joseph Meyer's library. Salomé's seizing John the Baptist's severed head and kissing and biting the bloody lips had fascinated me. It wasn't the sort of thing I thought Mother would appreciate.

Two or three days later I went downstairs to check the mail for a letter from Harry Valentine. I had written him several times recently without receiving a reply, and was beginning to wonder if he had disappeared or had become bored with our correspondence. There was nothing from Harry, but there was a letter addressed to me with neither a stamp nor a return address on it. Who would be delivering a message to me by hand? I opened it on the spot.

The note was from Frank Hern. *Meet me at 2:00 P.M. Saturday at the entrance to the Park across from the Plaza,* signed *Frank Romeo.*

I didn't know how I was going to escape from Mother. I spent most of the week trying to invent an excuse and came up with nothing. Fortunately on Saturday, just after noon, she left to do grocery shopping. I scribbled a note saying I was going out for a walk.

I sat for nearly two hours in the Plaza lobby, watching people and wondering how Frank had had the nerve to concoct this scheme. He had the reputation of something of a cutup at school, and was always being sent to Mrs. Nesbitt. PCS did not have corporal punishment; being sent to the principal was about the worst that could happen to you, other than expulsion. Frank's transgressions were on the order of laughing at the wrong times in class, passing notes, questioning why we were reading one book rather than another. What some of his teachers saw as arrogance appealed to me as independence. His father was in the diplomatic service, and while his parents lived in one exotic place after another, Frank stayed with his grandmother.

At a quarter to two I crossed the street to the park. Frank was already waiting for me. We went for a stroll, talking about the play and whether we would win our roles. Frank had heard that there were plans afoot to stage a scaled-down version of the play this summer, as a kind of dry run for the fall. He figured they were waiting to announce the cast until arrangements were complete. He had got wind of this by sneaking a look at some papers on Mr. Occhipinti's desk. I told him he was very wicked. He said he hoped this was true, and he took my hand. I thought to myself that there was nothing that I would rather be doing than walking through Central Park on a Saturday with Frank Hern.

Then he suggested that we go to see a movie.

"I can't," I said. "If my mother knew we were doing this much, she'd be furious. I'll have to get home soon."

Frank argued with me. He said that he had thought that I was a modern woman. Surely I could think up some kind of excuse. I could say that I had gone to a museum or to the library.

I didn't so much give in as eagerly agree. He knew a great film we should see, and it was showing only a few blocks away. He had already seen it, but he was anxious to go again. It was *The Queen of Sheba*.

Frank paid our way into the Capitol Theater. There could

not have been more than a dozen others in the audience. We snuck into the expensive, plush seats at the back just as the movie was starting. The timing was too exact; Frank must have had this in mind from the beginning.

The organ sounded an Arabian theme. The curtains parted. Credits, and then these words on the screen:

> And when the Queen of Sheba heard of the fame of Solomon concerning the name of the LORD, she came to prove him with hard questions.
>
> Kings 10:1

There isn't much about the queen of Sheba in the Bible, and there wasn't much of a story to the movie, either. She arrives in Jerusalem with a great train of camels and servants bearing spices and gold as tribute to King Solomon. The monarchs get on like a house on fire, with much feasting and dancing and energetic debauchery. That's about it until the queen departs laden with royal bounty.

But there was plenty to hold our interest. Spectacle would be the Hollywood flak-word for *The Queen of Sheba*, the sort of thing C. B. DeMille patented. Most spectacular of all were Betty Blythe's costumes. She must have had thirty of them, and if she had worn them all at once, she would still have caught pneumonia.

I shall never forget the first shot of Miss Blythe more or less naked. She sat in a big rococo chair, ankles crossed, leaning on one haunch, sandaled feet resting on an ottoman. Her lower half was wrapped in gauzy stuff showing plenty of thigh, and on her head sat a sort of cross between a toque and a lampshade.

Between her face and her waist, fishnet scattered with a few beads revealed all. With her breasts larger than life on the screen, her nipples the size of teacups, I wondered if I was supposed to be offended that Frank had lured me into such a display. I was not. We started laughing, linking arms and holding hands. Miss Blythe may have looked more burlesque than biblical, but she was one of nature's wonders. Her slave girls were no slouches either. Many of them I am sure went on to greatness as movie stars and prostitutes.

I whispered in Frank's ear that he had been very rude to subject me to such wickedness. My lips brushed him, and he turned to kiss me. We didn't know the movie was over until the music stopped and the lights went up.

Outside, we promised each other to go to another movie soon. I don't know whether Mother believed me or not when I told her that I had spent the afternoon feeding pigeons and browsing in bookshops, but it didn't matter. Her words floated past. All I could think of was what a daring, evil, terrible, reckless, wonderful boy Frank Hern was. I decided that if I didn't get to be his Juliet, I would kill myself.

When I told Rhoda what had happened, she was beside herself. She told me that I ought to have run out of the theater and that Frank Hern must be the most corrupt boy in school and that she had to find a way to see *The Queen of Sheba*. But how? It would never do to ask a boy. Her parents would never take her. Would I go with her? "I hate you," she said, "I absolutely hate you! I knew it! You were born lucky!"

"Born reckless," I said. It was the title of another movie Frank and I were scheming to see. I wanted to live up to it.

13

*R*hoda had reason to hate me when we learned that I would play Juliet opposite Frank Hern's Romeo. The cast list was announced in a letter telling us that, as Frank's detective work had discovered, four of us would enact scenes from the play before "selected audiences" later that summer, with the full-scale production scheduled for November. Besides the principals, the other two characters were Friar Laurence and the Nurse. I wondered whether Rhoda would be consoled or further disappointed and maybe furious that she had been chosen to play the Nurse. She had not even tried out for the role. No one had.

If indeed Rhoda's father had had nothing to do with getting the play put on, I bet that she was wishing he had. As much as I cared for her, I had to admit that she wasn't an actress. It may have taken Joseph Meyer's pull even to get his daughter the nanny's role. I wondered whether she would agree to play it or just quit in a pique.

Attending PCS was more of a diversion for Rhoda than, as it was for me, a matter of life and death. But I didn't want our friendship broken. I waited to hear from her. It seemed appropriate that she should congratulate me, rather than my offering her apologies, which she might take as condescension. When I didn't hear from her, however, I telephoned.

The maid asked who was calling.

"It's me, Irma. It's Margaret Spencer."

I was informed that Rhoda wasn't feeling well. She was not taking any calls.

Uh-oh. She was sulking. I waited a couple of days and tried again. When I got the same routine, I was angry, but decided to write her a letter. I must have done ten drafts. Finally I settled on a version that told her that I loved her and that I thought she was just as talented as I was but that for some unknown reason they had chosen me over her. On another occasion she would be the lucky one. I was happy for myself and sorry for her, but wouldn't it be fun to be in the play together? Surely she wasn't thinking of not playing the Nurse, was she? I would certainly have looked forward to playing Nurse to her Juliet, I lied.

At last I received a note inviting me to spend an afternoon at her house.

Rhoda received me in her bedroom. On the way up I noticed that her mother, with Mrs. Wong vigilant, was also indisposed, and wondered if Irma was in the doggie house again. Lying in her bed with an arm across her face, Rhoda looked as if she were in the last stages of a dread disease. I thought that she might have a future in the theater after all.

"You don't know what this has done to me," were her first words. "All my dreams, shattered. I am down, Margaret. Quite, quite down!"

"I know how you feel," I said, silently admiring what had obviously been a well-rehearsed speech. If she couldn't play Juliet, she was giving Ophelia a shot. I made noises about turning disappointment into triumph. I was sure she would be the best Nurse that ever was.

That was a mistake.

"Do I look to you like a nurse!" Rhoda screamed, bolting upright. "I tell you, that is just too much for a person to take! I never want to see you again! Go on, have your little fling with your Romeo! See if I care! I've got better things to do than watching you and Frank Hern make asses of yourselves!"

I started crying. I *think* it was genuine, at least from the shock of her words and her vehemence, if not from remorse.

130

She apologized. She hadn't meant to hurt me. We embraced.

By the time I left, we had a copy of the play out and were trading lines. She gave me her interpretation of how Juliet should be played, and I thanked her and resolved not to let it interfere with my own ideas.

Mother was worried that the play would hamper my modeling. I said that I didn't care whether it did or not. It was the most important thing in my life.

"That's all very well," she said, "but I have to think about putting food on the table. I have responsibilities."

In the end she acquiesced. Rehearsals were in the evenings. Performances, scheduled during August at various suburban estates, cultural diversion for PCS donors and potential donors, would require no more than a day's absence at a time.

As the play to see as part of my prize for winning the essay contest, I selected *Hamlet* starring John Barrymore. I schemed to let Frank Hern use the other ticket. We would benefit from seeing the performance together, I said; it would inspire us for our roles. Mother disagreed. Permitting me to attend the theater alone with a boy, unchaperoned? Ridiculous.

What if we simply invited him to accompany us? He could buy his own ticket.

"It's best to leave things as they are," Mother said.

During the first interval Mother expressed the opinion that this Prince of Denmark was drunk. She was probably right; nonetheless Barrymore entranced me; and the thought that I might one day be a part of the theater was so exciting that I was prepared to see merit in just about any performance or play. I note from my diary that Mother and I attended something called *Extra! Extra!* at the Knickerbocker. The subject matter is plain enough, but I remember nothing of the play; I doubt if it lasted a week. "Amusing," I commented in my diary. "Edmund Bigelow so clever! Frank would have enjoyed him." Whatever happened to old Bigelow? No matter, to a girl in New York he was genius itself for one afternoon. As for Barrymore, he was a legend and I accepted him as such, ham

131

or not; and I adored Rosalind Fuller as Ophelia, fragile and doomed with a voice like a flute.

We were sipping sodas in the lobby when I thought I spotted Harry Valentine. I started toward him, waving as I caught his eye, but he turned and disappeared around a corner as the lights began blinking. Had I been mistaken? Surely he wouldn't come to New York without telling me? It had been months since I'd heard from him.

At the second interval I rushed around looking for him and found him sitting alone in a corner of the second balcony just as the curtain was about to go up again. I threw my arms about him. He seemed shy, almost reluctant to talk. Before I went back to my seat, I got him to tell me where he was staying, a hotel I had never heard of. I looked for him again after the play was over, but he had gone.

After trying unsuccessfully to reach him several times, I went to see him one day after a modeling session. His hotel was a cheap place a couple of blocks from Underwood & Underwood. I knew there must be something wrong, or he would have called me. I guessed that he had been fired and was ashamed to talk about it. I thought I knew Harry pretty well.

I rang his room and he came down. He looked as if he had been up all night.

"Why don't you shave, Harry?"

"I'm growing this for a part. I'm playing a bum."

It wasn't the sort of lobby that serves tea. We went into the street and found a luncheonette.

I told him about Juliet. He was delighted and said he always knew I would succeed. This was just the first step. Maybe he could come to the play in the fall, if he wasn't working.

"Why are you in New York?"

"I came to see some friends." He knew this was not convincing. Here I was, his oldest friend, or one of them, and he hadn't bothered to look me up. "I have some business. There's a possible play." What play? "Play? It's a thing about hoboes. It takes place in a freight car. The trouble is, there's no love interest. It could be a stinker. It may be beneath me." He struck a mock-Barrymore pose.

Something was wrong. We sat in silence for a while; then Harry reached into his coat and brought out a bunch of clippings held together with a rubber band.

"This is my filing system," he said. "Here, want to read my notices? Some of them are pretty good." He had the shakes.

His files consisted of a dozen or so movie reviews from Los Angeles and trade papers. Wherever his name appeared, he had underlined it in red pencil. Sometimes he was merely listed as a member of the cast; three or four articles singled him out: "Harry Valentine was acrobatic as the policeman," or "Harry Valentine gives the marriage scene a lift with his impersonation of a preacher."

"The trouble is, you know," Harry said, "they give all the ink to the stars. But this stuff can be very helpful landing parts."

"They're very good," I said. More silence. Finally I got up the courage. "Why are you really here, Harry?"

He looked at the ceiling.

"You're too young," he said. "Let's just drop it."

"Come on, Harry! Haven't we had secrets?"

Into his coat again. What would it be this time? Another clipping. He hesitated, then laid it out before me. The headline read:

L.A. LOVE NEST TRAPS BIGGIE,
UNHAPPY VALENTINE, OTHERS

The story told of a police raid on the mansion of Mr. Alexander Pantages, movie-theater mogul and Hollywood heavyweight, who had been in trouble before on charges of rape and consorting with underage girls. According to the diary of a prostitute, Pantages had a virgin delivered to him every week. He and several other Hollywood figures, including funnyman Harry Valentine, were facing charges of rape, sodomy, contributing to the delinquency of minors, and violations of the Volstead Act. The article was dated about a month earlier.

"What is sodomy?" was my first question.

"Never mind," Harry said. "The point is, none of it is true. It's all lies. I mean, I was there, but I wasn't doing anything. I

133

was in the wrong place at the wrong time, is all it was. But it's got me in deep trouble."

Now, Harry couldn't stop talking. He had met Pantages at a nightclub and had made the mistake of accepting his invitation to a party. The situation was even worse than the papers had reported. There had been boys there, too, as well as girls. Teenagers. Maybe younger. Apparently everyone was supposed to take whatever they wanted. But somebody had tipped off the police. When they arrived, Harry, or so he said, was passed out by the swimming pool. He had been offered drugs but had refused; too many people he knew in Hollywood were gone on morphine and cocaine. Harry had to explain to me about drugs; I knew nothing about them. He also said that a number of compromising photographs had been confiscated. Thank God he wasn't in any of them.

Charges were still pending against him. Pantages, of course, had managed to get those against him dropped, not for the first time. He hadn't even gone to jail. Harry had spent a night in a cell with two other actors and a director, all of them insane. The studio had obtained his release; they had done at least that much.

Harry explained that Hollywood was doing everything possible to avoid this kind of publicity. There were so many people involved, the place was so corrupt, you never knew whom to trust. There had already been drug and sex scandals, even murders, and the raid had come right on the heels of the Fatty Arbuckle scandal. They had already made one fatty a fall guy; Harry might be next. Arbuckle would never work in pictures again, even though he had been acquitted.

I had never heard of Arbuckle, but I got the idea. Harry was in exile, the studio had ordered him out of town. Even if they got the charges dropped, he still might not be able to work again.

I didn't know what to think. Boys and girls? The pink tights in Harry's suitcase popped into my head. But I had to believe in him. A friend was loyal.

He described again how he had been sprawled there, comatose, with one foot in the water, when the police broke in.

I told him he didn't have to repeat it. I believed him. How did he think things would turn out, in the long run? When would he know?

"Maybe never. Maybe I should start looking for another line of work, something like a paper route. You're up early, finished by eight. Then the fun starts."

"I sell clothes," I said.

"No no, you're going to be a sensation. Look at you, you're gorgeous, sweetheart. You've already got style and class. Look at that hair, I wish you'd sell me some. You're so grown up, you could pass for eighteen and conquer Hollywood in a New York second. You've even got brains. Oops, they might not know how to handle that. Act dumb. I do. I can't help it."

"I don't think I want to go to Hollywood," I said.

"Good thinking. Aside from everything else, it's a hick town, full of nothing but con artists and Bible-beaters. There's a shortage of mammals. Everyone out there's a reptile."

I told Harry that everything would be all right. He was out of jail, wasn't he? Didn't he want to be friends always? I knew he did.

"I love you, Margaret," he said, his eyes watering and making him look even worse. I made him promise to contact me the minute he had news.

"Think about Juliet," were his last words to me. "Nothing else matters."

When I got home, I asked Mother as casually as I could if she knew anything about Roscoe Fatty Arbuckle. She refused to talk about such a revolting matter, and demanded to know how I had heard about it. I said that people at Underwood & Underwood had been gossiping.

"That is disgusting," Mother said. "Close your ears."

I let some time pass and then tested her to determine whether she had heard or read anything about Harry's troubles. I brought up his name and said it had been nice to see him at the play.

"He's a drunk," Mother said, and I left it at that. She had heard nothing.

I did not wish to believe that Harry had done anything

135

strange or wrong, but I worried more about his unhappiness. I thought the matter over seriously for several days, and the more I considered it, the less I cared whether he was guilty or not. I could not imagine his corrupting anyone. Anybody could make a mistake. How many novels had I read where somebody's life is ruined because of a single lapse in judgment? Women were always going to hell because they lost their virtue. Was virtue really something you could lose like a ring or a scarf? It didn't seem the least bit logical. Harry had never done anything to me except be wonderful and funny. I was going to stick by him, no matter what.

The next I heard from Harry was a letter posted from some place called Etiwanda, California. Everything was fine. He was back at work playing a timid sheriff in a comedy western. He said nothing about the scandal, probably because he guessed that Mother read my mail.

In his next letter Harry announced that he was engaged to be married.

Mrs. Cornwall trained us in Shakespeare's language, making sure we understood every syllable we uttered. When Juliet says that she had an ill-divining soul, she means that she foresees the tragedy that will befall her love—that sort of thing, so that we could display conviction in our speech and not indulge in the prattling, overrhythmical gibberish typical of ignorant Shakespearean actors. The more she coached me, the more I understood what had bothered me in other Shakespeare productions I had seen; I had been too stagestruck to figure it out. Many of the actors must not have had a clue to what they were saying or, more often, shouting. It was mere noise. Listening to Mrs. Cornwall made me remember how my father had tried to teach me Puck's words.

I began to see that learning, not emotion, was the key to acting, that one could hardly project the emotions of a character without first understanding the words she spoke and the world from which she emerged. Mrs. Cornwall lectured us about Elizabethan customs and conventions and beliefs. She told us to banish the modern world, to transport ourselves back three hundred years. What we lacked in knowledge of the period, our imaginations could supply. Acting was not mere self-expression. It was *acting*.

I needn't point out how unfashionable these ideas are today, when acting has degenerated into a branch of group therapy. But I digress. Suffice to say that I took Mrs. Cornwall's teachings to heart and believe in them still. And they made it easier for me to deal with modeling and with life on Fifty-fourth Street. I could flip a switch in my brain and be in Verona.

Guido Occhipinti staged our performances and coached us in movement and the sort of gesture that could cut through boredom. He was a tiny man with a big voice, dressed invariably in a dark suit with a bright silk handkerchief stuck like a bouquet in his jacket pocket. He would pull the handkerchief out with a magician's flourish and wave it about for emphasis, prancing on the toes of his mirror-polished black shoes and screaming at us in a voice that could penetrate the thickest back-row skull. He had started out as an actor in the Italian melodrama of the Lower East Side. He loved to roll his eyes and bare his teeth. His hands were butterflies. When I remember him, I think of colors, of his face that varied from green to brownish-purple, of his handkerchiefs, of the flash of his teeth, of the way he seemed to talk in colors, making syllables turn silver and gold. And I think of music.

"*Andante*," he would say, "*andante*, Frank," telling him how to walk toward me. "You are not in such a hurry. You are not a shoe salesman. Make your feet to walk like violins." He demonstrated, gliding and singing a few bars from some aria, seizing Frank by the waist and pushing him this way and that. "Elegance! Nobility!" Mr. Occhipinti did not seem to think that my movements required as much attention as Frank's, Rhoda's, and Buster MacEntee's—Buster was the kid playing Friar Laurence. I had the exuberant sense that my life had all been preparation for this.

Rhoda tried her best to be a good sport. Sometimes I caught her looking at me from offstage, stony-faced, as if maybe she wanted to kill me. She objected when Mr. Occhipinti told her that she would have to wear pillows strapped to her to make her look like the indulgent nurse she was supposed to be. "You want to be an actress, or a glamour girl?" he asked her. I don't think she knew the answer, but she gave in.

Mother attended some of our rehearsals. None of the other parents did, nor did Frank's grandmother. Mother would comment on my performance afterward, sometimes telling me what I already knew, sometimes indicating that she sensed how much I was interested in Frank. "You ought to tone it down a bit, dear. You don't want to look like you're going to eat the boy alive." When she was there, I had to struggle to shut her out of my mind. My delivery of the line "Some say the lark and loathèd toad change eyes" fell flat as an image flashed in my head of Mother's toad-green, unblinking eyes on me. My voice trailed off at the end, a failing that impelled Mr. Occhipinti to rage. As for whether I was overplaying toward Frank, I was content to let Mr. Occhipinti be the judge of that, and he had no complaints. It *was* acting, as I have said; then again it was not. It started as acting, but the more harmonious Frank and I became in word and movement, the more the gap between thought and action narrowed. I wondered what it would be like to play Juliet to a Romeo you despised. It could be done, but I preferred it this way.

One evening we showed up for rehearsal—Mother was at home—to find Mr. Occhipinti had called in ill. Buster took off, but Frank, Rhoda, and I stood around. All I could think of was that this was a chance for Frank and me to be alone for a couple of hours.

"I'll walk you home," Frank said.

"Okay," Rhoda said, "I get the message." I could hardly blame her for feeling miffed. Not only was she playing a frump, I was opposite Frank Hern. Did that mean that she was supposed to be stuck with Buster MacEntee? He was a potato-face.

She telephoned for her car; Frank and I left.

He had confided that his real ambition was to be a playwright. He maintained that there had never been a truly great American play, and that he intended to write the first. The only plays that captured American life were comedies, and most of these were mild and formulaic. The serious dramas were nothing but imitations of English and European warhorses.

First he would write a series of short stories about New York City. There would be one story for every borough and district—Greenwich Village, the Bronx, Brooklyn, and so on, even Harlem if he could manage it. The stories would hold a mirror up to the city and would reveal things that no one ever wrote about, the tragedies and comedies of separate lives. When he got finished, no one would be able to think about New York in the same old way again. The stories would make his reputation, and then he would set about conquering Broadway with plays about gangsters, socialites, shopkeepers, and salesgirls. The possibilities were limitless. The world was at our feet, if only we knew it.

"Look at that," he said as we walked through purple dusk. Or I walked. Frank skipped and leapt. He pointed into a tiny grocery store where we could see a man arranging shiny cans. "There's a universe in there! That guy might have found happiness or be chewed to a frazzle. Meanwhile we get a play about the South Seas and another about London society—fine, but what about us? What about that woman—does she know where she's going? Look! She's squeezing a tomato! What does it mean? Nothing! Isn't it great? There are apartments up there with people living side by side for years and they're strangers. People in this city are dying of stupidity! Listen, do you want to get some coffee or something?"

It was early. We hadn't been alone together since *The Queen of Sheba.*

"We could go to a movie," I said. "Who would know?"

"That's what I was thinking. Boy, are we alike!"

We went into the first theater and took seats in a corner at the back. I am sure the picture was wonderful.

14

We made a success of our *Romeo and Juliet* scenes, or so our teachers told us. The patrons of our appearances wrote fulsomely to us; checks poured in. Typically the four of us would board the train with our teachers one morning, be met at Dobbs Ferry, up at Newport, or somewhere out on Long Island by a car, and do our number before an audience of thirty or forty nabobs gobbling cocktails and canapés in some tapestried enormous room. We were permitted to mingle with the elite at a buffet supper, accepting compliments and chitchatting about tragedy and beauty. We returned by train or, if none was running, in a car provided by our host. These galas blend in my mind, one grand house and ice-encrusted hostess and her husband—some of them indifferent, some attentive and kind—merging into another. Except for our last occasion, which was in several respects different.

That final weekend in August, change was in the air. On the train out to Long Island Mrs. Cornwall as usual took it upon herself to tell us something about our hosts. She must have considered this part of her educational function. Like most of us, she cherished tidbits about the rich, and I think she wished us to believe that she was privy to inside information. I never knew her personal history, but she had that air of enthusiasm touched with sadness that suggests past betrayal and permanent damage and a woman who ever after took refuge in the vicarious: the ideal background for a teacher who wanted nothing more than for her students to triumph and to remember her with Christmas cards.

She told us that Mr. Edward Crupper, the oilman, had married the present Mrs. Crupper within the year. His previous wife had drowned in her swimming pool. Heart failure, the newspapers had said, but gossip intimated foul play in which Mr. Crupper's liaison with a Ziegfeld girl figured. That girl, Lydia, was the new Mrs. Crupper. Another version had it that the first Mrs. Crupper had been, well, free with her favors.

"You mean she was a nymphomaniac?" Frank asked brightly.

"That is not a nice word," Mrs. Cornwall said. It was only gossip, she didn't take it a bit seriously, but the rumor was that the first Mrs. Crupper, incensed at her husband's dalliance with a showgirl, had presented him with a list of her lovers. It was said to have numbered as many as twenty-five or thirty and to have included school chums of his, a gardener, business associates, and several polo players. It was obviously the attempt of a desperate woman to make her husband jealous. Unfortunately the list had fallen into the hands of a gossip columnist, no one knew how.

"Of course it's true," Mr. Occhipinti crowed. "A tale of passion!"

Mrs. Cornwall explained that the new Mrs. Crupper was the one who had invited us to grace her soiree with Shakespeare.

"Love and death!" Mr. Occhipinti said.

Rhoda, Frank, and I were so delighted with all this that we talked of nothing else on the way. Rhoda was all for trying to solve the murder. On this occasion we had been invited to spend the night; there would be opportunity to sneak about and turn up some clues. Frank was sure that Mr. Crupper must have confessed to his new wife. Only Buster MacEntee had nothing to say. According to Frank, Buster was single-mindedly devoted to masturbation.

"There'll be no sneaking about," Mrs. Cornwall said. "You shall behave yourselves. You are representatives of PCS."

Margaret in Hollywood

A liveried chauffeur met us at the Locust Valley station, and we proceeded through Glen Cove toward the Crupper house, which sat on a bluff overlooking Hempstead Harbor and the Sound. Viewed from several hundred yards down the driveway, the place appeared even grander than either of the mansions we had visited at Newport, perhaps because it sat alone on vast grounds. It had been built little more than a decade ago, Mrs. Cornwall told us, before the Great War, in celebration of Mr. Crupper's having struck it rich in Indian Territory, or was it California?

"In America nothing is old," Mr. Occhipinti announced with some disdain.

"That's what's good about it," Frank said. "My parents are living in China, and they say it's going to pieces."

"When you are old, you will feel different," Mr. Occhipinti said.

We mounted the steps and entered the great front hall where a butler led us up the branching staircase to our rooms. Each was slightly different in color and furnishing. Rhoda and I were placed next to one another and shared a bathroom, Frank and Buster across the hall, our teachers out of sight around a bend.

From my window I gazed out at a lawn that sloped for a quarter-mile down to a strip of beach and the sea, where a motor launch nestled against a dock, a sailing yacht moored beyond. In the middle distance, a gazebo; off to the left, an acre of burning roses. Hedges and walks and brilliant flower beds were scattered about. Close to the house classical statuary presided over a vast swimming pool shaped in the form of a crescent—or was it a *C* for Crupper?

At five we descended in full costume, except for Rhoda, who refused to strap on her pillows until showtime, to meet our hosts. The newlyweds were waiting for us at the foot of the stairs. Mr. Crupper stood with feet planted apart and bald head thrust forward, as if ready to charge and gore us. Lydia Crupper, half his size, canary hair in the latest bob, opened her arms and said that we looked like Arabian knights. As I drew closer, I got the impression that she had not yet lost her baby teeth, which had a bluish cast. She was in other ways cute— but was this a motive for murder?

Mr. Crupper caressed her flank. In his free hand he held a tumblerful of whiskey. He drank, peered at me over the rim, and turned to Frank.

"Do you play polo, son?"

"No, sir. I never have, actually."

"How about your friend, the padre?"

"What?" Buster said.

"Well, you ought to take it up. My sons all play. They're not any good, but they play. I didn't learn till I was forty-seven. Now, I'm three goals. They say I'm too old? Let me tell you something. The only reason a man would quit polo is if he was broke or dead."

His voice reverberated around the marble.

"Our guests are enjoying a cocktail," Mrs. Crupper said. "They all adore Shakespeare. I made sure of that."

"Anyone want a drink?" Mr. Crupper asked.

Mr. Occhipinti was about to accept, but Mrs. Cornwall said they would wait until after the performance.

"I always take a couple of belts before a game," said Mr. Crupper, casting a wink at Frank and departing with a slap to his wife's behind. "Give everybody what they want, god-damn it."

Mrs. Crupper and Mrs. Cornwall chatted about arrange-ments for our performance. "These people are mental defec-tives," Frank whispered to me. In my other ear Rhoda asked whether I had noticed Mrs. Crupper's ring: "Twenty carats and I swear it's cut in the shape of a horse's head!"

Because the evenings had begun to cool and the bugs to retire for the season, Mrs. Crupper had decided that we should put on our show on the terrace. She had ordered a stage set up beside the pool and spotlights mounted. It was also her inspiration to provide a harpist. With her husband out of sight, she loosened up, told Mr. Occhipinti that he reminded her of the maître d' at Delmonico's, helped Rhoda adjust her hair, told us that she hadn't been on the stage since *Spice of 1920* at the Winter Garden, where she had met Eddie.

"Such a *volgarità*," Mr. Occhipinti said when she left us. "How can I be expected to produce beauty for peasants?" He flicked his thumbnail out from under his teeth and bemoaned the artist's lot.

I was beginning to think Lydia Crupper endearing. Frank said that he wanted her to star in his first play. She would take the role of the girl living in a Brooklyn boardinghouse torn between careers as a showgirl or a nun, or both.

Getting into the mood for tragedy proved a challenge. From the library that served as our greenroom we watched the guests outside. Mrs. Cornwall recognized what she swore was an Astor and two or three other society types, but she pronounced the crowd a mixed bag. There were women wearing too many jewels and a man she identified as an usher from the Roxy Theater. Whoever, they were a noisy bunch. She reminded us that Shakespeare's own theater had welcomed everyone and that there had been bearbaiting outside the pit. I told Rhoda that I was more nervous than usual. All our performances had gone so well, I would hate to collapse now.

"You'll be fine," she said. "Just lean on Nursie."

When our audience—there must have been two hundred of them—had been seated as in a dinner theater at round tables ranged about the stage, Rhoda and I began with the scene in which I ask her who Romeo is, and she tells me, and I reply,

"My only love, sprung from my only hate!
Too early seen unknown, and known too late!"

That was all it took for me to lose my jitters. The language carried me along without a snag, and I was in that world of passion so delicate and so precise and fierce. It would not have made any difference if there had been an audience of ten or a thousand or no audience; by the time Frank joined me and we began exchanging those witty, extravagant, and erotic words, I was well-lost in the play and in him. Glasses must have clinked;

people must have whispered and coughed. I heard nothing but our voices.

I did hear a gasp and a small cry nearby as I stabbed myself with Frank's dagger—"O happy dagger! This is thy sheath; there rest, and let me die"—and, with no more words to say, I knew it was Lydia Crupper. How sweet of our hostess-in-the-rough to have been so moved. Friar Buster spoke the final lines (Frank's idea, since we had no Prince)—

"For never was a story of more woe
Than this of Juliet and her Romeo—"

and we were done.

Mrs. Crupper led her guests in standing applause that thundered in the evening air. We took several bows, and the swimming-pool lights went up. Mrs. Crupper, stumbling on a step, embraced us. Her powder was streaked with tears; she said that it was the most beautiful thing she had ever seen; it may have been.

Rhoda embraced Frank and me and told us that this night had been the best ever. I gave Buster a kiss as he stammered praise. I could scarcely look at Frank.

Mrs. Cornwall clambered up to congratulate us, while Mr. Occhipinti pranced about, preening like a popinjay. He had never been so proud, he said. We had shown these peasants a thing or two about art!

At dinner we were scattered among different tables. Imagine separating Juliet from Romeo! I drew Lydia Crupper's table, Frank her husband's. At least I got the better of that bargain. Of the four couples at my table, I caught only the Chester-Martins' name. He was in asphalt, he told me by way of introduction.

"Listen, honey," Lydia confided above the strolling violins as we spooned the cold consommé, "you've got it. I could spot that the minute you stepped onstage. Where'd you learn to walk like that? I heard a drumroll, I swear it. I'd give a million for what you've got. Make it two million!"

I thanked her but said the credit belonged to Shakespeare.

"Bullshit," she said, making me laugh. "Take my advice, don't give it away. Don't sell cheap. That's what Eddie says, and he knows what he's talking about. Another thing. Why don't you cut your hair? What is it, down to your waist? It's pretty, but it's old, know what I mean?" She flounced her bob. "With looks like yours, I guess you can do what you want. Tell everybody to go fuck themselves." She raised her water glass, which must have been filled with gin, and drank. "I never got a shot at Shakespeare, what the hell. Your eyebrows are a little heavy, honey. Come by my room in the morning and we can work on them.

"I'm so glad you kids could come. Of course Eddie doesn't give a damn. That SOB won't even take me to a play. I mean, you could go crazy just sitting around watching polo."

Waiters poured wine. From an upper corner of the terrace an orchestra struck up a fizzy version of "All Alone," driving out the strolling violins. I took some wine and thought to myself, This is some production. Where am I? I knew Frank was loving it. His table was maybe twenty feet away. We kept locking eyes, and with his thumb he gestured toward Mr. Crupper, who was carrying on a monologue.

Lydia looked at the heavens. "Not a cloud," she said. "We've got a tent they can put up in twenty minutes. You can do a lot with money. You can change the weather. Do you believe in reincarnation?"

"No," I said.

"I do. That's why I don't worry about anything. The next time, I'm picking a different husband. The next time, I'm going to come back as an independent woman."

"What does that mean to you?" I asked. "What does it mean, to be an independent woman?"

"Don't give me that. Independently wealthy! What the hell else would it mean?"

She turned to discuss an upcoming country-club event with the Chester-Martins, something about golf and bagpipes. I wondered how old Lydia was. If she was only three or four years off the chorus line, she couldn't be much past thirty, but earlier, in the harsh light of the hall, I had noticed quite a bit of wear and tear. Those were not laugh lines; nothing was that funny.

Across the way Mr. Occhipinti rose to propose a toast. It was his set piece. He would add and subtract flourishes, but by now I could have delivered it myself. Rhoda and I used to recite it back and forth. These gifted players, he began, these mere saplings in the garden of the theater, tender shoots scarcely older than the star-crossed lovers of Verona—these young thespians had brought Shakespeare to life in this domain of refinement, of taste, of aspiration toward the ideal. Juliet was Primavera herself, Romeo vigorous as a newly virile stag, Friar Laurence the soul of kindly faith, and the Nurse a symbol of maternal solicitude. Not since Lorenzo the Magnificent had such opportunity been afforded for the expression of the spirit. Without the patronage of noblemen and noblewomen such as those gathered here there would be no art, no beauty, no exalted passion, but only debasement—the noises of the street and the braying of jackasses.

"To the Cruppers!" Applause, applause.

When the orchestra began again, Frank came to my side. I thought he was going to lead me to the dance floor, but he guided me past the pool and out onto the lawn in the direction of the rose garden. I asked how things had been at his table. Mr. Crupper had gone on and on about polo, oil, and the stock market. Oil was four dollars a barrel and would go to ten. Steel was up. Everything was up, up, up. No one else had said much of anything, but there had been some compensatory amusements. At one point Mr. Crupper had leaned over and thrust his hand down the front of the dress of the woman seated next to him. Everyone had pretended not to notice.

I told him about Lydia, and I said I was feeling kind of a letdown after our performance. It would have been nice just to be alone afterward.

"Let's be alone, then," Frank said.

We walked hand in hand down toward the great gazebo. I

said I could hardly wait for the full production in the fall. Frank said that he looked forward to it also, but that I was the real actor, not he. He was acting only to learn about writing plays and for one other reason.

"What is that?"

"To be with you," he said.

We climbed into the gazebo and looked back at the house. The music drifted out. We spotted Lydia in the middle of the dance floor doing something resembling a Charleston, guests on the floor urging her on. When she fell, gentlemen rushed in to help her to her feet and set her spinning again.

We couldn't pick out Rhoda. Mr. Occhipinti was nowhere to be seen. Mrs. Cornwall remained at her table in earnest conversation. As for Buster, he was visible near the bandstand, looking like a Franciscan runaway.

"No one can see us," Frank said. He wrapped himself around me and we kissed. Lightning in the dark, light love in darkening night—my head was full of the play and my mouth of him.

We ran down toward the beach.

15

*T*he light on the dock drew us. When we saw the motor launch, we decided to climb down into it. I had to step carefully, not to get tangled in my Juliet gown. I nearly toppled him falling into his arms; we steadied ourselves and the boat. We picked our way to the cushioned seat at the rear and collapsed on it and started kissing madly, slithering onto the bottom. The boat moved us gently up and down and from side to side.

It was a question of what next and when. He had felt my breasts through my dress. He had opened my dress. The straps of my slip came down. I held on to the back of his hand as he cupped me. His other pressed me under the dress.

"Margaret, Margaret."

"Shh."

The difficult part was getting his tights down. Then I had hold of it, Frank's strong thing, all mine, and played with it. I swung open for him. He was over me, his hands on the deck, touching me with it. So finally, please, and—

Voices!

"Shit!" Frank said.

Laughter, men and women. A roaring male voice coming closer. Clatter of footsteps on the dock.

"Christ," Frank gasped. "It's Crupper!"

They were peering down on us. Frank was covering me as

if from enemy fire. I made out Mr. Crupper, another man, and a pair of women.

"Get the hell out of there!" Mr. Crupper bellowed at us. "We're going for a ride. Get the hell out!"

"Oh look, Eddie!" one of the women said. "It's Romeo and Juliet! How sweet!"

It was easier for me. All I had to do was drop my dress and fasten a button. I thought poor Frank would end up in the water pulling on his tights. They were laughing at us, except for Mr. Crupper, who mentioned trespassing. We made it onto the beach and watched them tear away in a streak, Crupper standing like a colossus at the wheel. They raced out to the yacht a few hundred yards out and climbed aboard, hullaba-loos reaching us across the water, the orchestra playing on behind us.

All at once the music stopped in midtune. A straggling sax-ophone sounded a last, lonely honk. We turned to see what at that distance looked like Mrs. Crupper standing in front of the bandstand, waving her arms and delivering a speech. We were too far away to make out her words. Suddenly the guests began scattering as if before a squall, and she disappeared into the house.

We ran all the way up the lawn to the terrace. Only a hand-ful of the guests remained to stagger up the steps and into the house by the time we got there. The musicians were packing up their instruments. Our cohorts had vanished.

Departing guests thronged the great hall, pushing their way out to their automobiles. A few chatted as if nothing untoward had occurred; most were gravely still. Frank, holding my hand, struggled through the front door. Either Lydia had discov-ered her hubby missing, or somebody had dropped dead from too much gin or culture.

But outside neither an ambulance nor a hearse was in evi-dence. Some were waiting decorously for attendants to re-trieve cars; others took off on foot for their machines. Chauffeurs drove up jockeying for position, one making an end run through the corner of a flower bed and clipping a topiary shrub in his eagerness to reach his employers. Versailles must have looked like this when word arrived that the mob was on the march.

Standing a step above and behind the Chester-Martins, I heard her say to him:

"It was you who insisted on coming."

I tapped her on the shoulder and asked whether someone had been taken ill.

"Yes," she said. "I have."

Frank spotted Mrs. Cornwall, who was talking to another couple. As we reached her, she was saying that she was most grateful for their offer to drive us back to the city, but that circumstances required we spend the night.

"Oh, there you are, children! Were you frightened?"

"Frightened?" Frank started to say. I gave his foot a kick.

"Yes," I broke in. "Especially when everyone started to leave. We were in the gazebo watching everybody dance. It was so lovely. We're not quite sure what happened."

Mrs. Cornwall took us aside to give us a breathless account. At the conclusion of the solo dance with which Lydia had entertained her guests but not, as it turned out, her husband, she had entered the house to refresh herself. Some minutes later she had returned in an obviously distressed condition. She had walked up to the bandstand, silenced the musicians, called for everyone's attention, and—Mrs. Cornwall closed her eyes and raised her eyebrows—announced in the most shocking language that she had discovered Mr. Crupper in a bathroom with another woman.

Mrs. Crupper had denounced her husband and the floozy. In the midst of what I gathered had been a colorful diatribe, Mrs. Crupper had caught sight of the motor launch cutting its path toward the yacht. She screamed at everyone to get out and announced that she was telephoning the coast guard.

"He may head for the Bahamas," Frank said.

There was only one thing I did not understand. Why had Mrs. Cornwall refused a ride back to New York? I had the sense that we were no longer welcome at Château Crupper.

"Let's go inside," Mrs. Cornwall said.

Under the staircase she whispered to us that Mr. Occhipinti, overcome by the success of our performance, had indulged in too many cocktails. He had got sick in the bushes during Lydia's Charleston and had made his way to bed. Mrs. Cornwall had tried to rouse him, but he was dead to the world. It would have been embarrassing and injurious to the reputation of the school to have him carried out in front of everyone. We were not to think for a moment that this behavior was in any way typical of him. He had been overcome by a strong weakness.

Mrs. Cornwall, to her credit, seemed more invigorated than distressed by events. She only hoped that our pleasure in our achievement had not been spoiled and that we would not think too badly of poor Mr. Occhipinti. She wouldn't want our parents to lose confidence in PCS. We would be away first thing in the morning.

I found Rhoda in our bathroom, brushing out her hair. She had run upstairs when hell had broken loose. I told her that Frank and I had gone for a walk. She didn't probe. She was upset, but not about our crazy hosts. For her, the evening had been ruined earlier. A horrible little man at her table had begun talking about the Jews taking over Wall Street and the world. She had tried to ignore him, but when he had started using ugly words like "kike" and "yid," she had left the table. She hated herself for not having said something. She had looked for me, and had gone up to Buster instead and told him about it. He had been very nice and had offered to punch the man in the nose.

"That would have made a beautiful scene," I said. "Too bad he didn't."

Rhoda said that it was the first time she had encountered anything like that. Her parents had warned her; from now on she would believe them.

Before climbing into bed, I looked out my window to check on the yacht. Its lights twinkled; it looked deceptively romantic, with no signs of a hostile boarding party.

I could not sleep, what with feeling bad for Rhoda and animated by everything that had happened. My thoughts soon flew past religious persecution and domestic drama and settled on the one thing that mattered to me that night. Surely, lying just across the hall, Frank could think of nothing but me and of what we had done and almost done? I made a feeble attempt to be glad that fate had intervened to save my virginity; that didn't work at all. I found myself wishing fervently that Frank would get up the nerve to sneak into my room.

Just in case, I got up to make sure the outer door was unlocked and to close the door to the bathroom. If only our rooms adjoined, I could signal him through the wall. He must be trying to gather courage, I told myself. I willed him out of his bed and into mine.

I decided I would give him ten minutes and then try to go to sleep.

I don't know how much time passed, maybe two minutes, it seemed like forty. I was not growing drowsy. On the contrary, I was becoming angry with Frank for lacking imagination and initiative as much as I was craving his company.

I got up, quietly opened my door, and checked the hall. No one, not a sound. I closed my door, crossed the hall, and tried Frank's. It opened.

He was sitting up in the semidark. I stood at the foot of his bed. He whispered my name.

"I wanted you to see me," I said.

I undid my nightgown and let it fall to the floor. I could feel the breeze from the window on me.

"You should have come to me," I said as I climbed in with him.

"That's all I was thinking about," he said.

"Don't think anymore."

He was timid at first. Not for long; nor did it hurt as much as books and girlish speculations had led me to believe it would. It was easy, so easy, and more wonderful the next time.

"We should have done this before," Frank said. "We should always be doing it. Do you love me?"

"Let's not worry about that now." I was sure I did, but I

didn't feel like saying it. All I was thinking was that we would have to find a way to be alone again and often and that the idea of going back to sleeping in the same bed with my mother was more than I could bear. On an impulse I burrowed under and kissed him on the tip of his diminished thing. That had quite an effect.

I hated to leave, but I didn't want to take the chance of falling asleep and getting caught.

Back in my own quarters I took a bath as I had heard one ought to do, although Frank had been careful. As I jumped into bed, feeling happier than I could remember and dying for the morning to come so I could see him again, I heard a distant, tinkling crash. I assumed that a servant must still be cleaning up on the terrace and had dropped a tray of glasses.

After a minute or so, I heard the sound again. I went to the window. The lights in and around the great C-shaped pool were still burning. There, standing naked beside a statue of some Greco-Roman god or other, was Lydia Crupper, alone, tipping back a champagne bottle. In the greenish, watery light she was beautiful, swaying under the bottle, angry and crazy.

I ran to get Frank.

We held each other in nightgown and pajamas as Lydia reared back, staggered, and flung the bottle at the god. It shattered against his flank. Frank started laughing. I put my hands over his mouth.

There was a case of the stuff at Lydia's feet. She popped open another and drank again. A few gulps did it this time, then the old heave-ho. She hit an ankle, and I thought I saw a chip fly off. But the god remained upright.

She opened another bottle and emptied it over her chest. This time she aimed high, and it sailed over the statue's head into the pool.

Rhoda came rushing in. She stopped when she saw Frank, but I motioned her over to us. I said I couldn't have let Frank miss this.

"Were you taking a bath just now?"

"Sorry if I woke you. I couldn't sleep. Isn't this incredible?"

Before Lydia could get off another heave, a maid appeared with a blanket and draped it around her mistress's shoulders.

"I think this happens every Saturday night here," Frank said. "This has to be in a play."

Whimpering, Lydia permitted herself to be ushered up the steps and into the house.

I did not disclose to Rhoda all the intimacies of that night, but before long she got the picture and even made it easier for Frank and me to meet. His grandmother's apartment was only a few blocks from the Meyers'; all I had to do was to tell Mother I was going to see Rhoda after school or a modeling session, and Rhoda covered for me if Mother telephoned. I told Rhoda I'd be delighted to do the same for her; she said she hoped she would be able to give me the opportunity before the end of time. When I did actually visit her or spend the night, her questions were endless and clinical. I couldn't tell whether she thought me a heroine or a slut or both. I don't think she knew, any more than I did. Her main worry was that I would get pregnant. Her idea that Frank and I would eventually marry was absurdly premature; and when I told her so, she was shocked in spite of her professed freethinking and knowledge of show-business types. Her own sexual experience at that point had progressed to necking with a boy at a charity ball and in the movies; she had yet to fall for anyone. I sensed that she was consciously saving herself for the man who would become the father of her children, a restraint with which I was not blessed.

I had at first felt sorry for Frank because his parents were living on the other side of the globe. The truth was that staying with Grandmother Hern and attending PCS had been his own idea; far from an abandoned kid, he was simply more of a free and independent spirit than anyone else I knew. He had lived with his mother and father when they had been posted to various places in Europe and in Washington; he had enjoyed Paris as much as anyone. All that moving around had given him his placeless, mid-Atlantic accent, but also a fondness for using the full range of his baritone in speech and for lively gestures uncommon in an American. But the idea of spending two years or more in the Orient did not appeal to him. He had the nerve to announce that it would interfere with his projected literary and dramatic development and alienate him from his material! When his grandmother, to whom he was very close, had offered to keep him, he had accepted.

Grandmother Hern, or Evelyn, as Frank called her, was a fanatical devotee of Margaret Sanger. She had presented her grandson with a packet of condoms on his fourteenth birthday. (He had not made use of them, or so he said, until he displayed himself ensheathed to me one afternoon when we were playing around in his bedroom.) "I'm finishing another letter to the pope," Evelyn said to Frank on the day on which I was introduced to her. "Do look it over and see if you think it's all right." She was constantly dispatching harangues on the subject of population control to heads of foreign governments, but especially to Pius XI, who infuriated her by delegating his replies to a cardinal.

Frank thought Evelyn only slightly nutty, and he adored her, not least of all because she let him do exactly as he pleased. He kept no set hours, was given an allowance to spend as he saw fit, and was free to conduct himself in any way he wished within the confines of his own room. That included entertaining me. "Hello, dears," she would say when we came in. "Have a good time." Frank had a quotation pinned up over his writing desk: *"Toute vraie passion ne songe qu'à elle."*—Stendhal. True passion thinks only of itself. Seeing it always made me want to fuck, not to put too fine a point on it, and we did quite a lot of that.

I don't know that we were extraordinary, but I don't see how we could have done it more, given the subterfuges required for me to get free of Mother. There was a limit to how often I could lie about visiting Rhoda or having a rehearsal or a modeling session run over. When we were apart for a few days, the tension was excruciating, and I swear I'd start coming the minute he touched me. Of course, I did worry about getting pregnant, and only Evelyn's supply of condoms (she handed them out like chocolates), her pamphlets on ovulation cycles, Frank's timely withdrawals, and the proximity of the bath to his bedroom must have saved us, though we took our share of risks. During the full production of *Romeo and Juliet*, we fell to the floors of empty classrooms, did it several times standing up in a clothes closet, in the seats of the darkened theater, in Mrs. Nesbitt's office one night when Frank found it unlocked—on the very couch where I had sat with Mother! More than once with frantic agility we managed it between acts behind the scenery, teachers and other students not twenty feet away, the challenge of speed and silence urging us on. Whether this activity helped or hindered our onstage performances I can't say. Frank thought it would play wonderfully well in a movie, Romeo and Juliet plighting their troth and then rushing off to consummate the union under a papier-mâché bush.

Frank promised that someday he would write a play for me, but that no one would believe in a girl as wonderful as I was. He had already made stabs at his collection of short stories—sketches, he called them—bits and pieces of characters he had observed and imagined in the city. Some of them were remarkably good, I would say reminiscent of Hemingway but no one had heard of *him* yet. One was about a bus driver who kept carrier pigeons on his roof; others about a girl whose one pair of new shoes is ruined in the snow, a minister with a mistress, a clerk who beats his son, a man sitting in a restaurant thinking about lost opportunities, an old woman living on Thompson Street who spends each day looking out the window with the radio playing behind her. This last I thought very clever because the music and dialogue from the radio were interwoven with the woman's thoughts of her absent children and the husband who has deserted her. It reminded me of my mother and made me feel slightly guilty—only slightly—for not trying to be closer to her.

Reading these stories put me in awe of Frank. He was only

159

a few months older than I, but he was already able to look at life with astonishing perceptiveness and maturity and empathy for other people. He happened to have a very large head, his caps were 7⅝, and I kidded him that this must be the source of his genius.

He had such a strong sense of his mission as a writer that I had no doubt of his ultimate success, nor did Evelyn, who had already announced that she was prepared to support him as long as necessary. Perhaps her generosity and liberal views of childrearing spoiled him, but I was envious of him. I already knew how overrated the virtue of "getting out to earn your own living" was; I had been doing this for some time and could think of few things worse. Years later I met a screenwriter doing what he regarded as hackwork. He had a house full of books with portentous titles and was sure that his own genius belonged on those shelves. He told me that his father had offered to support him until he got a novel published, but, of course, he had been too proud to accept a handout. "Then you're a bloody fool," I said, "and you will never amount to anything."

When we weren't carrying on or sitting around at Evelyn's or at Rhoda's, we devoured museums and haunted the Forty-second Street library; and Mr. Occhipinti took a group of us to see Jascha Heifetz perform the Beethoven Violin Concerto with the Philharmonic at Carnegie Hall, an experience Frank admitted was even more exalting than a Giants game. We hung around the basement at PCS, where there was a Ping-Pong table, discussing the arts and solving the problems of the world with other friends. Many of our cohorts, aping their parents, called themselves socialists or communists; Frank liked to argue with them that art had no purpose other than to capture the life of its time and the vision of its creator, whatever the consequences to social morale. The debates were heated, and Frank thrived on them. I let him do the arguing. My single ambition was to perform. When I was accused of using art as an escape from life and from myself, I pled guilty to the charge.

Alone we often discussed our parents. I don't think that Frank cared for my mother, but he was tactful enough to criticize her only indirectly. He visited my apartment occasionally—over my objections at first; I was ashamed of it and did not want him to associate it with me—on one pretext or another. He announced that he would in all likelihood write a play using our place as the setting. I said that the idea sounded extremely unpromising, and that I for one would not pay a cent to see it.

He referred to his own mother and father affectionately, but as if they were characters in some Shavian comedy, his mother a professional hostess and his father obsessed with schemes to upgrade the world's nutritional standards by such means as the preservation of unfermented fruit juices and the encouragement of a taste for peanut butter among the Russians.

Frank made everyone a story, everyone a character, and he gave me the sense that he would write his own life's script no matter what. Those would have been halcyon days entirely— if only I hadn't had to work!

16

*D*uring one of those evenings amid
the bronze and marble of the rich at Dobbs Ferry, I had attracted the attention of Klaus Knauer, the photographer. Dr.
Knauer had not yet reached the pinnacle of his fame, when
his portraits of Garbo, Verée Teasdale, Norma Shearer, and
others became icons for the millions; but he was already esteemed for his documentation of trench warfare and, among
the sentimental cognoscenti, for a series he had done on German folk art featuring the basket weavers of Schleswig-Hol-
stein. He had photographed Booth Tarkington, Lola Fisher,
Philip Barry, and numerous other theatrical eminences. A
portrait by Knauer was becoming a status symbol.

Dr. Knauer invited Mother and me to tea at the Gramercy
Park Hotel. He was in his mid-forties, with wavy, silvering hair
brushed straight back from a high, knit, and bony brow. His
deep-set gray eyes were full of *Weltschmerz,* and he continu-
ously widened and narrowed them as if adjusting a camera's
aperture. Full lips contrasted with what was otherwise the model
of an ascetic philosopher's face. He was elaborately courteous,
making sure we were seated comfortably, recommending this
or that delicacy. The pastries, he informed us, fell short of
Viennese standards but represented a hopeful sign of prog-
ress on this side of the Atlantic.

He poured the tea and withdrew from the inside pocket of

his gray suit a sheet of heavy, pearl-gray paper and presented it to me:

"I wish that you should have this, Miss Spencer, with compliments of the author. Please to understand. It is from one artist to another given. In the spirit of the inner life."

The page was headed "To Miss Margaret Spencer." In a graceful, ornate black script he had written out a two-line verse in German, followed by an English translation. It read:

> I have seen Juliet. Now I weary
> of the luxuriant summer trees.

Mother craned to read it. I handed it to her and could sense that she was suspicious. She began sucking on her upper lip, making that familiar wet, fleshy sound that I hoped was not audible to the waiter, who might think he was being summoned. I knew that she could not make heads or tails of the poem. I thanked Dr. Knauer and said that I would treasure his gift and that it was a great honor.

"It is only my little tribute," he said, addressing Mother. "Your daughter promises a wonderful future. Ethel Barrymore's Juliet was a failure, as of course you know, because she is, shall we say, a little too seasoned for the part. In Germany we believe that if the flower is picked too late, it will offend the nostrils at the Easter feast. Do you have that expression? Miss Spencer would by my opinion have made the production a success. In these matters I am an excellent judge. More tea, permit me, *madame.*"

I concentrated on my watercress sandwich.

To win Mother over, Dr. Knauer spent most of the rest of our meeting talking to her and politely answering her questions. Her lip-sucking subsided. She wanted to know what many of the famous people he had photographed were like in person. Was John Barrymore really a hopeless drunk? Was it true that Edwin Morgenstern had three wives and had divorced none of them? Did Carlotta Cardona use foul language? There were few things in the world more regrettable than foul language in a woman, didn't he agree?

Dr. Knauer said that he tried to capture his subjects' souls, not their personal habits. He discoursed on the absolutes of beauty and terror. At length he got around to the idea that I might pose for him. He had in mind portraits inspired by the friezes from the Parthenon.

I was now in demand for *Vogue* and *Harper's Bazaar* layouts, Mother said. My fee had gone up. She turned to me in her genteel, garden-party manner and suggested that perhaps I needed to go to the little girls' room so that she and Dr. Knauer could discuss grown-up matters.

I could tell you a thing or two about grown-up matters, I thought, but I bit my tongue and waited on a couch opposite the hotel cashier's desk, hoping that Mother would not drive Dr. Knauer away by holding out for more than he was willing to pay. I feared that to her he was just another shutterbug; I knew that having him take my picture would be a sure sign of my ascent, even before I landed a professional role.

They emerged arm in arm, he as if he were escorting King Ludwig's mistress, she looking smug as a farm woman who had just got the better of a turnip broker. Our first session would be a week from that day, Dr. Knauer said. He took my hand to kiss, bowing and clicking.

Our tea had been on Saturday. On Monday I left school at noon for a different sort of appointment. Norman and Chicki Kuppler, up-and-coming publicity agents, had landed the account of the Camp Fire Girls. To promote their new client, the Kupplers had decided on what they figured would be a surefire stunt, a contest for Camp Fire Girl of the Year. All over the country the Camp Fire Girls were locked in a fierce battle for membership against the Girl Scouts. The winner would have to have just the right combination of glamour and innocence, so that thousands would wish to emulate her and sign up for the Camp Fire Girls. The Scouts would never be the same. If the Kupplers chose the right girl, they would be able to place her picture in newspapers and magazines from coast to coast, a publicity bonanza.

All this my mother broached to me with her own brand of

boosterism. If there was something I wished to do on my own, its pitfalls gaped, perdition lurked at every turn; if there was something she decided I should do, it acquired overtones of a religious crusade.

In a matter of this importance, Mother said, no responsible organization would wish to take a chance on just any girl. The Camp Fire Girl of the Year would have to be poised, know how to act in front of a camera, be reliable and of verifiably impeccable character. A disaster had occurred recently at a Kansas City beauty pageant. Nell had written Mother about it. The winner had been discovered to be of mixed race. Something like this must not happen to the Camp Fire Girls. They required a bona fide professional. They had filtered word through the modeling world that interested candidates should submit their portfolios. The winner would achieve instant fame, appearing on the cover of *Everygirl's,* the Camp Fire monthly, and no telling where else. After Mother had hand-delivered my portfolio to the Kupplers, they had immediately scheduled an interview.

"But I am not a Camp Fire Girl," I said. "I've never even seen a campfire. I hate mosquitoes. Nobody at PCS is a Camp Fire Girl."

"Do not say 'hate.' Whether you're a member is beside the point. They can't take chances."

The next day I rode the subway from school down to Thirty-sixth and Seventh, where Mother was waiting for me. We cooled our heels in an outer office watching the secretary mark up a copy of *Variety*—publicity opportunities, I supposed. At last we were ushered into the other room, to be confronted by a peculiar trio.

Chicki Kuppler leaned her big self against a desk, her fist around a cigarette holder. She wore pounds of mascara, magenta lipstick that set off her mustache, heavy gold rings in her ears, a dark pinstriped tailored suit. You could have taken her for the matriarch of a clan of thieves, her tiny Norman maybe a purse-snatcher. Norman, his popping eyes giving me the once-over, introduced Mrs. Herbert W. "Buffy" Seymour,

Eastern Seaboard head of the Camp Fire Girls and vice chairman of the national board. Mrs. Seymour was the spitting image of Harry Valentine in drag. She even sounded like Harry doing his imitation of a social matron in a routine in which I had played a spoiled brat. Her bosoms were imperial.

"Take off your coat," Norman said to me. "Allow me." He hung my coat on a nail. "Well, what do you think?" he asked Chicki and Buffy. "Has she got it or hasn't she? This kid is another Mary Pickford, I swear to God. Let's see the teeth. Give us a smile, Maggie. So who did the dental work?"

"Those are her natural teeth," Mother said. With her gloved right index finger and thumb, she separated my lips. I shied away, like any beast with a sense of dignity. "Nothing whatever has been altered. Margaret is a genuine girl."

"You know what this is?" Norman said. "This is the girl next door. No, it isn't. It's, I should only be so lucky this is the girl next door, right? Ha! I tell you, it isn't every day you see a knockout with class. Am I telling the truth, Mrs. Seymour?"

"She seems charming," Mrs. Seymour said. "Can she speak? Do you know the English language, dear?"

Why are you wearing that ridiculous hat? were the words that formed in my mind. I managed to force myself to say that I was charmed to meet her and that I admired the work she did on behalf of such a wonderful cause, all the while despising myself for my flattery. There was something in me that tried to win every part no matter what. Mrs. Seymour was delighted. She gave a little speech about why she sacrificed her time, managing to invoke everything from God, her husband, and the Constitution to the American Indian tradition and principles of hygiene. Harry could have used every bit of it. Then she launched into a description of the requirements for the honor to which I aspired. I had to be a girl of impeccable moral character. Was I? Mother answered for me in the affirmative. Did I attend church regularly? Again Mother answered.

"In that case," Mrs. Seymour said, "you won't mind signing this form."

167

It was a pledge not to engage in any activity during the following two years that would bring discredit to the Camp Fire Girls, including drinking alcoholic beverages, smoking, engaging in immoral activities, lewd or lascivious behavior of any kind, or entering into a state of matrimony. Except for smoking and matrimony, it about covered my life. If notice came to the Camp Fire Girls or the Kuppler Agency that I had violated this pledge in any way, or that I had done anything to bring public disfavor to the organization, I would be stripped of my title, denounced as a fraud, and required to pay back with interest all fees earned by me. We would also be subject to a suit for damages.

"I see no problems with this," Mother said, and signed.

"Don't I have to sign?" I asked.

"You're a minor, dear. You may sign if you wish."

I let the privilege pass. I had a sense of having just witnessed the means of my ruination.

"I don't understand," I said, "how I can be Camp Fire Girl of the Year if I'm not even a Camp Fire Girl. Won't someone find out?"

"But you *are* one," Mrs. Seymour said. "I have the authority. Congratulations. As far as I am concerned, you always were one."

Mrs. Seymour, with handshakes all round, then withdrew.

Chicki explained gruffly that all this had to be on the QT. When they got everything organized, they would see to it that I was enrolled in a Camp Fire group.

"So you'll go to a few meetings and count pigeons, whatever they do. It's a snap. And listen, kid, you'll be on salary the whole time. What do you think, Maggie?"

"I prefer Margaret," I said with some intensity, anxious not to lose my name along with everything else.

"There is serious money in this," Norman said. "With this kind of publicity, you could become a star overnight."

"I've seen it happen," Chicki said.

"You are a very, very lucky girl," Norman said. "So what are you going to buy with all your money?"

Margaret in Hollywood

*   *   *

Rhoda and Frank differed in their reactions to my new jobs. Frank was immediately suspicious of Dr. Knauer and, from my description, said that he sounded like a pretentious fraud. He thought the poem about Juliet and the trees ridiculous and interpreted it as "nothing but a middle-aged fart reacting to a beautiful girl." He told me to make sure I didn't let the learned doctor get his hands on me. The Camp Fire Girls' promotion he thought funny. As to my fears of getting found out as less than virtuous, I had nothing to worry about on that score. Better to be involved with honest crooks than with a fake artist, was Frank's idea.

As a lawyer's daughter, Rhoda was more worried about the pledge my mother had signed. It sounded like a contract for servitude. Mrs. Seymour must be a genuine monster.

It turned out that Dr. Knauer had something other than individual portraits of me in mind. His plan was for group photographs, modern and living representations of a panoply of classical figures. He envisioned himself as a revivalist whose mission was to eradicate American provincialism with a New-World-Greco-Roman Renaissance, infused with intimations of Impressionism by the use of soft-focus, grainy photography. "The gods have not died," he was fond of saying, "they have only decided to take a little nap." Even as monks preserved the past and Renaissance artists rescued Europe from the Dark Ages, so he was taking up the task anew.

I received my indoctrination in this rationale while he drove me and the other models out to his shooting location, a beach cottage in the Hamptons, where we posed among the dunes. "Vandals are at the American gates!" he would declaim from behind the wheel. "Degraded races, the scum of Europe and Asia, are spreading their filth and slime. They have invaded the theater and have made Hollywood the capital of corruption. They hide behind the soft masks of democracy. Democracy? Pfah! Every dog must have its day." He would use the weapon of the enemy, film, to assault them with beauty, a Pythagorean perfection, plummet-measured, hard and cold.

The other models were veteran Isadora Duncan dancers inaptly called the Isadorables. They were a serious lot, at the opposite end of the spectrum from the fluffs I was used to in the modeling trade. They talked only of art, philosophy, and politics, and as ploddingly as they moved. A couple of them stank like badgers, as I found out cooped up in the car. They were less classical than paleolithic.

I gathered that Dr. Knauer was using me for contrast, or I hoped he was. He made me the centerpiece of every portrait. If I was Athene, they were my handmaidens. Of the muses, I was Music. I was the princess Nausicaa, tossing a ball to servant girls.

In order, Dr. Knauer explained, to mimic the miraculous qualities Greek sculptors gave to the folds of draped garments in marble, he doused our chiffon-clad bodies with buckets of seawater. He seemed to get a kick out of this, shouting and leaping about in the sand. It was mid-October; soaking wet, we shivered in the wind as he arranged us just so and had us hold our positions. Suffering brought wisdom, he reminded us.

Playing the lead compensated a little for the discomforts. It did bother me that the water he slopped made the costumes revealing, hardening nipples and showing every line of our figures. The others would have drowned themselves at his command, but when he brushed against me here and there as he adjusted my chiffon or moved against my thigh this way and that, it was like being nuzzled by a hound who had caught the scent of some bitch.

With winter closing in, after a few weekends he suspended operations until the return of Aegean weather, and I was able to switch my attentions to Frank and to auditions for *The Playboy of the Western World.* I didn't know if I would be robust enough for the lead—I was thinking of trying out for the crafty widow-woman—but I knew that Frank would be a great playboy. And oh, yes, there was that business of becoming America's outdoor sweetheart.

*   *   *

Margaret in Hollywood

By March the Camp Fire Girl scam was at full tilt. Hopefuls from Maine to California filled out entry blanks by the thousands, listing age, height, weight, hobbies, favorite outdoor activities, and writing a paragraph on what one most admired about a) one's parents or b) Indians. You enclosed a photo in Camp Fire middy uniform.

The Kupplers enrolled me in a Camp Fire group that met weekly in the Bronx. On Thursday afternoons I rode the subway to Van Cortland Park and spent a couple of hours drawing bugs and leaves in my notebook, gathering twigs and abandoned bird's nests if I was lucky. I was uncommonly inept, failing to earn my Wood Gatherer's or any other certificates required of the accomplished Camp Fire Girl. It wasn't for lack of trying, at least at first; I quickly learned how alienated I had become, probably from Garden days on, from an ordinary girl's life and its prescribed rituals. The other camperettes seemed so young, so pliant, so dutiful, and happy in their ways. I envied their simple lives, imagining the homes they went to after meetings, where Father sat reading the paper and puffing on his pipe while Mother attended to the pot roast and gravy and Brother helped Sis with her homework. I tried to avoid speaking to anyone because my diction, my entire manner, made me stand out; I mouthed the songs lest my stage presence and instinct to capture an audience take over.

When I told Frank about how much the freak I felt, he insisted that any one of those girls would trade places with me in a minute. When one day I would be hearing applause on Broadway, they would be in the audience, and they would go home to wash diapers and put up with a grumbling husband who hated his job. I agreed with him, he always cheered me up, until I had to go to another meeting, which brought the glooms again.

Several of the girls believed that they had a chance to win the contest. The consensus was that the candidate with the greatest number of merit certificates would be sure to make the finals. When one of them asked me if I was trying for the

title, I hesitated, then knew that I had to say yes. I down-
played my chances. She was so kind, this freckled pixie; she
offered to help me in my bumbling quest. She put an arm
around me when I failed to remember that WoHeLo stood
for Work, Health, and Love, when I identified a woodpecker
as a skylark (I had been reading Wordsworth), when my at-
tempts to glue leaves together in the shape of animals made
so much trash. I hid behind a tree when Action Beads were
awarded, and she tried to give me one of hers. When she discovered that I had won the ultimate distinction, I feared that
little saint would be soured on life forever.

One afternoon when I was birdwatching, I spotted Frank
loitering on the edge of the park. He had threatened to de-
scend on a meeting to tease me, and I had begged him not to
do it, afraid he'd make me give the game away somehow. He
caught my eye and waved; I turned away. His presence thoroughly rattled me and sent the most intense liquefying feelings coursing through me. He was like some pervert watching
a playground; I was his prey, but I wasn't frightened. Under
my starched uniform I was already his. I joined the others and
sat in a circle as our counselor, a wiry woman who could have
survived for weeks in wilderness, lectured us on how bacteria
liked to find a home in mayonnaise.

When the meeting broke up, I hid behind a tree until Frank
found me. The light was fading. I could hear the others' dwin-
dling chatter as they left the park for their happy homes. Frank
wore his tweed cap pushed back.

"What's your name?" he said. "Would you like to come home
with me?"

"No," I said. "Do we have to go home? Couldn't we stay
right here?"

"What do you have under that blouse?" He backed me to
the tree and touched me on my middy.

"You're very naughty," I said. "What would Mrs. Seymour
say?"

"You're the naughty one. I bet I know what you want."

"No, I don't. I don't want it."

He pushed everything aside. I had my arms around his neck, and he lifted me, backing me against the trunk all breathless. He could have carried me home on it, so swift and slick.

I wondered what I would tell Mother about my skirt. Ice cream, Frank said. A reward for good behavior.

One Saturday Dr. Knauer invited Mother and me to join him at the Metropolitan Museum. Frank and I had already made the Met our own. I knew I was in for some heavy analysis rather than the delight of just looking. Frank liked to say that the only true pleasure came without comment.

The doctor met us in the vast foyer. There were certain paintings and sculptures he wished to show us in order to gauge our reactions to a new project he had in mind.

He led us upstairs to contemplate Rodin's *The Kiss*. Mother averted her eyes from the voluptuous lovers. Dr. Knauer discoursed on the origins of the bronze, how it had been inspired by Dante's wind-driven lines about Paolo and Francesca, the guilty lovers murdered in the love act and condemned to drift in hell, remembering only their moment of ecstacy and death. It was just as Frank and I had read in the guidebook; Dr. Knauer spoke as if his knowledge had been acquired at the price of midnight oil. To Frank and me the lovers were ourselves, and we envied their fate, whatever Dante knew.

The doctor led us through the Greek and Roman nudes, in the galleries singling out nudes by Frenchmen from David to a newly acquired Renoir, its flesh tones glowing like a fevered child's, and a Bonnard, "Nude Against the Light," on loan from somewhere. It showed a young woman at an angle from behind, light from the window falling on what you could see of her breasts, as she held a bottle of perfume in one hand and applied it with the other. I was particularly attracted by the Bonnard, and Dr. Knauer noticed.

"You enjoy this one? Does she remind you of yourself?"

"I never walk around naked in our apartment," I said.

"I should think not," Mother said with a nervous little laugh.

In the museum restaurant Dr. Knauer informed us that he

173

wished to embark on a photographic essay in celebration of the female form. He hoped to achieve in photography what masters had accomplished in stone, metal, and paint: praise of the human body in works of inexpressible *tendresse.*

He went right to the point. He wanted to use me as a principal model, one representing perfection in adolescence. I kept my eyes on my teacup, waiting for the explosion.

"You wish to photograph my daughter *in the nude*?" Mother gasped. "Well, you can forget about that, Dr. Knauer! That sort of thing may be accepted in certain circles. We have different standards, thank you."

For once I was on Mother's side, though for different reasons. The idea of taking off my clothes in front of that Teutonic goat was repulsive. I would sooner have offered myself on a platter of *spaghetti alle vongole* to Mr. Occhipinti.

"I am prepared to double my normal rate of payment," Dr. Knauer said. "On the altar of art, and in obeisance to the exquisite beauty of this delicate creature, for whom I harbor respect as for the Mother of Christ, sacrifices must be made."

"Out of the question," Mother said.

"Three times my normal rate."

Mother broke the edge off a cookie and looked up at the ceiling. She contemplated me. Was she calculating my worth, or forming in her mind a rejection that would end the matter then and there?

"Contact me on Monday," she said. "I need to ask the Lord's guidance."

"Remind Him of Botticelli," Dr. Knauer said. "Have Him remember the women of Phidias who gave us dreams in ivory and gold."

We had it out when we got home. I told Mother that I was distressed that she had not flatly rejected Dr. Knauer's scheme. How could she so much as contemplate having me do that?

"This is a matter between me and God," she said.

"It is not! It's my body! And what if he puts it on exhibition or publishes it? How can you even think of it?"

"What would you say if I told you I thought I could get him

174

to quadruple his fee? Do you know what that would mean? Your rate would climb across the board."

"What does money have to do with it? What am I, a prostitute, goddamn it?"

"You sound like one! I won't have gutter talk!"

"I can't believe this. I won't do it. So forget it."

"I didn't say you would. Eat your carrots."

I refused her invitation to church the next morning. When she returned, I asked her what the Lord had said. He had been slightly equivocal. Thirty dollars an hour was nothing to sneeze at. If Dr. Knauer could make it forty . . .

"I'm leaving," I said.

"No, you're not!"

She grabbed at me, but I made it out the door and raced downstairs. She didn't follow. I telephoned Frank. Evelyn said that he had gone out and had not said when he'd be back. There was no answer at the Meyers'. I took a walk around the block. I thought of going to Central Park, but I felt lonely and didn't know what I'd do there. I circled our block three more times, gave up, and went back to confront Mother again. I had come up with the obvious argument. Surely that would finish this business.

I reminded her of the contract she had signed with Mrs. Seymour and the Kupplers. All Mrs. Seymour would have to do was get wind of this, and the entire Camp Fire contest would be down the drain. So there was no longer any question, was there?

"I don't know how," Mother said, "you could imagine that your mother could be so foolish as to forget about a signed agreement. Of course I haven't forgotten about it. I see no reason why you couldn't do both." All she would have to do, assuming she could make a satisfactory arrangement with Dr. Knauer, was to get him to agree not to publish or exhibit any such photographs of me until after the Camp Fire Campaign was over.

Speechless, I locked myself into the bathroom and ran the tub. I undressed and looked at myself in the glass above the washstand. It was a nice body, and Frank was always calling me beautiful. He said that my breasts were a perfect size, to him anyway, a little bigger than handfuls; they pointed up, and the nipples were pink. Rhoda had brownish nipples, but they matched her skin. There were so many different kinds of beauty. I held my breasts in the hollows of my hands. They belonged to me; they were me.

I climbed up on the edge of the tub to get a fuller view. Balancing, I spread out my arms to set off my figure, twisting and bending to examine myself front and behind. I paused in a side view of my breasts. I rested one knee on the basin to peer between my thighs. The hair there was darker than on my head, less auburn but still reddish in the light. I ought to be able to decide for myself who was going to look at that.

I climbed down into the water. I let the tap run on me, and I soaped and squeezed and rubbed at myself, trying to make everything dissolve into a reverie of Frank.

Drying myself, I came to a decision. I took my bathrobe off the hook and braced myself for the confrontation.

Mother had the radio on. I asked her to shut it off. I had something important to tell her. I had decided a few things.

"Oh, and what might they be?"

I told her that if she thought I could pose for Dr. Knauer and be Camp Fire Girl of the Year, I had another idea of how to deal with both situations. She already knew how I felt about Dr. Knauer. I also thought the Kupplers were creeps. The last time I had been in their office alone, Norman had put his hand on my rear. Chicki had called him a schmuck and told him that I was only sixteen and that he had better watch himself.

"Don't exaggerate," Mother said. "It's unbecoming."

"Is it? Well, guess what? I'm not posing for Knauer, and I am quitting the Camp Fire Girls. I'm sick of all of it, and that's that. You can go back to finding me some ordinary modeling jobs. I can put up with them."

"Oh, you can, can you? Well, let me explain a few things to you, young lady. You may think you're something, but I am reminding you that you are still my daughter."

Margaret in Hollywood

She must have had it all thought out. She told me that, yes, I was sixteen years old, but I was not eighteen, and I was a long way from twenty-one. I would do as I was told. And if I didn't, perhaps I needed to be informed that, according to the laws of New York State, she was no longer obligated to keep me in school. How would I like that? How would I like to be withdrawn from PCS? Oh, sure, I could run away if I wanted to. I could get on a train or I could go hang out in some saloon and become a prostitute. A lot of girls did it. Maybe that was what I wanted to do. I could see how far I would get without a mother to look after me and mend my clothes and manage my life and see to it that I stayed in school and got the training I needed for this grand theatrical career I supposedly had my heart set on.

Or I could do as she said. Stay in school and act like a decent daughter and do what was necessary to give myself a chance in life. The choice was strictly up to me.

17

I did not know how to tell Frank that I was going to have to pose in the nude, so I went to Rhoda first. She immediately said that I could move in with the Meyers, and she was so sympathetic that I felt like an idiot, became confused, and acted like an ingrate. Nursie was getting back, was all I could think. I could not stay with the Meyers, I responded to her kind offer. Mother might call the police.

I did not hate Rhoda, but I was far from wishing to become her instrument of salvation. I take that back. I did hate her, for a moment or two. I believed that she was justifying her existence by responding to my desperation. I didn't want charity, that sort of thing. If it weren't for people like her, the earth would be carpeted with aimless misfortunates, God knows, but at the time I ran off in a huff. She must have thought I was cracking.

I had the notion that Frank would be more understanding—how, I cannot imagine. At his grandmother's apartment I found him reading in his room. I ran fingers over his Harvard Classics, a gift from Daddy on his fifteenth, and I pulled out a volume or two for guidance but found none. He read me a letter from his parents, who would be coming home soon for a month's leave.

I took up a position on the bed.

"What's the matter?" Frank asked.

"Kiss me. No, give me a cigarette first." I lit up and leaned back against the pillows and forced myself not to cough. I was conscious of moving my legs back and forth like a scissors. He said I looked like Margaret Livingston. Always the allusion; I wanted to look like myself.

Frank touched me, and I let him. He pushed his fingers against my crotch so that the material stuck in there and got wet.

"You're soaking," he said. "I can't believe how soaking you are."

"What do you want to do, blame me? Do you want to tell me I can't help it?"

"Sure."

"Well, what are you going to do about it?" I took a drag on the cigarette.

There was still some of the cigarette burning when he was finished.

"There's something I have to talk to you about," I said, and I could see him getting angry as I told him about what Mother had agreed to; and when I had finished speaking, he said that of course I wasn't going to pose in the nude. Only cheap girls did that.

"I don't have any choice," I said. "Let's forget it."

I couldn't believe what he said next.

"What would your father think?"

My father?

"How the hell would I know?"

But Frank could see that he had struck a nerve. It wasn't that he was a prude, he said, God knew. It was just that we had a special thing together, and it would be as if I were giving myself to someone else.

I didn't mind his jealousy, but something in his manner bothered me and made me feel like an automobile he had decided not to loan out.

"You can't do it," he said.

"I have to. I don't have any choice."

"You're nuts! Your mother's just bluffing. She won't take you out of school!"

180

"You don't know her."

"So what if she does? You can pay your own tuition, goddamn it! I'll pay it! You pay it anyway. You work like a fucking dog to pay it! This is a joke. What do you mean, you have to pose in the nude?"

"You forget that all my money goes to her. Calm down."

He picked up a globe he had on his desk with a little flag stuck in Peking and flung it against the wall. Thank God the noise brought Evelyn knocking on the door.

"What on earth?" she said. "Mr. Hern and I had our disagreements, but get hold of yourselves."

When Frank spluttered the reason for his outburst, she saw nothing alarming in what I was being required to do. Only bluenoses, she said, objected to the human body. I was an extraordinarily beautiful child, I must know that, and women like me had made the world a more beautiful place since the beginning of time. It was a shame if I had to do anything against my will, but perhaps I should think about it philosophically. If I was truly dead-set against it, she would be happy to speak to Mother herself. Was I sure I couldn't stomach the idea? Klaus Knauer had the reputation of a serious artist.

I said I thought I should go through with it. She had made me feel much better.

"And you, Frank," Evelyn said. "Good Lord, you're behaving like a perfect little idiot."

She shamed him, but I don't think she mollified him much.

It was my body, wasn't it? Frank's possessiveness altered my perspective. As much as I resented Mother, his reaction made me feel like stripping in Herald Square.

I arrived at Dr. Knauer's studio on East Eleventh Street on a cold spring day. Formal in his gray suit, he helped me off with my coat and told me to sit in a chair next to the fire. The bookshelves, the Oriental rugs, the arcane journals piled here and there, the vases holding daffodils—it could have been the set for a play, about genius, of course.

He placed a disk, Debussy's *Afternoon of a Faun,* on the Victrola. "Our work will make us free," he said jovially. "Relax and allow your mind to venture into dark corners of the forest, into glens thick with ferns, where waterfalls splash." Would I care for a glass of sherry?

He poured me a drink from a decanter.

We would be engaged in the pursuit of Art as it had been celebrated since the satyr and the idyllic shepherd, in their rude, uncultivated state, first rested their eyes on the open limnings of nature. His mission was to restore an ancient, reveling oneness, to hoot owl-like at the darkness and to hear in response the echoing hoot.

I caught sight of a long rifle, inlaid with silver, hanging above the fireplace. He saw me staring and asked if I would care to examine it. It was so heavy that I held it across my knees. From a box on the mantel Dr. Knauer retrieved two silver-tipped bullets and gave them to me to hold. The gun and the bullets were handmade, he said, by a man in Bavaria.

"Feel the bullets," he said. "It is so nice how they break the bones. Life is the hunt. Death is beauty. We hunt in the autumn when the year dies. We shed blood on old leaves."

It went on like that. I said nothing.

The camera, mounted atop a tripod, was pointed in the direction of a freestanding mirror to the left of a tall window about fifteen feet distant. He told me that I should undress behind the screen in the far corner of the room.

Dropping my clothes, I surprised myself with my insouciance. It was as if an invisible shield were around me. I cared whether the pictures would be good or not, that was all. You could call it professionalism or merely self-protection. I felt selfish and implacable.

He was perched on a ladder behind the camera, his head beneath his photographer's cloth. That made it easier, too. He told me to pick up a bottle of eau de cologne he had left on the floor beside the mirror. I did my best not to let him gaze up my rear as I bent over. I figured he had counted on that, the old dog.

I realized that this was to be an imitation of the Bonnard we

182

had seen at the Met. Recalling the painting, I struck a saucy pose at an angle to the mirror, jutting my butt toward the learned doctor, holding the bottle aloft in my right hand and, to get into the role of Bonnard's model, applying a few drops in the region of my collarbone with the left. It was not my scent.

The light from the window was falling just as it had in the painting. I concentrated on my headless torso in the mirror, trying to position myself exactly as the painter's cocotte had done. Knauer emitted a bravo from under his cloth. I rather liked the way the mirror showed me. I knew that the camera would catch that image of me and another from the rear, contemplation of a girl contemplating herself. Bonnard had produced a masterpiece from this configuration; it might be that I would help Dr. Knauer do something worthwhile, too. I was no longer I, he was not he; we were the portrait. I forgave him his silliness and myself my own.

I had half-expected him to try to seduce me; I was prepared to threaten him with the police. Instead, still under his cloth, he said, "That will be all, thank you," and I dressed behind the screen.

"Do you think they will turn out well?" I asked when I came out.

"I have no doubt," he said. "You are young and exquisite, I am old but full of knowledge, how can we fail?" He bowed, clicked his heels, and took my hand to kiss, inclining more to slobber than I liked. "We have the saying, 'If it bleeds, it is old enough to butcher.' "

I got out of there. I decided that my next portrait by Knauer should be fully clothed. Let him commemorate my first Broadway role.

I headed straight for Frank's apartment. I was feeling rather jaunty, and I wanted to be with him and to reassure him. Without a word I undressed. What was that perfume? he asked, and I said it was a sample they had been handing out at Macy's; I thought it best not to go into details. It was too sweet, he said. I told him to kiss it away.

He knew where I had been, and he was rapacious. Then he wanted to know about Knauer. Nothing to it, I said; I had stood with my back to the camera the whole time. I suspected that when Frank saw the pictures, he might even discover that he liked them.

18

*I*n October 1924, timed for the new school year, I appeared on the cover of *Everygirl's,* wearing fringed buckskin and an Indian headband. I thought I had never looked so idiotic. If only the poor subscribers knew the truth! I studied my eyes in the photograph to try to detect whether what had been going on behind them showed through. They were impenetrable.

I told Mother that I despised the deception. Wasn't there something wrong with misleading thousands of girls?

" 'By their fruits ye shall know them,' " Mother said.

"What does that mean?"

"It means why should someone else get what we deserve? We have worked for this."

"I didn't even earn a single Action Bead."

"I'm sure you could earn as many as anyone else, if you set your mind to it. You just haven't had the time."

There was no end to the garbage printed. *The New York Times* "Mid-Week Pictorial" rotogravure section featured me on its cover wearing a Camp Fire uniform, the very one Frank had ravished, and described me as "A Winsome Queen of the Out-of-Doors: Miss Margaret Spencer, Chosen as the 'Typical Girl' of the Camp Fire Girls of America." My hobbies were listed as cooking, sewing, and canoeing. There was nothing I liked better than frying trout over an open fire and making corn bread in an oven constructed of stones. I knew how to dig a hole in the ground, line it with hot rocks, and produce a brisket that would make your mouth water. I also said my prayers every night, and at my church picnics I was known for my macaroni-and-marshmallow salad. I was destined to make some lucky man happy. Good looks had not counted in the competition, the *Times* assured its readers, but Margaret certainly had them.

Provincial papers lapped up the publicity releases sent out by the Kupplers and added their own touches. "Meet the new Queen of American Girlhood," the *Des Moines Capital* rejoiced in a full-page layout with a color illustration of me supposedly standing in a boat at Bear Mountain Lake holding up a string of fish. "Notice her long, shining locks—no perky bob, nor bizarre boyish shingle for her! No Cupid's bow to mar her smile! No mascara dabbed 'round her clear, fearless eyes! Beyond the fantastic foibles of flapperdom, the Camp Fire Girls found a friendly little figure in a middy and tam-o'-shanter whose stout walking boots contrasted strangely with the flimsy slippers worn almost universally by girls who prefer the rouge pot to the teapot. No painted face and no rolled stockings for Margaret Spencer, Camp Fire Girl of the Year!"

In an editorial headed TWO GIRLS AND ONE CIGARETTE—YOU DO THE THINKING, the *New York Evening Journal* contrasted my "starry-eyed innocence" with the sordid face of a girl described as the winner of the National Spanish Beauty Contest, a swarthy señorita depicted lounging on a settee smoking a cigarette. Lupi Sevilla, as she was identified, looked as if she had just entertained the U.S. Navy on shore leave in Barcelona. In a separate photo opposite, I smiled out from beneath my beret, sporting a Trail Seeker's badge on my jersey.

> You would travel many miles through Spain before finding the real beauty that you see in the face of this typical American girl. Pray that our nation may produce millions of girls like Margaret Spencer, with that same look in their eyes.

186

Pray that our nation may turn away disgusted from such a look as smolders in the eyes of a Lupi Sevilla.

Fortunate is the country that has such girls as Margaret Spencer, and the mothers to create them.

I wanted to throw all the Camp Fire publicity into the trash, but Mother pasted everything carefully into my portfolio and warned me not to touch it.

"Are you insane?" she said. "There are girls all over the country who would prostrate themselves for this kind of exposure."

Hollywood did not cast itself at my feet, nor did any Broadway producers show up at our doorstep. I don't believe I received a single job offer of any kind as a result of the Camp Fire campaign. It was successful only for the organization and for the Kupplers, who told us that membership had soared from coast to coast. There had been a few angry complaints from parents of girls in my group, but the Kupplers fended them off with the story that my real achievements had been accomplished back in Kansas City. Moving to New York, I had suffered from the shyness and modesty that were parts of my all-American nature. I kept thinking about little freckle-face and how confused and cast down she must have been.

But a real mess broke a couple of weeks later. Dr. Knauer published three studies of me in *Vanity Fair*. Mother always bought that magazine, and so was aware of what had happened the minute it was on the stands. Dr. Knauer had gone back on his word, she fumed. She had thought him a man of honor.

"Oh, he is," I said. I didn't care. I rather hoped there would be a scandal. I wrote to Harry Valentine, who had just written me that his wife had left him, that I might be the cause of an uproar equal to the trouble he had got into at the Pantages mansion.

Mother was terrified of what the Kupplers and Mrs. Seymour would do if and when they found out. I would be ruined, Mother would be ruined, the Camp Fire Girls would be ruined, and worst of all she would have to pay back all that money! I would have to quit school and work full time.

"I will not!" I shouted.

"You have no choice!"

"It's your fault! *You* go to work. I told you what you were asking for."

The only hope was that I was not identified in the magazine by name. The pictures were wonderful. I had to hand it to the doctor. They weren't Bonnard, but they had their own black-and-white beauty, and secretly I was damned proud of the way I looked. I didn't even mind that thousands of strangers would admire me. The trouble was, my profile was clearly identifiable.

"What you should do is, just deny it's me," I said. "Everybody has a lookalike."

Sure enough, the Kupplers summoned us. I was afraid Mrs. Seymour would be there, too, but we entered to find the pair alone. Chicki held up a copy of the magazine and slammed it down on her desk.

She shouted, "What the hell does this mean?"

"I don't know what you're talking about." Mother did her best. She looked at the pictures and asked, "What on earth is this? You're not trying to tell me this is Margaret, are you? I can see a resemblance, but my Margaret wouldn't pose like that, not in a million years."

"Alice," Norman said, "you're full of it."

"I beg your pardon?"

"I checked with the photographer, Knauer. Told him I was so taken by the dame in the pictures, I'd like to represent her. So he gave me her name, and guess who it was?"

"There's some mistake," Mother said.

"The hell there is. You're just lucky we haven't heard from Mrs. Seymour. Not yet, anyway. You can pray she doesn't make the connection. As it is, technically you owe us one hell of a lot of money. By the way, Maggie, congratulations, you've got the cutest little ass in New York."

"How about it, Alice," Chicki said, "when are you going to

pay up? You violated the contract. And by the way, the deal was exclusive, in case you didn't notice. I figure you owe us ten percent of whatever Knauer paid you."

"I can pay that," Mother said, and she broke down crying. It was not pleasant to see my mother like that. I took her hand.

"Can't you let up on her?" I said.

"I'm no son of a bitch," Norman said. "I'm too honest to be an agent. I play fair, I expect it from you. How do I know what other pictures Knauer's got of you? What did you do for him?"

"You shut up," I said.

"Hey, the gal's got a temper. That's good."

"I tell you what," Chicki said, "suppose we deal with Mrs. Seymour. Suppose we figure out a way we can smooth this over. A little money to Knauer, no more pictures for now, and he denies the model is Margaret."

"He promised he wouldn't publish them for two years," Mother said.

"Promised?" said Norman. "Alice, in this business, let me tell you, promises are worth nothing. You pay him some dough, you get him to sign a release, then you're talking. Put it in writing and be ready to sue the bastard, that's what it takes. You got to know what you're doing, Alice. You got to be a professional. Listen, I've seen people ruined for life. It happens every day. You wouldn't believe it, but there are unscrupulous people out there, a dime a dozen, believe me."

Chicki said Mother shouldn't be making these career decisions for me on her own. Look what already had happened. And how much had Knauer paid for these shots? Chicki said she could double it. Mother didn't even know the going rates. She was selling me at bargain-basement prices. She had a hot property on her hands, very hot, and she was giving it away. We needed a full-time agent—in other words, the Kupplers. They could make us deals we'd never regret, and we could forget the money we actually owed them. How about that for generosity?

Mother asked me to wait outside.

And that was how I became the regular client of Norman and Chicki Kuppler. Whenever people ask me, how do you get an agent, I tell them it's easy. All you have to be is desperate.

It was my last year at PCS. I had no idea what I would do after I graduated, try out for plays, I supposed, although I hardly felt ready and feared I could go on modeling forever. The school play that year was *A Midsummer Night's Dream,* and I decided to make the most of it. Frank, who had been a big hit the previous year in *Playboy*—as the widow I had been adequate, nothing more—was trying out for Oberon; Rhoda had given up acting. Her brother had graduated from Harvard, and she was concentrating on getting into Radcliffe. I felt I needed to make a splash as big as I had with Juliet, so I did something bold. I tried out for Puck. A girl playing what was ordinarily a boy's part would offer a possible tour de force and might attract notice.

Neither Mrs. Cornwall nor Mr. Occhipinti objected in principle, but they said I would have to show myself to be a more convincing Puck than Tommy O'Riordan, who was, I thought, a talented, athletic imp, well-suited to the role. When, years later, I saw Mickey Rooney in the film version, he made me remember Tommy; they were virtual twins. I don't know how I would have done against Rooney, but I beat out O'Riordan, earning, I am sure, his hatred. He had to settle for playing Starveling.

It was Puck himself who drew me in and on, witty Puck who could appear and disappear as he pleased, rub potions on dreaming eyes, cast spells and throw thick fogs around lovers, live on air in the forest, mock and taunt and philosophize and yet be all for love. As hard as I worked, poring over the meanings of every one of his words in Mrs. Cornwall's annotated version, bringing him to life in my mind, exercising to try to achieve a balletic weightlessness—for all my efforts there was a sense in which I had no difficulty at all in becoming Puck. I wanted to be him, more than anything else in the world, and wished that I could go on playing him forever.

190

Spontaneously, and to Mr. Occhipinti's delight, I invented a wicked little facial twitch, something like the lascivious contraction an oyster performs when hit by a squeeze of lemon juice. I thought it suggested the forest spirits who possessed this sprite and gave to him his magical powers. I introduced it at moments of Puckish glee to hint at unseen worlds. Mr. Occhipinti called it the bit of business that can fix a character and make a scene.

It was also my idea to have Puck deliver his "My mistress with a monster is in love" speech hanging by an arm, upside down from a vine, as if he had descended from the treetops and the sky. To this Mr. Occhipinti at first objected, thinking it too gimmicky; but I got up my nerve and sprang it on him during a rehearsal. I rigged the vine myself and delivered the speech in a monstrous little voice, swinging and twisting, wrapped around the vine-covered rope like a python. I did my best to emanate magic and I hoped a bit of sexiness. My rope trick stayed in. At the actual performance it never failed to bring applause.

Everything went perfectly those nights. I was so ready for this chance, and I identified so completely with the character, that I played Puck with absolute confidence, eager for my next speech and leaping about the stage with abandon. I was able to listen to the others as if I had never heard their lines before and respond with what appeared to be utter spontaneity.

I say this less to praise myself than to recapture the joy that kind of acting can bring. It is not *being*, but *acting*, less self-expression than escape from the burden of one's own personality. To convey the energy of becoming someone else to an audience with whom one must be in sympathy, that is acting.

Paradoxically it is also a license to egomania. I see that I have said nothing about the other performers. I am sure they were good, but I'm afraid I don't remember.

"Readiness is all." Theresa Helburn, executive director of the Theatre Guild, and Winifred Lenihan, director of the Theatre Guild School, were both in the audience. On the strength of my performance they invited me to audition. I was given bits of several plays to read, but my Puck had already convinced them. I was soon named winner of both the Winthrop Ames Scholarship and the five-hundred-dollar Otto Kahn Award. I would be given training in dramatic technique, movement, voice—even fencing!—and parts in school productions as well as regular Theatre Guild productions in actual theaters.

It was the chance of a lifetime. Mother was, I think, genuinely thrilled for me.

"There aren't many little girls as lucky as this," she told me.

"No, Mother," I said. "There aren't *any* others. I'm the only one!"

Frank was also admitted to the Guild School to study writing. I don't think I had ever been happier.

Act Three

19

*I*magine an actress's dressing room at the Garrick Theatre in November 1926. I was applying cream to remove my makeup. Amid the bottles and jars of powder and paint stood my dolls' box, still containing a volume of my diary—out of sentiment more than from fear of detection—and the stone from Father's grave that I had taken to touching for luck each night before going on.

Much had changed in my life, though not enough to suit me. I was still living with Mother in the same scuzzy apartment, still tied to her would be the correct phrase, as to a ball by a chain. Not a day went by without my dreaming of escape, but I was not yet making enough money to support us both separately. I had achieved the major move toward independence of an army cot in a corner. You would think that to have been a trivial-enough advance, but with Mother it was trench warfare, an inch at a time. She believed that she could read my mind when we were in the same bed. Looking back, I ought to have picked up my cot and lived in a tent in the park, but I kept believing that tomorrow would bring the big break. On her part Mother was showing signs of belief in my eventual success as an actress. The apartment was filling up with cheap books on investment—*How to Make a Million in Florida Real Estate, Secrets of the House of Morgan, A Christian's Guide to Profit.* She was even struggling through a correspondence course in high finance offered by a Bible college in Pennsylvania.

Rhoda was away at Radcliffe; we wrote back and forth regularly; the most recent exchange concerned the loss of her virginity to a law student in the backseat of a Franklin; at least it hadn't been a mere Ford, I reassured her. Harry Valentine was, from what he said, prospering in Hollywood, although his second wife had abandoned him for a Mexican jockey, depriving Harry of a daughter named after me. He had been sweet enough to come to New York to see me in my current run and had taken me to supper afterward, when he gave me my first martini.

And Frank and I were still an item, although as one might expect, we had our tiffs and rifts. He expressed his pique at the publication of the nude pictures by taking up with a nitwit from Finch College, a blond banker's daughter with a camel's hair coat and a vocabulary of five hundred words. He wanted me to think that he was trying to deceive me, when it was obvious that he intended me to know all about it. I refused to suffer. I was angry, but I wasn't about to let him know that. I pretended utter indifference, with inevitable results. He confessed to me one afternoon after we had made love in his room. He actually wept! He was contrite, abject, she was nothing to him, it was probably because of her coloring. He had never been with a blonde before, and as a playwright he had to write from experience. She had this amber skin—

"I don't give a damn about her skin," I said, "and I don't give a damn about what you did with her. Just be sure she doesn't have a disease. You'd better get yourself checked. Let me know when you decide to write about leprosy."

Still, I sympathized with him, not that I let on. We were too young for fidelity; better to experience the age of exploration early. I told him nothing about my own lapses, such as they were. There was Charlie Clement, a Theatre Guild patron, at thirty-five a pecan baron from Memphis who had moved to New York solely because he adored the theater. He was constantly sending me flowers and books, including the complete

Furness Variorum Shakespeare (I told Mother it came with the Kahn Prize); he implored me in his peculiar Southern way to introduce him to my mother or at least a cousin; and he asked me a dozen times to visit him in his suite at the Plaza. I gave in one afternoon.

I regretted none of it. If Charlie was living out a fantasy, escaped from his neurasthenic belle of a wife, spending an afternoon in wild abandon with "the most beautiful actress in these United States," as he called me, what was wrong with that? I thought it was worth it only to listen to his kindly, funny rolling accent, which turned the word ham into three syllables and made a scotch and soda sound like Haut-Brion. He was decorous, ceremonial, gracious, and six feet three. I had by that time reached my full height of five feet six and a half, and weighed 116; it was like coupling with a giant. The bed had been built specially for him by the Plaza's carpentry shop.

"I love living in this hotel," Charlie said. "It's gorgeous, the service is marvelous, the food's great, and you and I can be here without a damn soul bitching at us. I'm the happiest man in New York, bar none."

I think he was. It was a delightful afternoon. Well, make it two afternoons, or three. I didn't want any more, and I don't think he did, either. In the least insulting way, asking for the name of my bank, he wanted to give me money. I said no— not without some silent regrets! But good old Charlie: a note on Plaza stationery showed up in my box at the Guild School. In it he enclosed a receipt for a thousand-dollar bond purchased in my name, with the information that it would not mature until 1935, "when you won't even need it," he wrote.

There were a few other minor deviations. My fencing instructor, who shall be nameless because he may not be dead, embraced me one morning in the equipment room. He was a Romanian driven to paroxysms of lust by the sight and whiff of sweat. Everyone knew he preferred the young men, but a female with a sword in her hand worked nearly as well. It was most peculiar. Still with his mask on, he crushed me to his reeking bosom. "Look, S———," I said, "I am not a prude. I adore your muscles, but I really have no interest in you. Calm yourself, take off some of that padding, and I'll deal with it, all right?" I administered to him what is familiarly termed a hand-job, and he was delighted.

Then there was Phil Weinstein. It is fair enough to say that I was lightly, ever so lightly, in love with him for a month in the winter of 1925–26. I was angry with Frank for refusing to take me to the Follies; he was going through what I termed a brief attack of high seriousness, something like influenza, potentially fatal but in his case survivable. The Follies had become beneath him, garbage, tinsel, and so on. What had Ziegfeld with his big cigar ever contributed to the betterment of mankind? Nothing, I said, which was why he was so successful and why people flocked to his shows. The audience didn't want to be bettered, they wanted to be entertained; my father had thought otherwise, had gone bankrupt, and was dead, God rest his soul. I warned Frank that Phil had asked me to the Follies. Go ahead, Frank said, Weinstein is a vulgarian. So I did.

We went to the matinee and loved it, Will Rogers spinning his lariat around a group of girls, the curtain closing, the curtain rising again with Will still spinning as before, falling and rising again and again to the same scene; Ann Pennington in silver and salmon atop the Grand Staircase; a finale in lilac and pale green. It was spectacular and humorous and put us in such a good mood that—he was all of twenty-three—Phil took me to a speakeasy afterward, where we got fairly blotto. In the cab he was all over me, and we told the driver to keep going through the park. It was just a matter of getting carried away by the moment. We had to find a place for coffee afterward so I could go home to Mother without causing a war. Phil and I met a few times after that. He had a place in the Village not far from Dr. Knauer's. Phil was a comedy writer and kept me laughing, and prone, enough to make me believe briefly that I might be losing interest in Frank after all this time—but the laughs thinned out quickly, and so did the rest of it.

Frank's flirtation with Bolshevism bothered me more than the blonde. It set in after we had gone to see the Moscow Art Theatre doing Chekhov. They were all the rage that season; everyone at the Guild was talking about them; and I understood that back at PCS Mrs. Cornwall was jumping on the repertory theater bandwagon. At the Guild School, Cheryl Crawford, teaching theater history, was the Russians' most passionate advocate. Frank thought they were the ultimate in theatrical genius, the wave of the future. I told him honestly that I had no way to judge, since I didn't know a word of Russian, and that was all they spoke!

My attitude was as unpopular with my fellow students as it was annoying to Frank. That I couldn't understand what they were saying made no difference, he said. I had read the play in English, hadn't I?

I thought he, like most of the New York theater crowd, was fooling himself. He was afraid he lacked a coherent point of view or philosophy, he was embarrassed by the ease of his life, and at that moment anything Russian seemed the answer. He was giving up on the very thing that had sustained him, the belief in himself and in the details of ordinary life. He began to utter such drivel as that the egotism of the artist was nothing but a bourgeois convention, a symptom of the selfish individualism that sustained capitalism and kept the masses starving—this to me, technically speaking the real proletarian! I suggested to him that, if he felt that way about capitalism, he should stop living off his grandmother, and while he was at it, he could keep his paws off bankers' daughters—unless this was part of a conspiracy to undermine the establishment. But I knew he was struggling to find himself, and I believed that when he did, he would flourish happily on his own—and with me.

My faith in him was bolstered by the success he was already having with his writing—not money success but the acceptance anyone needs to keep going. His sketches had begun to appear in little magazines, one in *The Smart Set*, which wasn't what it had been but was still a coup for a beginner. His stories, ebullient and playful like the real Frank, bore no traces, that I could detect, of his newfound ideological claptrap, which proved to me that the Marxism or socialism or communism or whatever it was he thought he was professing would vanish with his first large royalty check. I provoked him by declaring that, in the eyes of the one irrefutable arbiter of literary worth, posterity, Cole Porter would prove to have been a greater genius by far than Karl Marx.

Frank said that I thought like a woman. Precisely!

I see that, just like a woman, I have nearly lost my train of thought. To return to my dressing room at the Garrick, if you will, we were in the last week of a limited run of Ferenc Molnár's *Liliom.* I was playing Julie, Joseph Schildkraut in the lead opposite me. The role never failed to reduce me to a state of exhaustion; by my last speech I was ready for the Home for Incurables. This was a new experience for me; normally final curtains left me in a state of nervous excitement.

Landing the part had come as a surprise, because I did not care for the play, which was to be reincarnated twenty years later as *Carousel,* greatly improved by the music. Winifred Lenihan had arranged my audition, to give me the experience of trying out in a professional situation so I could get used to the inevitable rejections. Up to then I had been in several Guild School productions, everything from light comedies to O'Neill to *Mrs. Warren's Profession,* in which I had played Vivie Warren and had irritated my mother by quoting at every opportunity my favorite line from Shaw's preface, that the world had more to fear from rich men without principles than from women without chastity.

These were only weekday matinees, however, done in theaters before audiences who wished to contribute to our training and who, like Charlie Clement, were curious about young talent. *Liliom* was the real thing, an actual Theatre Guild production of a play then regarded as a landmark of the modern theater, a work that had made Molnár a popular hero in Budapest.

Liliom himself is a sideshow barker whose rough, powerful appearance, crude jokes and songs, and general repulsiveness make him irresistible to young women. Julie runs off with him when he is fired—for being obnoxious, was the way I read it. The couple live in verminous, ecstatic poverty. He berates her and he beats her. She loves him.

My audition consisted in reading Julie's climactic speech for the director, Frank Reicher, assorted eminences of the Guild, and Mr. Schildkraut, whose reputation gave him a say in every aspect of the production. Summoning everything I believed about acting, I managed to get carried away and appeared to break down.

To give the gist of the scene: Liliom has been murdered. Julie, pregnant with his child, sits on the edge of the stretcher bearing his corpse and caresses its head as she says her final good-byes. She tells him that it was wicked of him to beat her on the breast and on the head and face, yet assures him that she loves him and, more or less, that he should get some sleep.

They ate up my portrayal of the waif who loves to suffer. The scene read to me like the depiction of a girl remonstrating with her Doberman, who, having run amok to the detriment of the furniture and herself, had mercifully been gassed. Against all reason I imagined myself as having loved this adorable brute, whose child I would in turn love without regard to its probable genetic deficiencies. Halfway through the speech, when my tears started splashing down on poor Mr. Schildkraut's face, I figured I might actually have a chance for the part.

Mr. Schildkraut arose from the dead and embraced me, saying to Mr. Reicher, "She must be our Julie." That was that.

I managed to reproduce those emotions night after night. The audiences had their handkerchiefs out every time. I had nightmares about being Julie, standing near Liliom beneath the Ferris wheel, whipping up meatless goulash for him in our hovel, and worst of all sleeping with him. I would awake to examine myself for bruises.

Frank, who was there most nights, said that I would not be

so hostile to the play if I understood that Liliom, whose name meant both "brute" and "lily" in Hungarian, should be seen as the oppressed worker, whose conditions of employment had alienated him and induced in him this crude, violent behavior. Julie was the saint who saw through to his pure soul. I told Frank that I thought the play nothing more than a sentimental brief for wife-beating, and that I had had sufficient experience of poverty to find it neither romantic nor an excuse for vileness. But I must say that his appreciation of my acting, in the face of my contempt for the character I was playing, made me overlook what I regarded as his temporary insanity.

Through all this my mother's behavior toward me altered. I was earning seventy-five dollars a week. She spoke of finding a larger apartment, something I discouraged because the next time I moved I intended it to be *out;* moving up in the world with her I regarded as a setback. She was anxious to bring Nell East to see me perform, and she busied herself collecting my reviews. Her favorite was the one from the *Sun,* which referred to me as "a milk-skinned Bernhardt."

Such was the state of my life on that Thursday night as I removed my makeup after another evening playing the girl for whom love meant an empty stomach and a punch in the face. I felt the way an athlete must feel after winning an exhausting race. The theater had become my home; all I wanted was to stay in it forever. Sometimes I dropped into the Garrick for no reason at all when no one else was there, using a key the state manager had given me. I loved everything about it, from the dusty flats to the banks of lights; I learned what I could from the director and the tech people and even the stagehands. Alone I would switch on a spot or two and sit in the empty seats to see things from an audience's point of view.

Even though I disliked the play, my experience of *Liliom* had been wonderful. Except for one secondary actor who habitually downed a pint of gin in his dressing room before going on and who muttered "bitch" under his breath and tried to upstage me and cross me during scene five, everyone had been kind. Mr. Schildkraut, full of good advice and encouragement, told me how glad he was to be back in New York after making a movie in Hollywood—a depressing experience, according to him, and a place with no cultural base or tradition. He had tried to start a drama group in southern California on the model of the Theatre Guild and had failed. He told me that I had a future.

I cherished the telegram Rhoda's parents had sent me after opening night:

> YOU ARE BEAUTIFUL AND A GREAT ACTRESS A RARE COMBINATION WE WERE MOVED BY SHALL WE SAY YOUR GENIUS AND WE LOVE YOU= BEST WISHES=
>
> THE MEYERS

My makeup was about half-removed when I answered a knock on my door. I was surprised to see Mother standing there. It had become our understanding that, because of the demands of the role, she would wait by the stage door, giving me time to recover. Here she was, smiling and aflutter.

She asked me to get dressed as quickly as I could. Some very important people were waiting to meet us.

"I can't meet anybody now, Mother, you know that. I need to go home and have some soup and go to bed."

Mother insisted I had to come. The people were already at the Waldorf and were not the sort to be stood up. My entire career could depend on them. She would not tell me who they were.

So much for delusions of autonomy. I threw on my clothes. Mother fussed at my hair. Who were these people?

"Is it Eugene O'Neill?" I asked half-facetiously.

"More important than that. Hurry up."

20

*O*n an upper floor of the Waldorf we knocked on double doors. Consider my disappointment when they swung back to reveal Norman Kuppler. That in the year and a half since I had seen him he had attempted to upgrade his appearance did nothing to raise my spirits. Formerly he had looked like an unsuccessful drug merchant; now, he was hidden in what may have been a hand-tailored suit, double-breasted with enormous lapels and high, heavily padded shoulders. The tailor was a sadist; the thing was several sizes too large. Norman peeked out of it like a turtle or someone miscast as the British ambassador. He was pleased with himself, stepping back a pace and holding out his wee hands as if to say, "So what do you think of me now?"

"And how is everything, Maggie?" He zeroed in on me, targeting my lips but settling for my cheek as I turned aside. "Wait. You don't have to tell me. Looking like several million as usual. I know. Everyone knows. With you, everything's coming up roses. Talk of the town. Good to see you, Alice. Looking great, and why not? Come in and meet a very important man. And a first-class gent, I might add."

Standing on the other side of the room with Chicki, *décolletée* in yellow silk, was a gentleman with a face the color of a poinsettia plant. Like Norman's, his clothes called attention to themselves, but they fit. A huge, square-cut diamond flashed from the little finger of the hand holding a cigar.

"This is Mr. Tommy Nolan," Norman said. "Mr. Nolan is right-hand man to Mr. Winnie Sheehan, whom, as you know, is nothing less than head of production at the studios of Mr. William Fox."

"Really?" I said. "Right-hand man to Mr. Sheehan? I should think your name should be Gallagher"—this in what I thought was a light, reasonably friendly voice, but Mr. Nolan started unsmiling past my joke. Doubtless I had not been the first to make it. Probably it insulted his ring, his pearl stickpin, his dignity. Oh, well.

"Tommy," Norman plunged ahead obliviously, "I would like to present to you Miss Maggie Spencer I've been telling you about, and you know her mother, Alice."

Know her? How would he know Mother?

"Delighted to meet you, Maggie," Mr. Nolan said.

"Margaret," I said. "No one ever calls me Maggie. Miss Spencer will do." I don't know what made me take that tone, but something put me on my guard. I figured I would hear about it from Mother later. Mr. Nolan, ignoring my response, was obviously not a man to let trifles deter him from the business at hand. I concentrated on his chin, which consisted of two red spheres parted by a deep cleft, a feature that made his face look as if it ended in a scrotum.

"Margaret is a beautiful name," he said. "It is my mother's own and her mother's before her. Won't you sit down, Miss Spencer? Will you take a drink?" He indicated a silver tray covered with bottles. "Gin? Whiskey? A glass of wine? I recommend the scotch. It's from Mr. Fox's private stock." Reverently he lifted the bottle by its neck. The label bore the Fox logo, the three letters filling a circle that represented, I suppose, the world. "Do sit down."

Mr. Nolan spoke with a slight Irish, or at least New York–Irish, lilt, each final consonant distinctly sounded, that lent to his voice a melodic quality combining light opera with the rattle of a Thompson gun. You did not miss a syllable. I had never heard of him, nor his boss, Sheehan. For that matter I had never heard of William Fox, although I must have seen a number of his movies. I had no conception of what a movie studio actually was, nor did it matter to me what studios made which movies or which men ran the show. It obviously did matter to Mr. Nolan and to the Kupplers. Although he was based in New York, Nolan was the first real Hollywood type I had met, and I quickly learned, as he dropped name after mysterious name, that to him the ins and outs of the parochial politics of that distant town were the most important subject in the world; the strong implication was that anyone who did not know about them or, worse, did not give a damn about them, must be a fool. Even the scotch: I had the sense that to refuse a sample of Mr. William Fox's private stock when it was being offered to you was like refusing Communion. Who but an apostate would do that? What a fuss Mr. Nolan made over a lousy drink! He hovered over the tray as if it had been heaped with money.

I considered asking for a scotch and soda, lady's drink though it was not, because I was thinking that I could have used someone like big Charlie Clement at my side just then and, in his absence, maybe his favorite booze would summon his spirit. I settled, however, for a ginger ale, as did Chicki. Mother drank ice water: American champagne, Mr. Nolan cheerfully called it. He, moving with all the deliberate ceremony of a priest, fixed himself and Norman scotches with a single quick splash of soda and no ice. To dilute the elixir further, he confided to us, would be a mortal sin. He himself preferred Irish whisky, but there was none available.

He seated himself and continued speaking of the picture business, naming more and more names that were Greek to me. He spoke of nets and grosses, of Mr. Fox's upcoming masterpiece that was being directed by a German with no expense barred. The sets alone would cost a million. They had constructed an entire city at the studio. He spoke of southern California real estate. You could buy up lots for nothing now and be assured of astronomical profits. It was a new world.

"This is the finest whiskey known to man," Norman broke

through the verbal torrent at last, holding his glass up to the chandelier. "Mr. Fox has it brought over in a submarine. The king of England won't touch anything else. They're personal friends from way back, the king and Mr. Fox. He gets it straight from the king."

Mr. Nolan threw Norman a sharp look. Norman had lost a couple of points with that encomium. This was a tough league for him.

Mr. Nolan proposed a toast to the most promising young actress in New York. I said that I was flattered and grateful for his good wishes and hoped that he could see *Liliom* before it closed.

"Oh, I've already seen it, Miss Spencer," Mr. Nolan said. "I was there tonight. Last week I was there with Winnie Sheehan. Before Winnie went back to the Coast, we agreed I should see it again. We don't believe in snap decisions at Fox. You want to have a good look at the horses before they leave the parade ring, I always say. A good train is punctual on departure as well as on arrival. I've already telegraphed him what I thought. I told him he was on the button, as usual. He can spot the talent, let me tell you. That is why Winnie Sheehan is where he is today, lengths ahead of the pack."

"You're buying the movie rights to *Liliom*?" I asked.

"Not at all, not at all. It's ten to one the play's not right for the screen, or not right for a Fox picture anyway. Miss Spencer, what do you think of when you think of a Fox picture?"

I drew a blank. Fortunately he went on.

"I'll tell you what I think of. Did you see *The Iron Horse*?"

I had, and I had enjoyed it, and I said so.

"Do you know that more than four years ago, when he was pursuing a study of Abraham Lincoln, William Fox himself came upon a fact in Lincoln's career which opened the gateways of inspiration? He found that it was President Lincoln who, with farseeing vision, brought about the accomplishment of the mighty plan to unite the East and the West of the United States by a transcontinental railroad which would run over plain and mountain from the Missouri River to the Pacific Ocean. Mr. Fox discovered that it was President Lincoln who made

208

possible that road which broke the power of hostile Indians, conquered nature itself, and opened up an incredibly rich empire to millions of future home-seekers. It was the central exploit of a thrilling and romantic phase of the Republic's history."

He took a drink.

"Mr. Fox saw in this heroic exploit limitless material of rich romance. He sensed the vitality and color of this epic of courage and toil and suffering and final triumph over all. Yet this great episode in the development of America had been ignored by the makers of screen drama.

"Mr. Fox moved deliberately and thoroughly. He personally selected the director and the principals of the cast. He personally supervised the writing of the script and selected the cinematographer.

"Production forged ahead winter and summer despite every whim and threat of nature, torrid heat and arctic blizzards, obstacles and disappointments almost equal to those which tried the hearts and spirits of the original railroad builders."

Another drink.

"The result, as I am sure you agree, Miss Spencer, was something that we of the Fox Film Corporation could present with perfect confidence first to the people of our own country and subsequently to the citizens of the world.

"That, if I may say so, is my idea, our idea, of a Fox picture. Do you see what I mean, Miss Spencer?" he concluded, patting at his brow with a cocktail napkin.

"I do, certainly," I said. "It was marvelous." I was referring to his speech, of course, but he did not have to know that. I wondered if he had written it himself. Probably not. It had sounded exactly like the sort of publicity material my mother gobbled up from the movie magazines. Mr. Nolan deserved full marks for memorization and delivery. I warmed to him as a fellow actor.

"That is the sort of picture we have always made and will continue to make," he added.

"It's an honor," Norman said, "just to be in this room with someone from Fox. They are a class organization."

"Fix Mr. Nolan another drink, Norman," Chicki said.

I glanced over at Mother. She was in a trance, as though she had undergone a religious experience.

It occurred to me that Mr. Nolan had an expensive face. It must have taken an astonishing number of bottles of the king's whiskey to achieve that color. His energy was prodigious. The way he talked on and on, he could have been a politician. He was one. He said that the most momentous change in the history of the cinema was about to take place. The Warner brothers, about whom the less said the better, had already successfully introduced a way of making the movies talk. Their process was called Vitaphone. With the foresight that had marked him as a pioneer, William Fox was already planning to introduce his own process, which would be called Movietone. It was only a matter of months now, and the movies would be talking. It would change everything.

As was true of every other ordinary patron of the movies, my only experience of talking pictures had been the occasional short shown before a feature in which, typically, a couple of dignitaries could be heard scratchily conversing. I had not found the phenomenon impressive. As Mr. Nolan expounded, I recalled having seen a talking film of Jack Dempsey exchanging witticisms with William Jennings Bryan, just before the death of the Great Commoner, who was my mother's favorite politician. His encounter with the Manassa Mauler was, to me, uninspiring; I had failed to recognize it as a harbinger of an Age of Wonders.

I had also heard rumors of the coming of talking pictures among the cast of *Liliom*. Mr. Schildkraut, although skeptical of the new developments, was already considering returning to Hollywood to perform in a talking role, in spite of his dislike of the place. He would use the money, he said, to buy himself greater freedom on the stage.

I had given the matter little thought, since I had no interest in the movies other than to be entertained by them. I had just succeeded in getting my foot in the theater's door and would not have dreamed of removing it. When Mr. Nolan said that Mr. Fox was now making every effort to obtain the brightest talents of the New York stage to act in his talking motion pictures, and that I had been singled out as one of these, and that he was prepared to offer me a contract with Fox Studios, I said nothing. I tried to think of the proper way to say no, as Mr. Nolan went on to explain that many of the silent actors had never delivered a line of dialogue, had voices too weak or in other ways inappropriate to the new medium, and that my voice and other qualities were ideally suited to this new phase in the history of screen drama. Many stars of today would soon be out of work. People like me would take their places. They were signing up only "certainties, odds-on favorites." I was one of the select few. I would be first out of the gate and into the stretch and heading for home before the also-rans were so much as saddled up.

I could not understand why he was giving me such a hard sell. Maybe he couldn't help himself. Was it something in my manner, an indifference, that must have told him what I was thinking? He had gimlet eyes.

It was time for a formal, polite refusal. I didn't want Mr. Nolan to waste his rhetorical talents further on me. He had begun to sweat, and his pulse rate must have been off the chart.

I said that I could not have been more flattered and delighted at the idea of being offered a job by such a person as he, the representative of so distinguished an entity as Fox. But I was too young, too inexperienced, and too attached to the theater. I was only just beginning to find myself. *Liliom* had given me my first real role. Besides, New York was my home. My friends were here, friends I hoped to keep for life who shared my loves and goals. I was sure that Mr. Nolan understood. I just wasn't one of those girls who longed to go to Hollywood. There was nothing wrong with it, but it wasn't for me.

"Of course I understand," Mr. Nolan said. "I understand and I admire your dedication, Miss. Spencer. These decisions take time and thought. If you don't mind my saying so, it is the sort of thing that prayer can help with. Do you pray, Miss Spencer?"

"Occasionally."

"Then I suggest you offer up a prayer. Will you do me this favor? Will you say a prayer and carefully think over what I've told you? I am sure you will."

"Fix Margaret another ginger ale," Chicki said to Norman. "Maybe she'd like some nuts."

"This is all such a surprise for her," Mother said. "She hasn't had time to think."

She wanted to throttle me, that was obvious. I was queering the agreement she had worked out beforehand with Mr. Nolan and the Kupplers.

A heavy silence invaded the room. No one knew what to say next. I thought of what I loved—the Garrick, Frank, the city. I believed that Mr. Schildkraut, Miss Lenihan, and others would applaud my loyalty to the stage. I was dying to see Frank. I would try to telephone him before I got home. Perhaps if I excused myself and said that I would wait for Mother in the lobby? The silence was making me more uneasy than Mr. Nolan's oration had.

Norman began to pace.

"Do you know what we're talking here?" he asked the ceiling. "I'll tell you what we are talking. We are talking three hundred dollars a week. *Three hundred dollars a week!* Fifty-two weeks a year. Work or no work. For seven years! What is that? It's until Nineteen Thirty-four, is what it is. Work or no work! I should have such a contract myself, I wouldn't worry." He faced a window, addressing the world. "Okay! Now I have told you. Why have I blown these negotiations? I will tell you why. Because I am in the wrong line of work. I am too honest to negotiate. That is the way I am. I am so honest I will tell you I have seen it in writing."

I said nothing.

"Do you know something?" Norman asked me. "What is it you know that I should know about this deal?"

"We needn't reach a decision now," said Mr. Nolan, smiling at me. "It's something we all need to pray about. I don't think what this means has sunk into Miss Spencer yet. It's very late, and I'm sure she's tired after giving such a magnificent performance."

Margaret in Hollywood

*   *   *

Downstairs I managed to slip into the ladies' and telephone Frank. I had time only to give him the facts, not the flavor of Nolan or the certainty of my reaction.

"You wouldn't do that, would you? You wouldn't run off? Not now? Jesus Christ, we're just—"

"Of course not. Are you kidding? Meet me for lunch."

Mother wasn't speaking to me.

21

An epic battle continued for maybe two weeks. I let loose with everything I had.

How was it, I demanded to know, that Norman and Chicki had come into my life again? I did not need them; I did not want them; I did not wish even to have to look at them. Here I was, getting rave notices, on my own as an actress at last, offers for other parts already starting to come in, my future assured, my life in order, and this pair of cretins shows up.

"You are an ungrateful girl, and you are sadly misinformed."

That was as far as we got that day. I stormed out to go find Frank.

To him I characterized everything as a joke, nothing to worry about. Neither of us had contempt for the films; it was none of the standard New York versus Hollywood clichés, or at least we didn't think so. It was that we were only beginning to establish ourselves, and to throw all of that away for something unknown, formless, chaotic, so distant that it may as well have been another planet, was out of the question. More than any of that, I had my own survival to think of. Going to Hollywood with Mother would be like stepping back six years. I would be her slave again.

We went to my dressing room and talked through the afternoon. Frank, looking rather down, said that if I did go to Hollywood, maybe he could follow me out there and become a screenwriter.

"You forget," I said, "I don't give up that easily. I'm not going. And besides, what would you do, rewrite *Robin Hood*? What about your New York plays?"

"Maybe I could write them there."

"No, you couldn't."

I did not care for his wishy-washiness, and he could see it.

"You're right," he said. "Both of us belong here."

Mother played snake-in-the-grass for the next forty-eight hours while I finished the *Liliom* run. Her silence made me nervous; she was acting too self-contained. We had to have it out and be done with it.

I brought up Norman and Chicki again. If I ever considered going to Hollywood, it would not be at their behest. They were out of my life, and she should get that clear.

I did not understand the business side of things, Mother said. I thought life was all culture and art.

"That is not fair," I said. "That's not me. I have that argument with people all the time."

I was being unjust to the Kupplers. She knew they weren't polished and didn't go around quoting Shakespeare, but I would have to agree that Mr. Nolan was a very intelligent man.

"Clever, I think, is the word," I said. "I wouldn't play poker with him, if that's what you mean."

"What do you know about poker? You have to realize that Norman and Chicki have contacts. They have your best interests at heart and always have." Didn't I understand that the more money they made, the more money we made, by a factor of nine-to-one?

"This isn't about money," I said. "It's about what's best for me."

"Are you aware that Norman and Chicki graciously waived their fee for *Liliom*?"

"What fee! They had nothing to do with getting me that role!"

"That is beside the point. They are your agents. We have signed a contract with them."

"Contract? You signed a contract? What kind of a contract?"

"There are many things you do not understand. I am afraid you will have to listen to those who know more about these matters than you do." The Kupplers had opened an office in California. They had become very important Hollywood people. How else did I think that Mr. Nolan had taken the time to speak to me personally? Didn't I know that there were people fighting tooth and nail just to speak to his secretary? Did I think I could obtain such a meeting on my own?

"I don't want it."

"That is your loss. And the Kupplers happen to have signed up some of the most important people in Hollywood as their clients."

"Who?"

She named four or five, all of them unknown to me. That was because I had my head in the sand, Mother said. I might know about a lot of things, but I didn't know about life.

We were getting nowhere. If I simply stood firm, I reasoned, all this would pass. I fell into a kind of lethargy. When I wasn't with Frank, I idled away days reading trashy novels Mother left around. There was *Sandy*, by Elenore Meherin, the story of a girl who defied life's conventions in her search for thrills. "With flapper-conceit she took everything and gave nothing. Her own happiness was her only goal, but in seeking it she lost herself." That was me all right.

I wished I could hear from Miss Lenihan, who had promised to help me choose my next role. It was important, she said, not to be miscast at the start of one's career or to become identified with a stinker of a play. It might not be your fault, but everybody connected with a failed production could get blamed. There were several possibilities, the most exciting a new O'Neill drama, a four-hour marathon, and the novelty of its length had its own appeal. Tom Powers and Lynn Fontanne had already agreed to the leads. Playing with them in something by the most respected American playwright would be fantastic for me. Meanwhile all I could do was wait until Miss Lenihan tried to arrange my audition. I felt sure that if I got that plum, even Norman and Chicki would back off. Hell,

I'd give them their 10 percent just to disappear. If Mother had signed something with them without so much as consulting me, it couldn't be binding.

At Mother's insistence, we met the Kupplers for dinner at the Plaza. Norman and Chicki must have been raking in the dough somehow. Or was Fox picking up the tab?

Norman and Chicki talked of California: the climate, warm days and cool nights, sun. It could be 90 degrees in February. Did they think I was some kind of a lizard?

"I bought a fur," Chickie said. "It always cools off at night. It is what they call natural refrigeration. In the daytime you sit on the beach no matter when."

"To think we work and slave," Mother said, "just to keep warm."

"You like theater?" Chicki said. "They have plays you wouldn't believe. How is five thousand head a night? I am not kidding. I am talking about one house. It's like a stadium. So do a stint between pictures, enjoy yourself. They have one play out there, it's been running twenty years. Is that some record or isn't it?"

"Animal acts?" I asked.

"Animal acts. That is very funny. No, what is it, Norman, that play they pack them in?"

"Mexicans or something," Norman said eagerly. "Pancho Villa, I think it is. They also got one about Jesus Christ. I am telling you, the cars are lined up for miles, night after night. You would think it was, I don't know."

"Judgment Day," I said.

"That's it."

"Everybody has a car," Chicki said. "I don't care who it is, they have one." She turned to Mother. "With the money this kid'll be making, she can buy a Rolls-Royce. Vilma Banky has one courtesy Sam Goldwyn."

"I've always wanted to learn to drive," Mother said. "I am anxious to see the Redwood Highway."

"Eat," Chicki said. "Mine was good." Her plate was scraped clean. Norman's was full. Maybe she ate for both of them.

"I look around," Norman said, swiveling his head with the

218

exaggerated gestures of the silent screen, "and I don't see any theater people eating here tonight. You know why? Because they can't afford it, that's why."

And Mother said, "A girl should feel pretty lucky being taken to the Plaza. You could live your whole life and not be so fortunate."

I excused myself to powder my nose. I was thinking about Charlie Clement. We had lunched together in that very room. I didn't know what drove me more nuts, the Kupplers or Mother.

I did not feel like returning to the table as yet. On an impulse I stepped into an elevator and asked for Charlie's floor. He had wanted to meet my mother. Here was a dandy opportunity. He would be wearing one of his houndstooth racetrack suits and two-tone shoes, and I would introduce him to them, and I would say, "This is Mr. Charles Shively Clement of Memphis, Tennessee, and one of the things we liked to do in his room upstairs was stand naked at the window looking out at Fifth Avenue wondering who could see us."

Maybe he wasn't in. If he was, I might just crawl into his bed and stay there. I could send word. "Miss Spencer has been detained on an upper floor. She regrets that she is unable to continue owing to her present position." I knocked. I heard his voice. *Won't he be surprised when he discovers it isn't the maid?*

He was wearing his dressing gown and a grin. I said why didn't he get dressed and come down to meet my mother. We were with some people who were boring me to tears.

That was a swell idea, he said, and he would do it, except that—he motioned inside. I peeked in. She was sitting up with the sheet pulled around her, smoking.

"Probably not the right time," he said.

I wasn't angry, don't misunderstand me. I thought it was funny. But I did feel ridiculous.

"Give me a ring," Charlie said. "Did you get those flowers?" He had sent an enormous bouquet to the Garrick. I hadn't got around to thanking him. "Next time, count on me, hear?" I might just have to do that.

I returned to the table, out of options. I would have to listen to whatever crap was dished out through dessert. Norman started talking about Fox Studios.

"Can't anybody get a drink around here?" I interrupted.

"You want a cup of tea?" Mother asked.

"No, I mean a real drink. I could use a slug of brandy."

"That's not funny," Mother said.

"I'm not joking. Anybody got a cigarette?"

After a weighty pause Norman said that he understood I had a boyfriend I was very attached to. Was that the reason I was so reluctant to leave?

"That has nothing to do with it," I said. "I'd prefer not to talk about that."

"This guy," Norman pressed on, "Hern, Frank Hern, isn't it? Some kind of a writer or thinks he is? Hey, don't take offense. We're all friends here."

Norman said that Frank Hern had found out about my offer from Fox. How he had found out, Norman didn't know. Maybe I had told him, which had not been a wise move, but that was all right. The trouble was, you should always keep a contract confidential, because once somebody found out, it was like the smell of hot soup. Nobody could stay away from it. Everybody wanted to stick in their spoons.

The sad part of the story was that Frank Hern had approached Fox on his own and asked about going there. A contact of Norman's, not Mr. Nolan, had tipped him off.

I asked Norman to say no more. I didn't want to hear anything about Frank from him. If Frank had indeed tried to see about working in Hollywood, what was wrong with that? Didn't he have the right? Maybe he wanted to be with me. Since I wasn't going anyway, it was a dead issue.

"Don't you see what I'm trying to tell you?" Norman kept on. "Don't you see I'm trying to save you grief? This Hern character is no good. My information is, what he wants to do is go out and ride on your coattails. He's out for himself. You got to get used to this, Margaret, you're going to be a star. Everybody wants a piece of you. The guy actually told Fox you won't go without him, so they'd better give him a contract, too, or else they don't get you. Supposing he flops, he can still live off you. Happens all the time. How many no-talent guys you think are living right now off big stars? I could name them.

"Believe me, it hurts me to tell you this. I don't want to see you hurt. That's what me and Chicki are here for, to protect you. There is a point you got to wake up, honey."

I left the table without bothering to excuse myself. In the lobby I broke down crying. A bellhop came up to ask if he could help. I rushed outside and ran home.

I didn't believe a word of it. It was just one of Norman's shameless lies. If they were trying to break me every way they could, they were doing a good job of it. Mother brought other arguments to bear. Grandmother Nell was getting old. What if she got sick? Who was going to pay her medical bills? My theatrical dreams were all very well, but the Fox offer was a bird in the hand. If we didn't grab it, some other lucky girl would reap the rewards. Why was I always putting myself first?

Every day Mother said it was time to make up my mind—or rather, to stop my nonsense and get packing. I was beside myself when the *Evening Journal* ran a story with the heading HOLLYWOOD BOUND?:

Word is out that MARGARET SPENCER, hot off her smash debut in LILIOM and Broadway's new wunderkind, is headed for stardom in the Metropolis of Makebelieve. Fox Pictures insiders say she's set opposite J. Farrell MacDonald in director John Ford's action period piece NAPOLEON'S BARBER, filming to commence February. The picture will talk, and so can scrumptious Miss Spencer.

In her letters Rhoda did not know what to advise me. Couldn't I get Fox to wait a year or two? When I talked to Frank, he vehemently denied having contacted Fox. He wouldn't even know whom to phone. But if I wanted him to, he would be willing to follow me out there.

Mr. Nolan issued an ultimatum. I had to agree within a week or the offer was off. Norman and Chicki were beside themselves. If I blew this chance, they said, I would have the reputation of being willful and petulant and an idiot, and nobody needed that, not with the money at risk in the picture business.

I had begun to wear down. Frank wasn't being as strong as I wished he would be. I was hoping that he would offer to let me move in with him and Evelyn, even if Mother called in the marines.

Then word came from Miss Lenihan that she had secured me an audition for *Strange Interlude*. Mr. O'Neill would personally judge the tryout, along with the director, Philip Moeller. I would be considered for the role of Madeline Arnold. Miss Lenihan sent the script; I read Mr. O'Neill's description of Madeline as "a pretty girl of nineteen" who "always knows exactly what she is after and generally gets it, but is generous and a good loser, a good sport who is popular with her own sex as well as sought after by men . . . " I thought I could handle that all right. A godsend! Madeline sounded too good to be true, but then Julie had been too abject to swallow. Acting would save me again.

I set about memorizing my lines before the audition, only a week away, sure this would impress them more than a mere reading. Frank rehearsed with me.

Suddenly things happened fast, too fast. Norman and Chicki announced with hysteria that Mr. Nolan had upped the offer to four hundred a week and added a clause raising that to five hundred after a year, seven-fifty the year after, a thousand in the fourth year, negotiable after that.

We were given twenty-four hours to decide. Mother screamed at me, tried to cajole me, conjured images of ease, comfort, extravagance, international fame. I still refused, and I grew cross with Frank, hanging up on him when he disappointed me by saying that, after all, it was a hell of a lot of money. What even Frank seemed to be losing sight of was that, apart from my emotional and artistic commitment to the stage—and to him!—I feared that going to Hollywood would only tighten the shackles that held me to Mother. What use would money be to me?

Then the bombshell.

Mother said that the decision was not really mine to make in any case. Under California law, I was still a minor. Mr. Nolan and the Kupplers had explained everything to her. As far as California and the motion picture business were concerned, I had no legal rights until I was twenty-one and, by law, had to abide by any contract entered into on my behalf by my parents. When I was an adult, I could make my own decisions; as of now, I was a child. It was only out of love and respect for me that she wanted the choice to be my own. She would be within her rights to sign for me.

Whatever *Strange Interlude* would pay, Mother argued, would be a fraction of the Fox offer; nor was there any guarantee that I would win the part, which wasn't even a leading role but only a small one in the final two of nine long acts. The audience would probably walk out before then. Norman and Chicki said that the word on Broadway was that O'Neill had over-reached himself this time, deluded by inflated ego into foisting more on his audience than even his most devoted admirers could endure. I would be throwing away the chance of a life-time for nothing.

I became confused. Did I have a choice or not? What did I know of the law? If I were a boy, I thought, this would be just the time to run off and join the merchant marine and come back a man, answering to no one. Unfortunately, I was capable of changing sexes only onstage.

Nor was my resolution strengthened by the unfortunate truth that the more I read *Strange Interlude*, the less enthusiasm I felt for it; the thrill of the prospect of being in an O'Neill play was being eroded by the astonishing tedium of the dialogue, interminable pretentious meanderings, soliloquies of unspeakable woodenness and phoniness. On the other hand, I hadn't liked *Liliom* either . . . I was beginning to wonder about my judgment.

Whenever I recall that evening when, with Mr. Nolan's deadline only hours away, Norman and Chicki showed up at our apartment contract in hand, and shoved it under my nose, I understand how people sign confessions to crimes they did not commit. You just give up. I believe I would have signed merely to get them out of there.

"I think Margaret should sign first," Norman said. "After all, she's the one who's going to be the star."

I contemplated bolting out the door, but I signed. Then I locked myself in the bathroom until they were gone and I could break down. I despised myself, especially when Mother said how proud of me she was.

I became an automaton. I let Mother pack my things and left it to her to tell Miss Lenihan, whom I could not face, that I was going to Hollywood. I felt that I was betraying her, the Guild School, the people who had sponsored and helped me so unselfishly. I remembered how, when I had written a thank-you note to Otto Kahn for the scholarship that he had donated, he had replied with a letter telling me how proud he was to be able to help me, and that he knew I had not only the talent but the kind of dedication and perseverance it took to become an ornament to the American stage. He and everyone else would now think me another greedy little opportunist who would do anything for money.

I didn't even have the nerve or the heart to call Frank. At least one of us should stick to what we had promised ourselves to do.

At Penn Station I did dial Frank's number. Evelyn answered. Frank was out. He had been anxious about me. She knew that I was having a hard time of it.

"Tell him I had to go," I said. "Tell him I'll write to him." I was going to say tell him I love him, but I couldn't get the words out.

22

The *Twentieth Century Limited* was supposed to be the finest train in America, but its splendors were wasted on me. I might as well have been traveling in a cattle car. I sat in the observation car facing backward so that I could watch the East recede. New York shrank to postcard size in my mind, buildings with everyone I knew at windows waving to me. Here I was, drawn along at speed, contemplating the blur of what was past and passing, unable to do a damn thing about it. When Mother came back to join me, I headed for our compartment. Rather than accompany her to the dining car, I nibbled on the basket of fruit the studio had thoughtfully provided.

"You should eat some solid food. You'll want to look your best when we get there."

No comment. I did my best to irritate her, but she was too happy to be fazed.

Grandmother Nell met us in Chicago and spent the day before we boarded the *Santa Fe Chief* for the long haul to Los Angeles. I had not seen her in years. She had not changed a bit. She was one of those creatures who look old and crabbed before their time and then surprise everyone by hanging on indefinitely in unaltered form. She seemed nearly as pleased as Mother at the turn in our fortunes and announced that she would visit us in Hollywood as soon as was humanly possible, after we got settled.

"It's too bad Grandfather isn't alive to come out," I said. "Do you think he would have liked California?"

She did not reply. Once Grandfather had been gone, he was gone, period. Mother hardly ever referred to Father, either; I was always bringing him up and receiving silence in response. Was there something in their backgrounds that told them it was bad luck to speak of the dead? Was Jesus the only one you were supposed to talk about?

Nell spoke approvingly of my cousin Hazel Mae, who would one day be one of the first women ever to graduate from the University of Kansas Medical School. When she thanked Mother for her latest contribution to Hazel Mae's higher education, it was the first I'd learned of our charitable activities. I supposed Mother must be sending Nell contributions for herself as well. What other worthy causes were we supporting? I thought that we had had barely enough for necessities. My new salary would open philanthropic vistas. Mother said she believed in tithing. Every penny you gave was supposed to come back to you a hundredfold. I guessed Norman and Chicki believed in it, too.

We wouldn't buy a house right away. Mother would have to get the lay of the land first, but she already had some helpful literature from promoters. People could lean out the window and pick grapefruit off the tree. She had also been reading up on investing and was beginning to get the hang of it. She checked the market fluctuations every day. She had never realized that even starting with a small amount, you could just sit back and watch the dollars multiply like chickens.

Chickens were always good to have, Nell said. If you had nothing else, you had eggs. She would be on the train to California as soon as possible.

Somewhere in Colorado or New Mexico the landscape got to me. For years I had scarcely been farther from Manhattan than Asbury Park. Here was infinity. The red earth showed through patches of snow; there were clumps of little pines,

226

weird formations I did not know to call buttes and mesas, more sky even than my memories of being at sea. Insignificant as I felt, I calmed down. Nothing seemed to matter as much, not even my loneliness and sadness. There was a kind of buoyancy in not caring. Anything might happen.

I could not remember seeing Mother so animated. When we stopped for fifteen minutes or so in what was then the village of Albuquerque, she wanted to get out to look at the Indians. I followed her. Navajos were selling the blankets and jewelry they made. I persuaded Mother to buy a turquoise ring for herself. She was thrilled slipping it on, it was exotic, and the Indians looked just the way they had in *The Iron Horse*. It had never occurred to me that any of this was real or still existed. The ring was to put away, Mother said, not the sort of thing a lady would wear in public, but she kept it on for the rest of the trip.

Mother was impressed that the meals on the Chief were catered by Fred Harvey. When E.P. had taken us to California, and I had been only a baby, she remembered that the train had stopped several times at Fred Harvey restaurants. Everyone had got off and eaten delicious meals served by friendly waitresses who lived there, way out in the middle of cacti and dust. Many of them ended marrying well-to-do passengers. She might have become a Fred Harvey girl herself, had she not married my father. Now, with refrigeration, you could eat the same food on the train. The meat course was always good. Vegetables. Fresh rolls with butter. The only difference was, no Harvey girls.

Her enthusiasm made me hungry, and I gave up my boycott. On our last night aboard we partook of Mr. Harvey's finest beefsteaks, sharing a table with a couple who were moving from Ohio to California. He worked for an oil company and discoursed on rotary drill bits. When Mother told him proudly that I was going to be a movie actress, he and his wife were mightily impressed. I couldn't help mentioning that I had played the female lead in *Liliom*. That was all very well, but Hollywood counted more.

They must have assumed we were going to be millionaires. The man said that we should stockpile shares in Standard Oil right away. The stuff was flowing out of the ground at the stick of a pin. Wait till we saw Los Angeles—there were forests of oil derricks all over the place.

"Don't you think I should have a diversified portfolio?" Mother asked.

I nearly fell into my steak. Where had she picked that up? I had no idea what it meant. The man said it was a good idea, but not to fail to invest in oil immediately.

"Margaret Spencer," he said. "We'll remember that name. Congratulations," he said to Mother. "It looks like you've got your own little oil well seated right beside you! She's a regular gusher, I'll bet, and a darned pretty one, too!"

I had already gone from being an artist to a hole in the ground.

"We'll look for your name in lights," the woman said.

"Don't be a salary slave," the man said. "Take all that money and put it in oil. Then you can sit back and count it. Oil's going to double in two years, mark my words."

The wife asked for my autograph. In flamboyant script I signed the menu right across the appetizers.

"You don't look like the kind of girl who'll get into trouble," the woman said. "I don't suppose your mother worries you'll fall in with the wrong crowd, does she?"

"My mother knows that I'm as pure as the driven snow, don't you, Mother? Why, there's nothing I like better than hiking through the woods and cooking over an open fire. When I'm not acting, I'm birdwatching."

"Who's *your* favorite actress?" the woman asked.

"Mary Pickford," I said sweetly.

"I read where her brother dynamited his mother's house to get at the liquor, did you hear that? Blew the roof clear off."

"How enterprising," I said. "I don't touch liquor, of course. Oh, maybe a martini cocktail now and then before lunch."

"Margaret," Mother said. "Please."

* * *

Margaret in Hollywood

When the porter woke us the next morning, the landscape had changed again. Under a blazing sun, orange and lemon groves rolled out. The windowpane was hot, and it was December. At least the Kupplers hadn't lied about the weather. If there really was a play about Christ out here, I might have to reconsider my opinion of them.

At breakfast mountains to the north rose up snowcapped and broad-shouldered beyond the groves. The waiter said the mountains would be with us all the way to Pasadena. Some of them were eleven thousand feet high. He sang out the names— San Jacinto, San Gorgonio, San Antonio—as if we were all aboard for Gloryland.

23

After a few nights in a fleabag on Hollywood Boulevard (it was called the Plaza) Mother took an apartment on Ivar Street, a ten- or fifteen-minute streetcar ride from the studio. We hadn't been there two weeks when I was jolted by a letter from Rhoda. I had written to her and Frank more than once, but this was the first reply from either.

She didn't know how to say what she was about to write. She wasn't sure that she should be telling me at all, but our friendship had always been based on honesty and trust. At least she could continue to be honest, although she was not sure that I would ever trust her again, and she was beside herself with worry about that.

She had come down from Cambridge for the Christmas holidays. With me suddenly gone, a void had come into her life in the city. She was glad to see her parents, but she had been lonely, and her boyfriend was with his family in Boston. One day she had been sitting around looking through some old photographs and had come across the pictures taken of us when we had been in *Romeo and Juliet*. There she was with me, and there was Buster, and there was Frank, looking so young and cute, and the two of us obviously already in love. It had made her very sad, and out of sorrow, not for any other reason, she had telephoned Frank. He felt deserted, and—she was reluctant to tell me this—he had actually contemplated suicide! He had a revolver of his father's and was thinking about playing Russian roulette!

That didn't sound like Frank to me. Well, it did sound like Frank the dramatist. I felt bad for him, but he was too ambitious to shoot himself; so was I. It was part of why we got on.

Rhoda admitted that it had been her idea that they get together, just to talk about old times, so she could cheer him up. They had gone to a deli; then they had ended up at his place. Frank's grandmother was very sort of *different*, wasn't she? (Oh, no. I could hear Evelyn: "Have a nice time, dears.") Things had just happened. Yes, they had made love. Please, could I try to understand, they had talked about me the whole time.

The whole time? How revolting.

Could I ever forgive her?

Not on your life, was my first thought. No wonder Frank had not written, the sniveling bastard! I didn't know which one of them I despised more. I hadn't been gone two weeks when this had happened. And was it just once? Rhoda cleverly hadn't said, one way or the other. For all I knew, they were coochy-cooing at that very moment. He was probably making a regular milk run up to Cambridge.

The thought of Rhoda's actually . . . drove me wild.

I wrote her a letter acid with sarcasm, saying that it was just fine with me that she had screwed the one person I cared more about than anyone else in the world. I was grateful to her, because I had entertained fantasies of Frank's coming out to California, and she had done me a big favor by waking me up. Now I would not be distracted by false hopes and could get on with my life.

But why had she been so niggardly with the details? I asked. Had it been good, bad, or indifferent? She had mentioned her boyfriend. Had she told him? Maybe I could save her time and write to him myself. And by the way, wasn't he supposed to be her future husband? Frank could be the best man. How had Frank behaved? Had he groaned when he had his orgasm as if he were having his appendix removed without benefit of anesthetic? I had always found that impressive. Had she enjoyed the way he held her afterward instead of rolling off the way other men did when they were done? Oh, I had forgotten. She had not had much experience. It was good that at long last she had been to bed with an honest-to-goodness man instead of the stuffed shirts she was used to.

I did not send the letter, I am relieved to say. I admit that I cried a lot. I had to face that some of my sarcasm rang true—boomeranging against me. Let them enjoy themselves; I was gone, and there was no going back. It took a while for me to see it that way.

Rhoda finally telephoned. After we hung up, Mother asked what it was that I had been forgiving Rhoda for over the wires.

"She stole something from me," I said.

"That doesn't sound like her. What on earth of yours would she want?"

"It wasn't much of anything. Something old."

Weeks later Frank did send me a chatty, empty letter about himself. I sent him a postcard showing the Malibu Pier. People jump off the end of it, was my message; I added that much had happened since I had seen him, more than I could say.

In those days the Fox lot still stood on both sides of the street at the intersection of Western and Sunset. On my first day there I was taken on a tour of the five big indoor stages and the western town—saloons, a bank, a whorehouse, a hotel, and a church—where Tom Mix held sway. I watched him leap from the hotel balcony onto Tony. I was as impressed as any fan to discover that he actually performed the stunt himself. I lied to my escort, a secretary, that I could ride, and said I would happily learn to shoot to kill. I hoped they would look around for the role of a girl who had just got off the stagecoach from the East. As long as I was going to be in Hollywood, I might as well try something different from Broadway. But it would be a year before Raoul Walsh figured out how to shoot outdoors with sound (*In Old Arizona*, based on an O'Henry story), and I had been brought to the Coast to talk.

Sol Wurtzel was second in command at Fox and ran the

studio when Winnie Sheehan was in New York to see Mr. Fox and the money men, which was more often than not. Mr. Wurtzel was a sad-faced, worried-looking man, dressed in a rumpled brown business suit, who came around from behind his desk to shake my hand and welcome me. I had heard so many Hollywood stories, I was relieved that he did not have his fly open. He reminded me of an uncle who had assumed the burden of supporting a large and profligate family.

His telephone rang constantly during our brief interview, and he was always saying something like "No, we can't afford it," "Elephants are nothing but trouble," "Mr. Sheehan says no," "Don't give in to the son of a bitch unless he shows you Zukor's offer in writing," "The schmuck can't act worth a shit." A large bottle of Pluto Water stood on his desk. In fifteen minutes he poured himself three or four glasses of the stuff, belching softly behind his fist. He talked about the studio and himself, how they had made eighty-five pictures last year, how the cheaper pictures made more money, no matter what the critics said, how his brother Harry was now an agent and was robbing him blind with his demands, how Janet Gaynor was the most cooperative actress on the payroll, how Harry Cohn over at fly-by-night Columbia never had an idea for a picture he didn't steal and would be broke and ruined in six months, how the Warner brothers would break a contract just on principle, but they didn't work that way at Fox, how a certain actor was the laziest drunken son of a bitch in Hollywood and if he didn't watch it he would be out in the street and starving to death and if a car ran over him it would be too good for him. I found the monologue instructive, to the extent that I could follow it; I had the impression that it would be better to stay on Mr. Wurtzel's good side. I also grasped how much this business ran on gossip and power and manipulations of people: I was too green to be able to state it that clearly to myself, but I got the idea.

I do not believe that I uttered a syllable. I waited for Mr. Wurtzel to ask me about myself, my ambitions, what sort of roles I hoped to play. As I was getting up to leave, he did tender me a piece of advice:

"Take care of yourself. Keep your bowels open."

At the publicity department a youthful flack named Kowazanik, all wild black hair and eyeglasses half an inch thick—he would have made a perfect mad scientist—showed me the collection of my photographs they had assembled. Several from *Liliom* made my heart take a dip. Kowazanik had prepared a biographical sketch that he said would soon be released to the press and asked me to read through it while he phoned Louella Parsons about some dirt he had dug up on a star at a rival studio. In exchange for that, Kowazanik explained, Miss Parsons would run an item for him the next time he needed a favor. It was a lot cheaper than having to pay a writer under the table to print something.

"You mean you bribe people?"

"I hear you're an intellectual," Kowazanik avoided answering.

"I wouldn't say that. You mean somebody says I actually read books?"

"Who's your favorite novelist? Mine's Tolstoy."

I said that was a pretty good choice. What was a young man like him doing here? Shouldn't he be in a library or writing in a garret? He said that he wrote scripts on the side. There was terrific demand for them. I asked him what kind of story he was working on. Was there a part for me? No, he said, he was adapting *Robinson Crusoe* to modern times. In his version, Crusoe is a kind of Thomas Edison figure who gets shipwrecked on an island. To escape, he invents a time machine that runs on breadfruit. The machine takes him back to the Old West. He knows where he is when he sees lariats and six-guns and cowboy boots floating by in space, and all of a sudden you cut to a saloon where he is surrounded by outlaws, who beat him up and throw him into a stable. But from stuff lying around in the muck he puts together a Gatling gun and blasts the outlaws to smithereens. At the end you see him driving off in a wagon he has converted into an automobile. What did I think of the story?

I wished him good luck and turned to my biography.

If Kowazanik had not spelled my name correctly, I would

have assumed he had given me the wrong biography. I learned that I had been born in 1906 in San Francisco during the earthquake, the daughter of one of the richest men in the world, a nephew of the czar. My father had discovered the largest vein of gold in the mother-lode country and had built the most luxurious mansion on Nob Hill.

At the height of the earthquake, my parents were crushed beneath a marble column thought to have been personally designed by the emperor Nero. I had been stranded in a refugee camp at Twin Peaks beyond the city when Mr. William Fox, who had rushed to San Francisco to aid the victims, saw me in the arms of a nun. Mr. Fox had been in the clothing business at that time, and he presented me with baby clothes and, never forgetting my beautiful face, sent me a new wardrobe every year thereafter and personally supervised my education by the Sisters of Mercy. On my eighteenth birthday, the man who had become the most powerful studio head in Hollywood threw a lavish party for me and asked me if I'd like to be in pictures. Other than overlooking the vast financial empire I had inherited, I was now devoting myself to a screen career.

When Kowazanik finally got off the phone, I told him that this was the most preposterous thing that I had ever read. No one would believe it. I'd be surprised, he said, what people would believe.

"But it has nothing to do with me! It doesn't even mention my work on the stage!"

"We can add that," he said. "Glad you reminded me. Anyway, I have an alternate version. See what you think of it."

This one had me as the daughter of the duke of Chorley, whoever he was, and a student at the Royal Dramatic Academy. I preferred it, but I asked Kowazanik what on earth was the matter with my own life? I had not been born on a dungheap. My father had been a man of the theater, successful in his day. I had won scholarships and prizes.

Kowazanik said that, come to think of it, there was nothing wrong with that. He would have to apologize, he had not even so much as glanced at the biographical questionnaire I had filled out. What I had told him now was perfectly good, even if it was true. He hoped I understood. Putting down the truth was not his job, and he wasn't used to it. There was one star on the lot who had come straight to Sunset and Western from a New Orleans whorehouse. He had personally been assigned to locate and destroy the negatives of photographs of another star who had an unnatural affection for her Alsatian dog. Of course, if you were really notorious, an honest-to-God gangster, for instance, like Al Jennings, that was a different matter. Jennings had been hired because he was actually an outlaw and a killer. That kind of publicity you couldn't buy.

"You mean they would hire a real killer?"

"Sure, just as long as he didn't go around shooting up the lot. Then again, it would depend on who he shot."

Kowazanik said he would get cracking on another bio for me right away, if I cared to wait around and check it out.

I did wait. In the end Kowazanik was as good as his word, or nearly. I am sure to the frustration of his mythomania, he produced a fairly straightforward account that fudged only by saying that my father had produced nothing but Shakespeare and Greek tragedies and had owned theaters in Manhattan before his untimely demise in a railroad crash. I figured E.P. would probably have approved. Kowazanik also threw in that my mother had been the daughter of a Kansas cattle baron. I did not think she or Nell would mind that. Nor did I object that he described me as "gracious, aristocratic, and refined."

The first interview with me after I had arrived in Hollywood appeared in the *Los Angeles Examiner* and ran in Hearst papers across the country. The reporter talked to me in an office on the lot. It taught me a lesson.

GIRL STAR WOULD OWN THEATER
FOR HIGHBROWS

A lowbrow reporter has no business interviewing "a lady in every sense of the word," as Fox Studio's biography of their latest hotter-than-hot property describes this visitor from the rarefied air of New York's Theatre Guild.

Margaret Spencer is one of the army of Eastern thespians who have arrived in our little frontier town by the
Pacific to teach us about art.

Sorry, but I forgot to bring my fingerbowl.

So as not to risk taking the shine off her polish, I guess,
Miss Spencer would like to use some of the spare change
from her more-than-poverty-row movie salary to build a
theater for some of the actor friends she left behind in
Gotham. They would play "nothing but the classics."

Miss Spencer, as she prefers being addressed—Lady
Spencer would probably do—doesn't care for jazz either,
she says. Nothing but the three B's for her. And I mean
Bach, Beethoven, and Brahms, folks, not beans, biscuits,
and Buster Browns.

By the way, wasn't that Earl Burnett's orchestra I heard
on the radio as I entered Miss Spencer's Beverly home?
Well, it doesn't matter.

Margaret Spencer does have a warm handshake, and I
thought I could detect a little mischief behind those dark,
serious eyes. Maybe after a little fun in the Southland sun
she'll figure out there's more to life than they taught her
in school.

Come to think of it, maybe she was putting me on about
all that highbrow stuff. Maybe that's what the biggies over
at Fox told her to say. You never know in this business.

What would a lowbrow reporter know anyhow?

The lying son of a bitch. His name was Freddy Schultz, and I
vowed never to talk to him again.

I made an effort to loosen up in interviews after that. I made
a point of saying I liked jazz; I had never said otherwise, only
that I had not had a chance to hear much of it. I began throwing in that I read the funny papers and that there was nothing
I enjoyed more than to wake up on a Sunday morning and
rustle up some scrambled eggs and flapjacks.

I came off a bit better subsequently, but I was unable to

bring myself to sound like one of the gals or guys. I always seemed a bit of a snob, no matter what. Maybe I was one.

I couldn't do anything about the papers' saying that I lived in a Beverly Hills mansion with a swimming pool or that I kept a town house on Park Avenue or drove a rare Italian car. The studio wanted that. Money was glamour, and vice versa. The highbrow stuff turned John Q. Public sour. It was okay in a man, Mr. Wurtzel and others told me. People liked associating John Barrymore with Hamlet. But a girl ought to make sure she came off, well, feminine. Sophistication was all right. You could get away with being streetwise. A girl could even look as if she had a few miles on her. But bookworm females scared people off. Besides, everybody thought they were frigid.

The studio did not suggest a lobotomy. They did cut off my hair and pluck out my eyebrows, or most of them. I protested, but the hairdressers and makeup people said they had orders from Mr. Wurtzel himself. I guess he had been studying me more closely than I had thought between gulps of Pluto Water.

Dolly, the woman who did my hair, was sympathetic and nice. Too nice? Sycophantic might be the word. She told me I had the most beautiful hair she had ever seen, that my features would knock them dead, that I was surefire box-office material, that every other star would be jealous. I wanted to tell her to lay off. The sincerity quotient in this town was low enough already. But she *was* nice; better her than some grump, and besides, she was getting paid to flatter me.

I had to admit that I liked the new look. It felt cool and light, and it was, how shall I say, Californian. And it called for a new set of publicity stills, scores of them, in dozens of different costumes and settings, requiring every variety of expression I could manage. They put me in ball gowns, furs, bathing costumes, pioneer calico, nurse's uniform, tailored suits, an Eskimo jacket, sailor middy, yachting garb, tennis whites, jodhpurs. In one shot, clad in harem pajamas, I held up an enormous transparent ball and made kissy-poo lips at it. Turkish delight.

It was amusing some of the time, different from my old modeling career because I was selling myself, not the clothes; but it went on for weeks. Some of the grips and technicians were vile. I did not run to Mr. Wurtzel, because nobody laid a hand on me, but perfectly audible remarks about tits and pussy and ass upset me. Rather than cringe, I looked daggers at them and assumed my snottiest, coldest air, which helped. One day when a gravelly-voiced grip asked another to take a bet on whether Miss Spencer had a "fire pussy," I stomped out and refused to return until the foul-mouthed creep was fired or transferred. To my surprise, he was gone when I resumed posing. It was a battle, but maybe I could win if I fought savagely enough.

I looked so different in every picture, no single image of me came through. I regarded this as proof of my abilities, but I came to understand that to the studio it presented a problem. They would have to decide who I was.

One of the photographers, Max Autrey, was extraordinarily talented, with none of the pretentiousness of a Dr. Knauer. When I admired his work, he brought in some of his favorites to show me. There was talent in Hollywood, Mr. Autrey said. It was a matter of how and whether it was used.

"And what are they going to do with me?" I asked him.

"Who knows? Right now they're trying to define the Margaret Spencer mystique. We'll see what they do with the most beautiful woman in Hollywood."

"What about acting?"

"Oh, you can forget about that!"

*A*fter that big buildup, you can imagine my disappointment when, as my first picture, they decided to put me in a four-reeler that starred a washed-up vaudeville team, Clark and McCullough. It was called *Cloud Ten* (get it?) and was set in a mythical kingdom where I was the princess. Four-reelers were shown before the feature film to give the audience their two bits' worth and to make them suffer through something awful so they would appreciate the virtues of the main event. Nonetheless, some wonderful four-reelers were produced, with Will Rogers and Laurel and Hardy and the like. *Cloud Ten* was not one of them. There was no story; the gags were shopworn; my part consisted of standing around looking dumb and pretty and uttering a few inane lines.

Why had they done this to me? I suspect it may have been to take down a peg this snotty Broadway import who insisted on being called Miss Spencer. Or maybe there was a less sinister explanation. Maybe they simply had not figured out what to do with me and did not want me drawing a salary sitting idle while they made up their minds. You never knew. You did what you were told.

Fox's Sunset and Western studios were outmoded by the advent of talkies. Mr. Fox was already building his enormous soundstages out near Westwood Village; but until they were completed, we had to work at night on the old indoor stages that were fine for keeping out the occasional rain and had once seemed advanced but were useless against the traffic noises, even though the walls were draped with heavy felt. My call was at 4:00 P.M. for makeup; we were rarely finished before two or three in the morning. Then you were supposed to try to sleep.

I wasn't alone in bitching. The theater had been a breeze compared to this. Everyone complained and prayed for the completion of the soundstages. So much for lying on the beach!

There was a certain camaraderie, but I must have cut a lonely figure, sitting by myself in my dressing room and wondering what I was doing there. When I learned that *Strange Interlude* had become the critical and commercial hit of the season in New York and was expected to run forever, I was bewildered. I had thought the play a dog and had left telling myself I wasn't missing much; maybe I wasn't so smart after all. People tended to keep their distance from me, except for one young assistant director, Sammy Maltzman, who tried to cheer me up. He would come over and chat, and he called me Princess.

I confessed to Sammy about my frustration at not having at least auditioned for the O'Neill play. He was from New York and knew what the theater meant there. He told me not to worry, that I would do something grand. As for him, he was only making seventy a week, but was determined to move up and become a director. Before landing this job, he had been working as a cabin boy on the night boats that ran between Los Angeles and San Francisco. One was called *Harvard,* the other *Yale,* and they were nothing but floating brothels. Gambling and booze and scads of girls turning two-dollar tricks until somebody put them in the movies. He would rather be where he was, and maybe I shouldn't feel so sorry for myself, Sammy told me in the nicest possible way.

We started meeting for lunch in the commissary, then at spots he knew. (Mother, of course, thought I was at the studio.) I told him about Frank, and about Rhoda and Frank; he said that he had already lost two girlfriends in Hollywood to men who were making more money than he. One afternoon

he asked me if he could drive me up to his apartment in the
hills before we had to be at work. It was the silliest building,
gingerbread with a fake windmill attached. We were like bud-
dies, Sammy and I, making love in the early afternoon and
then at ten or eleven in the morning, nothing serious, but it
did take the edge off loneliness. He had the flat roof fixed up
like a porch, with a table and an umbrella, and sometimes we
would drag the mattress up there and screw away the morning
and sit naked drinking coffee in the shade, watching the city
below get busy. Occasionally we fooled around in my dressing
room, as everyone else did during the endless waiting around.
You could only read so many books.

"Someday I'll brag I *shtupped* the great Margaret Spencer,"
Sammy said.

"And someday I'll say that the great Sam Maltzman was my
demon Hollywood lover."

"And nobody will believe us."

No, he was not handsome. You could call him ugly, in a
cuddly Quasimodo sort of way; I preferred to think of him as
rugged-looking, outwardly a thug and inside as soft as a grape.
He was built like a short wrestler, and he was losing his hair.
Maybe I ought to have gone after someone like Rex Ingram,
who was an important, powerful director and so good-looking
you could faint, brilliant and dashing as no damned leading
man ever was. But Sammy was my man; he made me feel as
if I belonged, a little.

After *Cloud Ten* my parts improved. I am not suggesting
that the films were great, even compared to the junk of today.
I'm not sorry that the early ones have all been lost or turned
to goo or burned up. But I began to get good notices. *Bad
Intentions,* in which I had the lead opposite Phil Spode, was no
worse than the typical Broadway comedy, nor was *Penny Ar-
cade* with Stanley Burgess. A mystery, *Murder by a Blueblood,*
was clever. I saw none of these in final cut, and I found working out of continuity, as is always done, maddening. A movie
actor never gets the chance to build a character scene by scene.
You might begin on your deathbed. This factor, more than

any other, has always made it difficult for movie actors to get thorough satisfaction from their work, whatever many of them say. I have heard Bob Mitchum joke that the greatest movie actor of all time was Rin Tin Tin, because he always did exactly as he was told and kept a sense of modesty about his work.

When I watched the daily rushes, as we were sometimes able to do, I was not particularly pleased with myself. I could see that I needed to tone down my theatrical style. The gestures I had cultivated were too broad for the screen, and I was still trying to reach the back row with my delivery. But no one, including my directors, had figured out the difference between stage and screen acting, and most films were shot as little different from a photographed play, the camera motionless as a spectator glued to his seat. To my alarm I saw that the camera is a microscope and that even primitive Movietone picked up every nuance of sound, as we were never more than a couple of feet from the microphone, hidden in a vase or a piece of furniture. There was way too much dialogue: you could convey just about everything you needed through your eyes. Critics praised my hands, but I thought they fluttered about absurdly, mannerisms cultivated for the stage.

The possibilities of film acting intrigued me, but most of the other actors loved chewing the scenery as if playing to a house of zombies. When I restrained myself, the directors told me to give more. And who were they? How about Reuben Guthrie, Sigmund Parr, names deservedly forgotten. I once told Parr I thought there was too much dialogue. What was the point in all this talk, when half the words could be conveyed visually?

"Stick to your job and leave the fucking directing to me," was his reply. "I didn't notice your name on the script." I kept quiet after that.

This was at a time when John Ford, whose pictures had less than half the dialogue of anyone else's, Howard Hawks, Raoul Walsh, Alan Dwan, and other immortals were on the Fox payroll. I do not know why they never wanted me. Maybe they heard I was difficult, a self-important know-it-all, or maybe it was bad luck.

The more I did mediocre pictures or stinkers, the more I longed for at least one great role. If I was going to work this hard and be in Hollywood for years, I wanted to make the best of it. Others must have felt the same way, but you could get used to merely doing your job and picking up the regular checks. You had no say whatever in your roles; if you balked, you were put on suspension and blackballed by the other studios.

I kept at it, night after night, in five or six pictures that first year alone. You made friends and enemies, working so closely with people for three or four weeks; then you might never see them again.

And, working nights as we were, we had no social life. Hollywood has always been peculiar, but never so much as during that period of the earliest talkies. It was the night shift in a factory. One Saturday when I was not needed on the set, a junior executive named Eddie Garvin, a relative of Mr. Nolan's, did ask me out. We had dinner at the Ship Café on the Venice Pier, oysters and barracuda, which I thought exciting. The place was designed to look like a galleon and was noisy and fun, with a band and a big dance floor. Unfortunately my date was a dope. I think he had spent too much time with the Jesuits. On the dance floor he rubbed up against me as if he itched.

At the door to our apartment building I made the mistake of permitting him to kiss me good night, and he began his writhing anew, and emitted a sort of grunt.

"Well," he said with satisfaction, "I guess you're no longer a virgin."

Home life was another world entirely. True to her word, Grandmother Nell appeared. I gathered that she had more than a holiday in mind when two steamer trunks followed her.

She moved into our two-bedroom apartment on Ivar, a few blocks below Hollywood Boulevard and above Sunset. The arrangement would save us a great deal of money, Mother said enigmatically. I am sure that she had had it in mind from the moment Mr. Nolan made his pitch to her. Three could eat as cheaply as two, she said, Nell took up so little room, and long-distance charges would be cut to the bone. We would also save on postage, as Mother no longer had to mail Nell a check but could slip her cash in the wink of an eye.

As my schedule required that I try to sleep at odd hours of the day, hanging sheets and bath towels over the window against the relentless light, I was permitted my own bedroom and I was grateful for what peace and privacy I managed to preserve there. If it had not been for that blinding, monotonous southern California sunlight, I would have been almost cozy with my books and trinkets from the past.

The apartment, on the second floor of a two-story faded green stucco nondescript, was small; but it was clean, had a separate kitchen, and was, compared to the one we had left behind in New York, positively cheerful. For this much people uprooted themselves and spoke of paradise. The other occupants of the building included a policeman and his wife and two children, a bachelor screenwriter, and a tough thirtyish "actress" who was actually an energetic prostitute. Mother and Nell pretended that the woman's visitors were out-of-town relatives. It was a prime location for hooking, just down from Hollywood Boulevard where tourists swarmed, and so I am sure she was able to feed herself well. Those were the sorts of people who lived up and down Ivar in those days, middle-class folks, more or less, on a street of wooden and plaster bungalows, Spanishy duplexes, a few oddities: a house built to look like a miniature fortress, castellated with a fake drawbridge over a dry moat; a witch's house with crooked windows; an auto court with a sign proclaiming its special attraction, SLEEP IN A WIGWAM! The screenwriter could be heard at all hours reading aloud from his masterpieces, a kind of melancholy mumble like a noise in the pipes; he walked around with eucalyptus leaves sticking out of his nose. A remedy for nasal drip, he told me when I could not resist asking.

We had windows that faced the street, and from my room I could look west down into a small yard, a couple of square feet of which were shaded two or three hours a day by a squat

palm tree. The yard, or garden, as Mother and Nell euphem-
ized it, was for the communal use of tenants. In practice only
the whore was ever in it, sprawled brown and slick with a mixture of olive and wintergreen oils whose scent wafted up and
through my window. She was quite beautiful, slim and sleek
as she lay there soaking up the sun and flicking ants off herself, except for a deep scar between her shoulder blades, where
I suspect someone had taken a broken bottle to her.

With my long hours I did not see much of Mother and Nell.
When I was not at the studio, I was with Sammy or, later and
briefly, with Richard Merwin, my leading man from a picture
in which I played a college-educated gun moll. (Richard looked
so much like Valentino that women had been known to faint,
thinking they had seen a ghost; he was just this side of impo-
tent, and therefore a melancholy fellow. He could function
only by reciting dialogue from his pictures—"We sail by the
full moon" and so on—and our affair quickly ran out of lines.)

From the material that stacked up all over the apartment, I
could see that Mother was spending a good deal of her time
boning up on her galloping obsession with getting rich through
investment, or with *How to Retire in Deluxe Style in Six Months,*
as one pamphlet offered. She was impatient for the year to
pass, so that I could get my first big raise. I had my own ideas
about what to do with that money, moving into my own place
first of all, but the question was how to get my hands on it. As
in New York, everything went straight to her.

She was busy with other projects, too. Soon after our arrival,
she joined the Motion Picture Mothers Club, an organization
I believe to be unique in all the world. Certainly there was
never a Broadway Mothers Club? Vaudeville Mothers? Stevedores' Mothers? To qualify for membership, your child had to
be in the movies, that was all. Theoretically directors' and producers' mothers could join, but it was actors' mothers who
swelled the lists.

What did the Motion Picture Mothers *do*? Well, there were
the usual committees, one for gardening, mah-jongg, canasta,
the promotion of decency, as well as charity-directed groups

supervising the care and feeding of lunatic actors, drunk actors, dope-fiend actors, senile actors. Primarily the club functioned as a forum for the mothers of actors to boast about their children, to bitch about them, or to exchange trade secrets relative to the promotion of their progenies' salaries and careers. Mary Pickford's mother, rightly regarded as the shrewdest, most ruthless agent in Hollywood, in historical truth the guiding light of every agent to come after her, a genius at squeezing the last dollar out of moguls and standing toe to toe with Goldwyn and Zukor and their peers—Mrs. Pickford was at the top of the Mothers Club heap, the Genghis Khan of filmdom's moms.

The mothers of actresses far outnumbered those of actors. It was Mother's membership in that company of venal matriarchs that made me recognize her, as well as myself, as a type. I was only one among the numberless hordes of fatherless girls who had descended on Hollywood as the fruit flies on the citrus groves. I differed from the mass mainly in that I had arrived with a studio contract in hand; most settled in tatty apartments waiting for a break, attending bogus casting calls, pursuing producers, directors, or, if the girl was an imbecile, screenwriters, in the usual way. (There was a joke going around: What did the moron who wanted to be an actress do? She screwed the screenwriter.) Boardinghouses near Gower Gulch teemed with starstruck girls and their mothers. It was exactly as in war. The directors and producers were the officers; they could hardly be expected to do anything but comply when swarmed over by camp followers. The idea of the rapacious film executive fiendishly attacking female prey was a halftruth. Everyone was fucking everybody, to be sure, but it was a mutual and natural phenomenon, as ordinary as the way all species behave in struggling along the food chain: in Hollywood the mothers were the panders. I went to bed with whomever I pleased only because I already had my deal sewn up. In this sense Norman and Chicki Kuppler had indeed protected me and preserved my freedom of choice. God bless them.

Margaret in Hollywood

I say fatherless girls because that is what virtually all of us were. Why, if there was a viable and prospering papa, would any mother bother entering what amounted to the pimp trade? Name the female star of yesteryear and you will find that, nearly without exception, her father had died before she came to Hollywood, or he had deserted his family, or he was a failure. In the last instance mother and daughter left him behind at his lathe or down a mine shaft and forgot him. He may have been stuck with the other kids, or they trailed along to watch Sis rise to stardom and to live off her. If Sis failed, Mom married someone else, a prop man or a real estate agent.

Young men, by contrast, were apt to come to Hollywood on their own, looking for adventure and bucks, or they arrived by chance. Somebody spotted them riding a horse or hanging from a rigging; or they landed as roustabouts on the studio lot. Those who did show up with apron strings attached never undid them.

Best of all, the women who joined the Motion Picture Mothers Club could make friends and accomplices in a world that would otherwise have been alien to them. In New York, Mother had had no friends after Father's death, no life outside our apartment. Now she was at one with many, as was I.

Mother achieved for Nell an associate membership in the club, a *force de main* that rankled not a few mothers and caused the passage of a bylaw specifying how and if a grandmother merited admittance. They had that commonality now, and shopping, movies, regular visits to Clifton's Cafeteria, a shrine to democratic culinary standards downtown that boasted an interior waterfall that could make you believe you were in Yosemite without having to drive there through the inland heat. They went to movies and to what passed for theater but would have made my father glad to have joined the heavenly choirs at an early age. They adored the outdoor dramas of which Norman and Chicki had so glowingly spoken. When they brought home a program from *The Mission Play*, I read that this extravaganza, a kind of Hispanic-flavored tent evangelism disguised as drama, was performed in an amphitheater equipped with the largest pipe organ in North America, featuring a cast of four hundred people and countless farm animals. Conveniently located refreshment stands offered Mexican delicacies. The arena, seating twenty-five hundred (Chicki had exaggerated), nestled in the shadow of Mission San Gabriel, twenty minutes from downtown via a scenic highway once traveled by conquistadores; two million souls had witnessed this extravaganza since its inception in 1912. The ritual, enacted year-round, told the story of how Father Junipero Serra and his doughty band of flagellants had instructed the California Indians—a feckless lot!—in the virtues of Christian piety and the Protestant work ethic.

Depending on how you defined it, theater boomed in southern California, although the Pasadena Playhouse was about the only entity recognizable as such. Mother and Nell were regulars at Aimee Semple McPherson's Echo Park temple, where the doors were locked once you entered and clothespins descended on lines stretched across pews to accept donations of no less than a dollar. But Aimee offered salvation only on the installment plan. Avid for quicker results, Mother went gaga over Chauncey C. ("C.C.") Julian, a former Texas oil-field worker who held rallies at the Tar Pits to raise capital for his Julian Petroleum Corporation. Famous for giving cabbies fifteen-hundred-dollar tips and driving his roadster through the plate-glass window of the Bank of California when he had been denied a loan, Julian was not what I would have thought of as Mother's type. She could not, however, stop talking about him. She kept one of his flyers by her bed, stuck in the Bible:

> Come On In, Folks, The Water's Just Fine. I'll Tell You, Folks, You'll Never Make a Thin Dime Just Lookin' On. I've Got a Sure-Fire Winner This Time. We Just Can't Lose. We're All Out Here in California Where the Gushers Are and Why Shouldn't We Clean Up Too? Come On, Folks, Get Aboard For the Big Ride. Thousands of My Investors Are Already Cleaning Up. When We Get The

Margaret in Hollywood

Julian Petroleum Corporation Under Way We'll Make That
Standard Oil Crowd Turn Flipflops. I'm Not Kiddin', Folks,
You're Lookin' Opportunity in the Eye. For More Infor-
mation Send Two Dollars to The Julian Petroleum Cor-
poration, Loew State Building, Broadway, Los Angeles.
Chauncey C. Julian, Founder and President.

When I had the temerity to ask Mother whether she was actually thinking of giving money to C.C. Julian, I got the cold
shoulder. She would take care of the future, she said; I ought
to tend to present business, which meant looking pretty in front
of the camera. Meanwhile why didn't I attend to those black-
heads she noticed on my nose? A subcommittee of the Mothers Club had formed an investment discussion group. She was
head-to-head with some of the most astute minds in western
America.

Fleeting though our contacts were, Mother and Nell and I
were often thrown together on Sundays. A vengeful God had
decreed that, no matter what, my efforts to escape would be
thwarted on His day. They would go to church while I slept,
and then it was off to the San Fernando Valley in search of
vegetables.

The car was a new Model T Mother had bought. I hated
the dusty drive over Cahuenga Pass and the hot, dull expanse
of the Valley. However, since it was either that or make her
sullen, I chose appeasement. It was the weekly repetition that
did me in. Somehow driving with the windows open to the
beanrows, picking over vegetables, and prodding fruits and
bantering with farmers at roadside stands gave her and Nell
happiness. They liked to point to the girl dozing in the car
and say she was in the movies.

The trouble with California was, some damn thing or another was *always* in season. The Valley, all truck farms and
ranches then, must have reminded Mother and Nell of their
youths. They delighted in the dirt-cheap prices and brought
home more than we could eat. The surplus gave Nell oppor-

tunity to indulge her passion for home canning. Hardly a day went by when she wasn't boiling and preserving something in Mason jars. In a curious way it was touching to see her storing up against the Apocalypse; I knew in my soul that people like her were the ones who would forestall the plunge toward inevitable extinction. The kitchen shelves filled up with peaches and tomatoes; the hallway closet was stacked to the ceiling with hoarded comestibles.

"We've plenty of pickled watermelon now," Nell would say.

"My, yes," I assured her, "plenty indeed. You're short of apricots, though."

"Next week I'll get some. Remind me of it."

Women like Nell represented the backbone of the country, before everybody went soft, like me. Watching Nell can, you didn't worry about petty, personal anxieties. If the Mexicans had decided to take back California, we would have outlasted the defenders of the Alamo. I stole dozens of jars and handed them out to grips and extras; if Nell missed them, she must have guessed that they were doing good, because she never complained of the theft. There were always more than enough remaining for the long, hard winter that one day might visit the southland.

Often Mother drove back from the Valley via Sepulveda and out Sunset, a narrow track then, to Highway 1 and the ocean. Overlooking the water not far from the Malibu Pier was a restaurant called Louie the Sea Lion. The parking lot featured a cage where old Louie sat forever on a rock placed in a few inches of seawater. I always tried to avoid looking at him or smelling him as we came in for our fried mackerel. Sometimes he barked mournfully at us, and I would throw him a sign of recognition.

It was pleasant to watch the sun sink into the Pacific, a novelty dazzling to Easterners. If the fish tasted rank, it didn't matter; Mother and Nell filled the fatty air with talk of this wonderful new life, of how elsewhere people were shoveling snow or fighting the boll weevil. After dinner we would take a brief constitutional along the beach, removing shoes and stockings and dipping our toes. The Pacific was wilder and colder than what I had imagined. I had expected lukewarm lagoons, ukeleles, and bronzed youths tipping back coconut shells. The movies.

There came that first Christmas on Ivar. (Our very first California Yuletide had been passed at the Hollywood Plaza, the smells of hot turkey-and-gravy sandwiches mingling with Lysol.) We had a tree and what was left of the family united after a decade. I talked to Rhoda on the phone; Frank was going with a City College girl now, she said; he had always wanted somebody to talk books all night with; I had probably been too interested in dross like fondling his balls. I had a great urge to call him, but satisfied myself by squeezing my legs together as I watched Nell stuff the bird.

When Nell unwrapped her present that was tagged from me, who hadn't a clue to what it was since Mother had done the shopping while I worked, I was surprised to see how generous I had been. It was a mink jacket, worth a week or two's salary at least.

I thought she would be delighted with it, tell me that I should not have done it, and so on, although she must have known that Mother picked it out. I was prepared to tell her how much she deserved it. Mother said that it would be just the thing to wear to the *Pilgrimage Play*, the al fresco Eastertide drama that Norman had hyped and that by every account was more moving than the New Testament.

But Nell donned her mink without enthusiasm as if she had been presented with a hand-me-down. Had she been counting on Russian sable?

"What's the trouble?" Mother asked. "There's flu going around."

"To tell you the truth," Nell sighed, "I was hoping for a car." Had I heard her correctly? "Oh, well, I've lived long enough to know that you can't have everything in this life. I never had a car in Kansas City. Of course, I didn't have a lot of things."

"Maybe you can have a car in the next life," I heard myself saying. "Maybe Jesus will give you a Stutz."

"Don't say such things," Mother snapped. "I can understand how Mother feels."

"It's just that, for shoot's sake," Nell said, "when you're off to your mah-jongg or somewhere, I'm stuck here. I don't play cards, you know. I have learned to drive. It seems such a waste."

I wanted to point out that there was a streetcar on Hollywood Boulevard. I rode it to work, and I got rides home from Sammy Maltzman or some other kind soul at 3:00 A.M. But Mother was too quick for me.

"We could take the jacket back, would you like that? I'm sure Margaret wouldn't be offended."

"Who, me?"

"We could let you have the Ford, and I could get a Chevrolet. They're very nice."

"What the hell," I said, "get her the car. She only lives once. What the hell, give her the damned Ford."

"Margaret! Your language! Apologize to your grandmother!"

The word "apologize" got to me:

"Apologize for what? For working like a dog? You pair of— old crows! Bitches!"

There were other words welling up that I managed to choke back. I had absorbed quite a colorful new vocabulary on the set. I might have given them both heart attacks. Even in my fury I sensed that calling one's grandmother a cocksucker would be excessive. As it was, they cowered. They had never seen me this way. It had been years since I had thrown a decent tantrum. Something in me had snapped.

I spotted my Christmas present under the tree, a cellophane-wrapped, beribboned basked of fruit and dates and nuts called a Mission-Pak—the perfect item to send to relatives back East to let them know what they were missing in the Land of the Padres. How thoughtful it had been of Mother to give me one. It showed that she cared about protecting me from scurvy.

I snatched up the Mission-Pak and ran out the door, down

254

the stairs and into the bright Christmas heat with it. Blindly I headed toward the Boulevard. I didn't know what I was going to do with the Pak. I wanted to give it to the first person I saw, but no one was on the street. It occurred to me to board a streetcar and present it to someone who looked as if he or she deserved it, maybe a maid heading home after assisting a producer and his family on this holy day. Or I could give it to the conductor.

Then I got a better idea. A Mack truck was lumbering down Ivar, one of those big old chain-driven ones that were always waking me up in the middle of the day. Whenever I came home from work, I fixed myself a glass of warm milk and fell to sleep about dawn. Soon Nell would be up rattling jars; Mother would turn on the radio; the policeman's children would be off to school; the tap-tap of the dream merchant's typewriter would begin; if the whore had been lucky enough to snare an all-night stand, he would stumble down the stairs, maybe belting out a sea chantey; the light would stream in, and sooner or later a Mack truck would grind its way past.

I stepped to the curb, waited until the last possible second, and heaved my Mission-Pak under the wheels. A perfect shot. Grapefruit and oranges rolled and squished and splattered all over the street. Dates were mashed to pulp. There were nuts everywhere.

The driver never stopped. He must have thought he had hit a cat.

I hoped Mother and Nell had been watching from the window.

25

Question: What did Alice Spencer, Norman and Chicki Kuppler, Harry Valentine, Louis B. Mayer, numerous southern California banking officials, stockbrokers, real estate brokers, U.S. Senator Frank Flint, a tailor named Abe Getzoff, District Attorney Asa Keyes, Tijuana racetrack touts, bootleggers, Pasadena socialites, Santa Monica beach-combers, a close friend and associate of President Hoover's named Henry M. Robinson, Rabbi Samuel W. Nussbaum, Monsignor Patrick McGrath, Judge William Rhodes Hervey, the postmaster of Los Angeles, the potentate of Al Malaikah Temple of the Mystic Shrine, the locker-room attendant at the Hollywood Athletic Club, Erich von Stroheim, movie studio attorney Mendel Silverberg, the headwaiter at the Brown Derby, the owner of a wiener-shaped hot-dog stand on La Cienega, the curator of the Los Angeles County Museum of Natural History, the swimming coach at USC, and forty thousand other southern Californians have in common?

Answer: Shares in the Julian Petroleum Corporation.

I didn't know this until later. I certainly never suspected that Harry Valentine had anything in common with Alice Spencer, except a mutual dependence on show business. But one day I visited Harry at his house and began to make the connection, along with some others.

I had contacted Harry as soon as I could after coming to

California, and we had managed to meet for lunch a few times. He was working at Paramount; we usually went to Lucey's on Melrose, one of the "in" places, where Harry enjoyed the favor of the owner, Rico, and was coddled by waiters with fake Italian accents and occasionally was greeted by people such as Ernst Lubitsch and even Jesse Lasky, the mogul with taste. Harry was happy to let people think I was his date, especially because he never had one. He had never had any wives, either, nor a child, he soon confessed to me. He said he had written me that nonsense because he couldn't think of anything else to say and wanted me to think that he was a normal person. I didn't give a damn about that; I had given up on normal people long ago.

Harry ordered more than even he could eat and kept his double and triple gins going. He claimed that he performed better when he was in the bag, and who was to contradict him? He had found directors who let him ad-lib, his forte, and he was pulling down fifteen hundred a week. Was he happy? Don't be ridiculous.

As his spirits rose on the tide of gin and the mountain of lasagna, he would talk of blowing this town for Pago-Pago. Except for what he referred to misleadingly as dining out (Rico could have paid off the cops on the Valentine bar tab alone), he had no expenses. When he wasn't in something from Western Costume, he dressed exclusively in bib overalls held together at the sides with big safety pins; he drove a battered truck with S. HERMOSILLO, VICTUALLER painted on the rear; and he said he lived rent-free in a house in the middle of a lemon grove that I was anxious to see for myself.

One Sunday I managed to avoid the vegetables and headed for Harry's in Nell's Ford. (Mother had her black Chevy sedan by then, big enough to haul a gross ton of onions.) Etiwanda was a hell of a long drive, east on 66 through Pasadena, Claremont, Upland, and Cucamonga, but a pretty one along the foothills and past groves and vineyards once attached to wineries but then reduced to producing raisins or wine grapes shipped to criminal enologists in more civilized parts of the country. Harry said the trip was good for his hangovers.

Margaret in Hollywood

It had rained the night before, so it must have been April; everything smelled good; there was snow on Old Baldy. The route paralleled the railroad tracks that had brought us to Hollywood. I had an impulse to forget Harry and keep driving and pull into New York in a couple of weeks and call a press conference, announcing my triumphant return to the stage. But, in truth, I was getting used to California. I had yet to be given a great part; I had become aware that most actresses never were; but I was established, and something better might happen. More than anything else I wanted to split from Mother and Nell, but I still had not got my hands on my own money, and until I did, I could not figure out how to abandon them without leaving them or me or all three of us indigent. I had the vague idea of staging a coup when I was twenty-one, only a few months off. Sammy Maltzman was urging me to do it, and so was Dickie Barnes, a character actor with a house in the cool hollows of Laurel Canyon where he demonstrated yoga positions on a bear rug before the fire. I could not tolerate yoga, or the vegetarianism that accompanied it, but watching his erection defy gravity as he stood on his head was a novelty that led to fascinating experiments in high-energy physics. The soundstages out at Fox Hills had been completed by then, and I had more time for what every healthy American girl craves.

I turned at the derelict Diaz winery, as Harry had instructed, and about a mile up toward the mountains I spotted the mailbox painted with a big red heart. I plunged into the grove on what was little more than a muddy footpath. The still-wet trees gave off a wonderful scent; there were white blossoms and green nubs of fruit and here and there dots of yellow among the leaves that brushed the sides of the car.

His house, a cottage made of rounded granite stones that must have been gathered when the grove was planted, stood in a clearing. Beyond it you could make out the swaying tops of eucalyptus and the mountains gray-green with chaparral. When I cut the engine, there was birdsong. This was what California meant. Why was I living on Ivar?

Parked next to Harry's truck was a blue, almost a royal-purple, Bugatti, which I figured must belong to a friend Harry had said he wanted me to meet, an Englishman named Adrian Percy. That was a name dreamed up by a publicity department, or I was descended from the duke of Chorley.

But Adrian Percy turned out to be the real thing, whatever else he was, a genuine English aristocrat, albeit one without a penny to his name. That was a hazard of Hollywood: I had grown used to everything and everyone's being fake; it got so that, if you happened to encounter the real article, you didn't recognize it, you didn't believe in it, or, worst of all, you didn't care one way or the other. People actually preferred the bogus. It was the beginning of the Disneyland mentality. Standing in the doorway, gin in hand, Adrian introduced himself in a voice that had been meant to order troops to hurl themselves into enemy fire. He wore espadrilles without socks, rolled white flannels, a red-and-blue silk necktie for a belt, a dark blue linen shirt with the top two buttons undone. Harry in his overalls made quite a contrast.

"You are every bit as lovely as Harry said you would be," Adrian said. "Have a drink."

"What do you do in Hollywood?" I asked. It was a bit rude of me, but I could not resist.

"Very little," Adrian said. "My uncle tells me that I am a voluptuary. I think that's rather a good thing to be, don't you?"

"Suits me," I said.

I enjoyed hearing Adrian talk. He had come to Hollywood because he had been nearly everywhere else in his thirty years. His father had been ambassador to Portugal, his uncle adviser to the viceroy of India. After he had been expelled from Eton—for general recalcitrance; he had not cared for being beaten—he had bounced about the world, got married, and returned one evening to his house in London to find that his wife had packed two suitcases for him and left them on the doorstep. As all the family money and property had gone to his elder brother, he decided to spend his last few pounds on passage to America. He checked to make sure that his wife had included his dinner jacket, and he had a splendid crossing, staying drunk the entire time. By the time he reached Hollywood, he was penniless, and he secured employment as a waiter at the Beverly Hills Hotel, where his accent inspired enormous tips.

An English screenwriter friend of his with a sense of humor had spread word at MGM that Adrian Percy, the genius novelist and playwright, had arrived in California to escape the London fog. The next thing Adrian knew, he had been invited to lunch at the commissary with Louis B. Mayer.

"He's a terrific Anglophile, you know. All the moguls are. He offered me a thousand dollars a week."

"To write? Can you write?"

"Of course I cannot write. I can't do anything at all, though I'm a damned good waiter. They give me a screenplay to read, and I tell them what's wrong with it. I don't actually have to do anything. The other day I ran into Mayer and he told me to be sure to change a scene in a script he had assigned me. I asked which scene. He said, 'I don't know. I haven't read it. Just get it changed. It stinks.' That's the way it is."

"I tried for the same job at Paramount, but they wouldn't believe I can read," Harry said. He picked up a shotgun and announced that he was going outside to shoot some lemons. In return for living in the cottage, he was supposed to run lemon rustlers out of the grove. There never were any, but he liked to practice on the fruit.

"Jolly good idea, Harry. Make yourself useful. The charming Miss Spencer and I will stay here and get sozzled."

I asked Adrian if he was afraid of losing his MGM sinecure. He laughed at the question. Of course he would lose it. Thalberg or somebody else with brains would find him out and chuck him into the street. Until then, he intended to enjoy himself to the fullest.

We heard the boom of Harry's shotgun, not too far off. Adrian said that shooting and drinking were Harry's favorite ways of passing the time in the pastoral splendor of Etiwanda. He was very like some of Adrian's cousins that way, although they favored grouse over fruit.

Adrian professed to believe in absolute freedom. He owned
nothing and spent everything. He was paid in cash on Fridays
and considered himself a failure if he had not got rid of all of
it within the next week. The Bugatti would go soon; he was
already behind on payments to the previous owner, an actor
overfond of morphine. Wasn't it a marvelous machine while it
lasted? He was not, like Harry, an absolute maniac about saving money and investing it. Harry believed that he would end
up an oil tycoon. He was always talking about this extraordinary charlatan C.C. Julian, who was going to make him rich.
Had I heard about Julian?

I told Adrian that I was afraid my mother might be suffering from the identical dementia.

Everyone he knew was throwing money at Julian. It was like
a religious mania. His screenwriter friend had extended his
mortgage to invest. It was all quite mad and wonderful, terri-
bly Californian, didn't I agree? He hoped my mother was already very rich. Julian was a bubble.

"It's my money," I said. "She has nothing."

"Oh, dear. You'd better have another drink. Here comes
Harry. If you ask him about it, you'll never shut him up. He
thinks Julian is the Messiah."

Adrian was right. Harry became rapturous, bringing out his
stock certificates and fondling them. He had bought them at
ten, twenty, forty dollars a share, and when they hit a hundred
he was going to sell out and retire. He couldn't say how much
he had put in, something around a hundred thousand. It had
already more than doubled.

Mother could not have been in the same league—I wasn't
making that much; but I was very curious about how far in
she was.

Adrian said that the only sane way to live was to have nothing at all, no savings, no property and, most important of all,
no responsibilities. It was the free life and the happy one.

"What do you plan to do in your old age?" Harry
asked him.

"There won't be any. I'm counting on some devastating disease to carry me off. Cheers!"

Of the two, I favored Adrian's view; but I preferred to have the option, and I did not care for the idea that Mother might be depriving me of it. I would have to do something.

Harry put a Bing Crosby record on the phonograph and passed out. I was not used to drinking very much; the alcohol went to my head along with images of my salary flying out the window. If Mother did lose my money, it would be even more difficult for me to wrench free of her. What if we ended up in debt?

Adrian and I danced. I told him about my worries. "Come live with me," he said. "We'll be carefree and foolish and go live in Paris and Marrakech. I have a rich cousin living on the Bosporus who'd let us stay forever. She's married to a Turk, isn't that peculiar? I mean, a lot of people are married to Turks, but most of them are Turks, for God's sake."

"I won't live with you," I said, "but you may kiss me if you wish."

He was a superb dancer. We put another record on. He fox-trotted me right into Harry's bedroom, and we fell into that bed—not the most romantic of locations, Harry's twisted and unimmaculate bedsheets—but I could have been anywhere, my head was spinning so. I know, it sounds so loose and amoral and degrading. It was, and what's more, I liked it so much that I knew I would see Adrian again, and that made everything all right. We could hear Hollywood snoring in the living room. I asked Adrian how he had met Harry—at the bar at Musso & Frank's, not surprisingly—and were they good friends? They were, Adrian thought. Harry was quite odd, as I must know, but Adrian rather favored odd people, although he wasn't altogether prepared to give special favor to those of Harry's inclinations. Almost everyone drew the line at that, and he supposed he did, too.

"I don't know what Harry's inclinations are," I said. "Tell me about them. I only have some suspicions."

"Really? But you've known him so long."

"I was a child."

"Indeed. Well, I'm not sure that I should say. . . ."

"I can't be shocked. . . ."

"In that case . . ."

Adrian turned over and opened the drawer of the bedside table and pulled out a pile of photographs and showed them to me. They were pictures of naked girls and boys, postpubescent mostly, or barely, but some younger.

"I was wrong," I said. "I *am* shocked." I also began to feel sick, partly at my own stupidity. Of course I ought to have known. Harry had lied about the Pantages party just as he had lied about his marriages. Had his affection for me been nothing but a perversion at the beginning? Adrian could see how upset I was.

"It's not my kind of thing, but we all have our little peculiarities. Here, I'll put them back. I thought you were aware. You've known each other for ages."

"At least there aren't any of me in there."

"No, he talks of you as if you were the Virgin Mary. But I daresay that's just the problem, isn't it. We'd best have another drink."

Since Adrian had known where the pictures were, had he slept with Harry? It was not a pleasant thought, if for no other reason than that it would bring me that much closer to having had sex with Harry myself. I chose to believe that at most Harry had shown them to Adrian as a way to gauge his interests.

In spite of my revulsion, it was difficult not to have feelings for Harry when I saw him slumped in the chair. He had done nothing to me, though he must have wanted to. Unregenerate Shakespearean that I was, I thought of the sonnet "They that have power to hurt and will do none . . ."

"Poor Harry," I said softly.

"I think that's why he's so keen on piling up all this money," Adrian said. "He wants to be able to get away when he gets caught. He's afraid of being trapped."

I could identify with that.

Adrian started the phonograph again. Harry woke up and immediately began babbling, to no one in particular, about how he was cursed with having a small penis. He was always doing that. He said that it was so small he couldn't see it under his stomach. He hadn't seen it in ten years. It was the size of a mouse's dick, it was smaller than a bumblebee's stinger, a cocktail wiener, a midget's pinky.

"Show it to us, Harry," Adrian said. "Let's have a look at the offending member. Maybe we can help. Out with it."

"Bring the magnifying glass!" Harry shouted.

I headed for the door.

"Will I see you again?" Adrian asked. It seemed a rather strange question after the way we had passed the afternoon.

"Of course," I said, but I was no longer entirely sure.

I searched through the apartment for information about Mother's investments. I was sick to death of being in the dark about everything and anything. I found a stack of Julian certificates hidden behind the Mason jars in the hall closet. I counted more than a thousand shares, all made out in her name.

She and Nell were returning from a club meeting when I confronted her. I said that I had been suffering from an overpowering lust for stewed tomatoes and had blundered into the evidence.

Nell looked terrified and betook herself to the kitchen. Mother, hard as nails, accused me of snooping and yelled that I knew nothing whatever about high finance and that it was none of my business.

"It *is* my business. It's my money!"

"You're a selfish little nit, aren't you. I never would have thought that after all—"

"How much did you pay for these!" I demanded, flapping them at her. "How many more are there? Don't you realize that Julian is a crook?"

"You don't know what you're talking about. You don't even know that the brother of a United States senator is on the Julian board of directors!"

"What does that mean? Did you never hear of a senator who was a crook?"

"Norman and Chicki Kuppler—"

"Norman and Chicki! Are they in on this, too? Jesus H. Christ, we are doomed!"

"I won't have that language!"

The next day I called Adrian Percy—I don't know why I trusted him; I guess it was because of what he had said about Julian and because he professed not to care about money and obviously did not—which made him unique among my acquaintances. He was extremely kind and pleasant, offering to help me find a lawyer and asking me to dinner that evening. I accepted the dinner invitation, but I wasn't sure that I was prepared to bring suit against my own mother. I went instead to see Mr. Wurtzel, told him my troubles, and asked about having my contract rewritten so that at least from now on I could control my own money.

"Julian!" Wurtzel shouted. "You don't know how many people believe in this schmucko Julian! Mendel Silverberg which it is I thought he was one smart cookie talks Julian, he wants I should join a pool! I told him I'm jumping in the lake first!"

Mr. Wurtzel told me that C.C. Julian himself was in the hands of a couple of shysters who should be behind bars. The word was getting around. People were finally starting to get nervous. The stock was slipping. He heard Mayer was trying to get out, but nobody would buy. There was going to be a panic. He hated to say this about anybody's mother, let alone the mother of such a fine upstanding young woman as myself, but my mother was *meshuggeneh*. She should put money in a bottle and throw it in the ocean, it would do her as much good.

And he could do absolutely nothing for me.

"What do you mean you can do nothing? You've got to help me!"

Mr. Wurtzel had his secretary bring my file. I appreciated his going this far. No one had ever shown me my contract before. Unfortunately the file included a copy of an agreement that Mother had signed with the Kupplers. They were named as my agents in perpetuity, *for life*! They and only they were authorized to deal on my behalf with Fox or with any other studio, producer, photographer, you name it. I must have

266

looked like a prisoner in the dock. Wurtzel let me sit there
forever. I could feel his ferret eyes on me.

"So there's nothing you can do?" I asked plaintively.

"Nothing."

I still sat there. I knew it was time to go. He took a call and
told somebody to fuck himself. Then he launched into a
monologue about how he and his wife had been married for
twenty-five years, how their children were nearly all grown,
how sacred marriage and the family were, but how when his
children reached twenty-one, they were on their own. He was
grateful for his long marriage, with so many people in this
business getting divorced and marrying four and five times.
But when a marriage went sour, there was no other choice,
unless you wanted to die of misery. In a rotten marriage people could get sick and never go out of the house. He had seen
it happen. He had to take another call.

I got up to leave and thanked him.

"Nothing in this business is for life," he said. "That is so
much dreck."

Adrian took me to a hole-in-the-wall in Venice. The wine
was poisonous, but the lamb chops were good, and I didn't
care to drink anyway. I was thinking of how appropriate it was
that I was with the one person I had met who seemed to have
no ties to anyone or anything—no real job, no family anywhere on this side of the planet, no country, really, and to all
appearances no cares. Maybe I had something to learn.

At the table Adrian presented me with a crystal bottle of my
favorite perfume, Jean Patou. I had not told him; he had recognized it when we were at Harry's. I put some on. It cut
through the smell of grease in the most attractive way, he said.

We went to his apartment, which had a balcony on the sea,
and made love out there; I tried for oblivion with the moon
misty over the water. Afterward all the disagreeable things
came back.

He wanted me to stay the night. I said that when I did that,
and I might, I did not want to be living on Ivar. All I would

have to do would be to come tripping up the stairs in the morning light. Mother would be waiting for me with a meat cleaver.

We spoke of Harry. He would be all right, Adrian said. What he ought to do with his money, if he really had any, was to move to some other part of the world, where people were more tolerant of that sort of thing. There were any number of beautiful Arab boys and girls who would be happy to accommodate a big fat American who wanted to throw dollars at them. They would be charmed by a man wearing overalls with his testicles hanging through a rip in the crotch. Harry would be king of the Casbah.

Well after midnight, when I got home, Mother was up reading something profitable.

"Your hair is a fright," she said. "What is that smell?"

I held up the perfume. "Present from an admirer."

"You smell like a streetwalker."

"Maybe you'd like me to sleep with Miss Hollywood Boulevard next door."

"Who gave it to you?"

"Louis B. Mayer."

"A likely story."

"Ten thousand a week and all the brandy I can drink."

"I saw your name in Louella Parsons, my dear. You cannot fool me. You are going to ruin your reputation. Have you been carousing with Adolph Menjou?"

Kowazanik had been at it again.

"No," I said. "With Adolph Menjou's gardener."

She stood up and walked over to me. With surprising feline quickness she snatched at the perfume. It fell from my hand and shattered.

"Slut!" she screamed. "Nothing but a slut!"

She went for my hair, but Nell poked her head out of their bedroom and I got away and slammed my door.

I lay on my bed panting. Maybe on the weekend I would head for Adrian's or something.

26

I remained indecisive—no, weak is the word. I did everything *but* move out, trying to delude myself into believing that Mother would kick me out, when I knew that she would never do that. She was too old to give birth to another daughter.

My affair with Adrian became wild. Everyone wanted to know who the Englishman was waiting for me at the studio gate. "Haven't you read *South of Suez*?" I'd say. "You should try his *When the Going Was Good*." When I had the Ford, we would meet like some adulterous couple at his place or some other rendezvous. It would be dinner and dancing at Fatty Arbuckle's Plantation Café or at Frank Sebastian's New Cotton Club with its Creole Revue and Lionel Hampton—Los Angeles was provincial, but there was plenty to do if you had the gasoline to find it. Off the Santa Monica Pier we hopped a motor boat out to the *Rex*, one of several gambling ships anchored beyond the three-mile limit. Tony Cornero, fresh from a stint up the river for rum-running, operated a couple of these floating casinos safe from the law. It was diverting out there, being a fugitive for the evening, watching Adrian shoot craps or play blackjack, looking every bit the lord in his evening clothes, chatting with the movie people and gangsters and whores as if he had known everyone forever. He usually lost, and did not mind in the least.

He was equally at home in the Negro jazz clubs down on Central Avenue, where everybody greeted him like an uncle returned rich from afar. Mother and Nell referred to the area with dread as Niggertown. Mother had made a wrong turn one afternoon and had panicked when she found herself surrounded by savage darkies with blood in their eyes. She and Nell ought to have nipped in for a couple of pops at Stanley and Sally's Bourbon Street West or the Tuxedo Club—everyone was welcome.

According to Adrian, the reason he fit in so well down there was that Negroes, unlike most Americans, had a sense of style. They were upper class at heart, the difference between them and the British upper class being that some Negroes had talent and worked at it and most of them recognized talent when they saw it. By style he meant good manners and clothes and laughter and lighting up a room with flash and talk. They were the real American aristocrats. There were four kinds of aristocracies: that of birth and blood, of which he was one; that of money and power; that of beauty, of which I was one; and that of talent, of which I and every member of the Tuxedo Club Trio were ones. How he talked, and the way Adrian and I parted the floor was like the Bugatti doing ninety!

I loved his tiny bedroom with nothing but the bed in it so you could concentrate on matters at hand. At work, my nerves were shot; I snapped at people more than usual. It didn't seem to affect my status, and may have improved it. I thought that if I could let myself go to the point where I became a real bitch, I might finally land the good part. That was how the big female stars seemed to do it, or many of them, except that I was not going to bed with the right people.

At home, life was a standoff.

Just at this time, when I was doing my best to live up to my mother's worst opinions of me, Providence at last smiled on me in the form of disaster.

I was awake early one morning with the day off work, trying to think of a way to get out of the apartment, lying in my room staring at a painting Harry had done for me about a year before. I had told him about the vegetable-hunting expeditions, and he had sent me this picture of a carrot with a long, sad face on it. I had not seen Harry since learning about his secrets, and I was feeling guilty about it. Maybe I would call him for lunch or spend the morning writing him a letter suggesting he go see a psychiatrist. Adrian had ridiculed the idea, saying Harry was beyond help and that shrinks were all crazy anyway. I suspected he was correct on both counts, but one had to try something. Every time I had telephoned Harry at his cottage, he had been too drunk to talk.

In the kitchen all was hustle and bustle. Another day glorious with sunshine in the entertainment capital of the world. I went down to fetch the paper and sat at the table reading the whole story before I said anything. I wanted to savor every syllable. The banner headline announced:

STOCK SWINDLE ROCKS L.A.
FORTY THOUSAND INVESTORS FLEECED,
MOVIE MOGULS AMONG VICTIMS

Trading in Julian Petroleum Stock had been suspended indefinitely on the Pacific Exchange. Bogus certificates had been issued to raise cash and inflate the price of shares, which had plummeted from fifty dollars to nothing yesterday afternoon.

Mr. C.C. Julian, the colorful founder of the company, known for his penchant for forcing himself behind the wheel of taxicabs and engaging in fisticuffs with Hollywood celebrities such as Mr. Charles Chaplin, had lost control of Julian "Pete" last year, and was believed to have fled the country. Wire reports indicated that Julian may have committed suicide by taking poison during a glittering dinner party at the Imperial Hotel in Shanghai. Other sources claimed to have located him in Oklahoma.

Losses among investors large and small were expected to exceed $150 million. The various investment pools that had been formed to bamboozle get-rich-quick believers covered

271

every social, financial, and geographical aspect of southern California, from Pasadena to Beverly Hills, from the bungalows of Glendale to the mansions of Hancock Park.

Questions had arisen as to the involvement of the district attorney and other state and local officials. It was thought that the scandal would be found to have spread into many quarters of the banking and financial community and would prove to be the most devastating economic calamity since the collapse of W. C. Ralston in San Francisco after the Gold Rush.

I read everything several times. I wanted it all to sink in. Then I called to Mother:

"How much money did you say you had invested in Julian Petroleum?"

"I didn't. We agreed that those kinds of things are in my department."

"Well, it doesn't matter. It's all gone anyway."

"I don't appreciate that kind of humor."

"Here. See for yourself."

For a while I was afraid that I would have a couple of corpses on my hands. When Mother finally had the strength to switch on the radio, we learned that things were even more chaotic than supposed. Senator Flint's brother, a lawyer for Julian interests, had been shot to death by an irate investor who had ten cents in his pocket. A mob had burst into the Pacific Exchange.

"This bulletin just in. The body of a prominent Pasadena philanthropist has been discovered at the bottom of the Arroyo Seco. He is believed to have jumped . . ."

The telephone rang, and Mother grabbed it. I could hear a woman's hysterical voice on the other end. Mother could not get a word in, hung up, and announced that several club members had been ruined.

"It must be nice to know you're not alone," I said. I demanded to know how much she had gambled and lost. She stonewalled. But I found out soon enough.

When the phone rang again, I reached it first. The excitement was too much for Nell, who shut herself into her room.

It was Chicki Kuppler on the phone, sounding deranged. She said it was the biggest flop since D. W. Griffith's last picture. She had to speak to Mother.

I told her Mother was indisposed, and when Chicki insisted on talking to her, I held firm. I wanted to hear the facts for myself.

"Did you get my mother into this?"

"Stick to acting, honey. You'll need it."

I did my best imitation of Wurtzel's telephone manner. Finally Chicki said I might as well face the truth. My mother had been putting two thousand a month into Julian for the past two years.

"That's half my salary!"

"You better be sitting down, Maggie, because what I'm going to tell you is going to make you understand that you are up to your pretty little ass in hot water."

"Don't speak to me that way. What are you talking about? What does this have to do with me?"

Mother was up from the table and trying to take the receiver out of my hand. I pushed her away, hard enough to send her reeling. She looked shocked and kept her distance.

"You owe me and Norman fifty thousand bucks, sweetie pie. I want it by the end of the week. I don't care how you get it. Just get it."

What was she talking about? In tones that would have taken the skin off a gangster, she told me that Mother had borrowed fifty thousand dollars, at 19 percent interest, from Norman and her in order to buy more Julian stock. Her total losses were thus something like ninety-eight thousand, of which fifty was owed and due immediately. The Kupplers had taken her Julian stock as collateral. At one point it had been worth nearly a quarter of a million. Now, it was toilet paper. The Kupplers had been heavily into Julian themselves. They, too, had gone down with the ship, and they owed plenty on their own. I was to beg, borrow, or steal, but I was to get them their money by Friday.

"Don't be ridiculous," I screamed into the phone. "I don't

owe you anything! This has nothing to do with me!"

"It has everything to do with you, Little Miss Perfect. And you will pay up pronto."

I slammed down the phone and found that Mother had joined Nell in their bedroom. Apoplectic with rage and fright, I stormed back there. Nell was lying on her bed with her face to the wall, trembling. Mother was in hers, with the sheet pulled up over her face, whimpering, "I'm sorry, I'm so sorry."

I had no idea what to do. I thought of everyone I could call and tried Sammy Maltzman, who had quit Fox for Columbia. Couldn't reach him. So for no good reason whatever I called Adrian, the least powerful, least influential person I knew.

"How are you?" I asked pointlessly.

"Never better."

"Have you heard about Julian?"

"My dear, how could I not? It's all anyone's talking about. How is your sainted mother holding up?"

"I've got to see you."

"Meet me at my place in an hour."

Adrian was surprisingly sensible. Surely, he said, certain principles of Anglo-Saxon justice still obtained, even in Hollywood. I should ignore Norman and Chicki until I got some legal advice. So far as he knew, both extortion and indentured servitude had been outlawed. And 19 percent sounded like usury to him.

"Why aren't you a lawyer?" I asked.

"Have a drink. It's a lovely day. Absolutely stunning, don't you think? We'll sit on the verandah. We should sail to Catalina, is what we should be doing. It's cocktail time in Avalon."

I put my arms around him and started crying.

"Now, now, there's no need for that. I can't bear it when people get all blubby."

We tried to reach Harry Valentine at Paramount. He had not come in, but was expected. He was not at the cottage, either, so Adrian and I discussed what I should do about my life. I had already made up my mind that I would not return to

Ivar. It was not so much a choice as a realization that a decision had already been made for me. He offered to help me move whenever I was ready. He would go into the apartment himself, if I preferred not to face the witches of *Macbeth*.

When we learned from Paramount that Harry had not shown up for two days and was in danger of being fired, and when he continued not to answer his phone, we decided to pay him a visit. He had probably drunk himself into a stupor over the Julian fiasco and would need assistance sobering up.

We stopped on the way to retrieve my belongings. I did not bother with formal introductions. Mother and Nell sat stonily watching us carry things out. Of course I was nervous, but I managed to to say in an even voice that I would be in touch with them and would make arrangements when matters settled down, whatever that meant.

"Chicki has been trying to reach you," Mother said.

"I'll bet she has."

"She says you've refused her calls at the studio. Do you think that's wise? They are still your agents, you know."

"You must be kidding."

"Where shall I say you can be reached?"

I turned to go.

"You are making a serious mistake," Mother intoned gravely. "Do you know that I put my head in the oven last night?"

"She forgot to turn on the gas," Adrian said when we were in the car. "It never works that way. My ex-wife tried it."

When we reached the cottage after the long drive, we noticed an empty gin bottle lying between Harry's truck and the steps. Otherwise the place was as idyllic as before.

"You see," Adrian said, "poor old Fatty is in there absolutely dead drunk."

Adrian was half-right.

"Oh, dear," he said as we stepped inside. "What a nuisance."

He held me back, and told me that I should wait in the car while he phoned the police.

27

*H*e had pulled the trigger with his toe, shooting himself through the heart. The note was to me, saying only that he had two thousand dollars left in the bank and wanted me to have it.

Five hundred people must have shown up at his funeral, everybody from Paramount and many fans. Harold Lloyd placed a heart-shaped wreath of orchids on the grave. From the way a wardrobe lady wept, I figured she must have been sweet on him. Even Adrian blubbed a bit, but he kept me from falling to pieces. The minister said that Harry did the crazy things everyone else wished they could get away with. What a peculiar way to have phrased it.

I told Adrian afterward that I was surprised he had shown so much sentiment. I was touched, but after all he had not known Harry very long.

"I am a man of wax," he said.

Norman and Chicki were up to their necks in the Julian debacle; Mother had been far from their only victim. They were indicted on usury, extortion, and other charges; but then so were Louis B. Mayer and other Hollywood figures indicted on various counts, and none of them ever stood trial. They came back stronger than ever, the usual story in the movie business, as with the studio-boardroom genius of later vintage who discovered that it was far more profitable never to pay people what you owed them, to let them sue you, and to settle for half or less. This insight made him the most powerful man in the Hollywood of his time; he was known as a great philanthropist, so generous with other people's money that worthy causes honored him with banquets. Norman and Chicki, in addition to defrauding Mother and trying to extort money from me, had often cashed for their own use the salary checks owed to me, or to Mother at any rate, knowing that she trusted them to make her rich, serving their own greed by exploiting hers. They were far from unique; they learned by example.

But at least they were out of the agenting business and my life. Their resurrection came as producers; they specialized in gangster pictures praised for their authenticity. When I did hire a new agent, a man who became a lifelong friend, he won me over by telling me that he would never make a deal for me without assuming that the other guys were out to cheat us, and that he would show me step by step how they were trying to get away with it. He also renegotiated my Fox contract, on the grounds that it had been forced on me by parties not acting in my best interests. The lying and fraudulence had been there from the beginning: Mother had lied to me, or perhaps the Kupplers had lied to her, about my still being a minor when I had signed back in 1926. California had not changed the age of legal majority from eighteen to twenty-one until the next year, and the new law had not even gone into effect until 1928. If I had refused to sign, Mother could have done nothing about it. I had been free without knowing it—emancipated one year, and made a child again the next; and all the while I had been oblivious. I still wonder what I would have done had I known all this at the time. It's probably better that I was ignorant. I might have shot a few people.

I only wish Harry Valentine had been sober enough to think of shooting the Kupplers before he killed himself.

Once I began receiving my own money, I sent Mother a certain amount a month. I dropped by to see her and Nell every once in a while, but I would not call the atmosphere cordial. Mother quickly regained her pride, however, when the Motion Picture Mothers Club elected her president.

Not long after Harry's death, I found that I was pregnant. No one had to tell me that I was. Women know what I am talking about. Even before I missed my first period, I felt it. You see it in the mirror, in your eyes, in a luminescence of the skin. You may try to pretend otherwise, but it's no good; you know. The doctor merely confirmed it.

It should hardly have been surprising, but I think that I had begun to assume that I must be infertile. I had equipped myself with the latest female device and had believed that I was being cautious, but there were careless instances, and one of them must have been it. I presumed it had happened on an afternoon when I had been feeling despondent about Harry and at loose ends about my future and thinking about death. Adrian and I had made heedless love as if we were the last couple on earth, and we had fallen asleep in each other's arms, joined together. I remembered waking up and thinking, I don't care.

Panic mixed with relief that I was after all capable of conceiving, as well as with reveries in which I believed that I could live for my baby and my husband and manage to work, too. What husband? Adrian's abilities as paterfamilias were dubious, but he would change, wouldn't he? We must have wanted this to happen, to bring us together. I thought of how we would raise the child with love and kindness and indulgence, and make sure that its maternal grandmother had as little to do with it as possible.

We were already living together. The publicity department had got wind of that and was urging me to marry or separate. Love and necessity could now combine.

I told him one night at dinner. "I'm pregnant." Just like that.

He finished pouring the wine, put the bottle down carefully, lifted his cup, swished some wine around in his mouth as if it weren't filthy, swallowed, patted his lips with his napkin. Only one other couple was in the restaurant; we were at a table in the back corner.

"Say something," I said.

"How far along are you?"

"Not far. Three weeks maybe."

"The thing is, I believe in dealing with these sorts of things briskly."

"Briskly?"

"Quite right. As briskly as possible. It's the best way to avoid, you know, things dragging on and a lot of needless wringing of hands and that sort of thing. Don't you agree?"

I did not reply. I did not want to hear what I thought he was saying. Of course, I had considered it myself, and I had rejected it. I had begun to want the baby rather badly.

"It's a very simple operation, don't you know," he marched ahead. "It can be all fixed up in no time, and you can forget all about it. It's no more than an inconvenience, as a matter of fact."

"What if I don't want to forget about it? What if I love you?"

"Now, now, there's no point in getting sentimental."

"You sound as if you've had some experience in these matters."

"No need to get into that, is there? I do have the proper contacts, that's the important thing. I'll take care of everything. You've got nothing to worry about."

I kept silent. I felt like such a fool for having believed in him. We all have to believe in something; that's where the trouble starts. So he's not the sort to run away at a time like this. He'll run away later, is what he means.

"Now don't look so glum, Margaret. I promise you, it's nothing more than getting one's teeth cleaned. I know you think I'm being crass, but I'm not. I'm simply being practical."

"Practical? I've never thought of you as *practical*. I was hoping for something else. I always do."

He launched into a lengthy disquisition about himself, his background, his failed marriage, his peccadilloes such as sailing off to here and there without notice and refusing to hold a job. I had heard most of it before. Why had I discounted it? He had not misled me. I had been forewarned every step of the way. Reality descended.

He added one bit that was news to me. He already had a child, a girl nine years old—or was it eight?—living with her mother and her new husband in London. Surely I could understand that since it had been proven that he could not manage one marriage and child, he could hardly be expected to assume another.

"What's her name?" I asked.

"Katherine."

"Not the wife. The child."

"Oh. Laura. Laura Elizabeth Desmond. She's taken her new father's name, and quite rightly, as he supports her. He is a barrister, I believe."

"What does she look like? Does she resemble you?"

"Does she? Hm. Difficult to say. She's blond, actually, or not really. Sort of kind of brownish, I think her hair is. Yes."

"How long has it been since you've seen her?"

"A year. Two? When was it that I left? Let's see. It was just after Pegasus won the Irish Derby. What year was that?"

Actresses did not give birth to little bastards with impunity in those days. The prospect of my child's being cared for by Mother and Nell while I clerked in a department store to support everyone was not a welcome one. I would be giving my child a start in life less auspicious even than my own after Father's death; at least I had had a father the memory of whose love had sustained me.

Let's see, Mother could stick a cowboy hat on it and land it a part in a Will Rogers picture or put taps on its shoes and try for Eddie Cantor, and we could all live off it, the cycle starting over again. Or I could give it away, losing my career and my child in one swoop. I had the notion that if I was going to make the choice to bring a child into this world, I owed it a decent start—not to speak of what I owed myself after everything that had happened.

For a couple of days I sleepwalked through work and sat on Adrian's balcony asking the sea for answers. I made the mistake of guessing the sex of what was growing in me and decided I would name him Edward, after E.P. I struggled to stop thinking that way.

Finally Adrian's absolute indifference convinced me that, whatever I decided, I did not want any child of mine to have a father like that. I was all too aware that, if I was paying for my own behavior, it was up to me to set the price.

"You're being damned sensible," Adrian said when I told him that I had made up my mind. His cheerfulness was beginning to get on my nerves. If he had any negative feelings about what we were about to do, he hid them well.

"Let's just get it over with," I said.

"Exactly. We'll be back and forth across the border in no time."

"What border?"

"The Mexican border, of course. You don't think Dr. Menendez works out of the Brown Derby, do you?"

We hit Tijuana about noon that Sunday. We drove along honky-tonk streets smelling of sewage and thronged with gringos buying trash and beer and having pictures taken with donkeys that had geraniums behind their ears. Adrian kept up a relentlessly cheerful chatter. There was the nightclub Harry Cohn favored. It featured cockfights and a lesbian show. I wished he would shut up, but I hadn't the strength to speak. I felt much heavier in my heart than I had ever thought I could.

Adrian seemed to know exactly where he was going. Dr. Menendez practiced the art of healing in a shack adjacent to the Lower California Jockey Club, under some trees that separated the Monte Carlo and Sunset Inn casinos—famous places, Adrian assured me, favored, along with the Hotel Agua Caliente, by all the Hollywood elite. He himself preferred the Agua Caliente, because it was closer to the racetrack. We would have to visit it soon, under other circumstances.

282

Thank God there were no other customers waiting in the little room where Adrian peeled off some bills and gave them to a señorita dressed up as a nurse. On the wall behind the card table where the cash box sat, a calendar featured a picture of Our Lady of Guadalupe. The señorita beckoned me into the next room. Adrian said that it would all be over shortly and that he was going to step outside for a breath of air. I suspect he headed straight for the Jockey Club bar. I couldn't blame him for that.

The next thing I knew, I was lying on a table, and the señorita was placing a cloth-wrapped cone over my mouth. I took a couple of gasps and was out. I never did catch a glimpse of the distinguished surgeon.

By the time Adrian helped me to the car, the sun was going down. I was woozy, but I heard him say that everything was fine, had gone well, not to worry, and so on. I would need a couple of days to recover.

I passed out again before we crossed the border.

When I awoke, I did not know where I was. There were other beds, one occupied with a coughing old woman I at first was afraid was Nell. It was a hospital. I prayed I was not in Tijuana. I tried to sit up, but I had a terrific pain in my abdomen and between my legs. I was no longer one for prayer, I had thought, but I was ready to try anything. I asked for forgiveness—there was no immediate response. Where was Adrian? Had he dumped me someplace? Maybe he had hopped a freight.

Then a nurse was standing beside me, holding my hand. I was at St. Vincent's in Los Angeles, she said. I should try to lie still. I had lost a lot of blood, but I was going to be all right. The doctor would be in to see me. My brother was outside. She would tell him that I was awake.

My brother! That was clever of Adrian, appealing to family feeling at a Catholic hospital. He had probably told them that I had been left by some cad to be butchered and that fraternal love had rescued me.

Adrian told me how sorry he was about what had happened. He had not noticed the blood until he had stopped at a filling station in Laguna. Then he had rushed me to a local hospital. Idiots, they were, but his good sense had prevailed. He had me taken by ambulance to St. Vincent's, which was run by the Daughters of Charity, wasn't that perfect? The nuns and the doctors had been exemplary. No questions asked, once they understood. Entirely professional, and very kind as well. I would be up to snuff in a few days' time. As far as the studio knew, I had been done in by a spot of ptomaine poisoning, bad luck and a spoiled holiday into the bargain. Happened all the time in Tijuana.

If I didn't mind, he would just as soon retire for the moment and tend to pressing business. He would be back to visit me tomorrow and make sure everything was tip-top. Would I care to have him bring me something to read? Some magazines perhaps? The selection in the waiting room was wretched. Nothing but drivel about nutrition and saving pagan babies. He would bring me a novel, that was the ticket. Anita Loos had a new one out, not as funny as the first, he had been led to understand, but still probably just the thing to while away the hours. There was nothing in the world more boring than hospitals, didn't I agree?

28

*A*s soon as I was able, I moved out of Adrian's apartment and into one of my own a block or two away. It did not have an ocean view, and the hot water was irregular, but what with keeping up the Ivar place and supplementing Nell's pittance of a railroad pension, my resources were limited. Nonetheless, it was my own. I had never realized how important that was until I had it.

I hung Harry's carrot and foraged in junk shops for things I liked. In spite of the Tijuana memories, which came to me often in the middle of the night—not the sleaze and the pain so much as what I had done—I favored Spanish-looking plates, furniture, mirrors, flowerpots, because they fit California and reminded me of Buenos Aires, where I was convinced I had spent the happiest years of my life. The idea was to bring good luck. I still had the Argentine dolls; they went on the mantel next to a photograph of my father and another of me as Puck.

Adrian had not tried to hold me; we did not have to tell each other that it was over between us. Occasionally we had a drink and a meal together. Mostly I just worked, which was all that I wanted to do, and soon enough I was damned glad for having that.

When the Big Crash came, William Fox went under immediately, losing his entire $300 million empire, which he had mortgaged in an attempt to snatch MGM from Mayer. Fox

then went to jail for bribing a bankruptcy judge. Like everyone else, I took a cut in salary. But within a couple of years,
Fox Studios merged with Twentieth Century and was making
more money than ever under Winnie Sheehan and Darryl
Zanuck. Bread lines lengthened, and Hollywood flourished.

Adrian, however, was axed at Metro and went back to being
a waiter at the Beverly Hills Hotel. Once Prohibition was re-
pealed, which was bound to come soon, he was counting on
being appointed sommelier. In that position he would not only
be able to impart civilized knowledge to people sorely in need
of it, he would have unlimited access to drink. The prospects
were dazzling.

"Would that be the height of your ambition?" I asked him.

"Ambition?" he snorted, not, I think, without some self-
mockery. "Ambition? A gentleman has no ambition. A gentleman has not the doctrine of *getting on*, nor the habit of it. The
contest is not against material things, but between those who
want and those who don't want to *get on*, having more important things to attend to. I was taught that ambitious was a very
vulgar thing to be."

To thine own self be true, I urged him from the depths of
my vulgarly ambitious self.

Rhoda and her husband, Howard, came out for a visit. As
they were not suffering much from the Depression—Howie
was a partner in her father's show-business law firm—they
stayed at the Beverly Hills. I thought she was going to choke
on her hearts of palm when I told her that I had had an affair
with our waiter. Howie, whom Adrian afterward termed a se-
baceous youth, looked nauseated and wiped the rim of his water
glass with his napkin. Rhoda grew solicitous, patting me on
the hand and chuckling about how I had always been the
wild one.

"Yes, I was always fucking everybody, wasn't I," I said, trying
and failing to bring color to Howie's jowls. "Speaking of that,
whatever happened to Frank Hern?"

"Frank who?" Howie pretended interest.

"How would I know?" Rhoda said. "No, wait a minute. I

read about him. I think he's become a radical or a communist or something. His grandmother died."

"Did you read about his grandmother, too?"

"There was an obituary," Rhoda said testily.

Could she still actually be carrying on with Frank on the side? I was dying to know, but Howie never left us alone. She had found a dutiful one there, all right. I imagined her sneaking off with her Red lover, screwing dialectically while Howie was in the office negotiating the movie rights to a musical. Well, from the looks of the husband, she needed and deserved something on the side. I only hoped that Frank was writing well, whatever his philosophy. I would hate to have thought that my judgment had been wrong there, too.

They spoke endlessly of their children, both boys, who had been registered at birth at exclusive schools and, at ages two and three, were showing incontrovertible signs of mathematical and artistic genius. Did I think I'd ever get married and have children, Howie wanted to know, or was it too difficult to manage that and a movie career? I said I had no idea as yet. I had been working since the age of twelve and had been on my own for only a short time. I was still supporting my family.

"You've always had a tough go of it," Rhoda said.

"I wouldn't trade it for anyone else's."

"I admire your spirit," Howie said. "I think we should call it an evening."

When she got back to New York, Rhoda called to say that *by chance* she had run into Frank Hern at the Russian Tea Room and had told him about seeing me and how radiant and wonderful I looked and how we had reminisced and how much I missed the stage. I didn't remember talking about the stage at all, nor had I been thinking about it much lately. But I told her that if she ever ran into Frank Hern again by chance, to give him my love and to tell him how much I always admired his talent and that I wished him the best. I said that I understood that she had had to leave after only a day in L.A. because they had had to visit Howie's relatives in San Francisco, but that I hoped that the next time she came out, or I visited

New York, we could have time alone together because I had personal things to share with her, and she might even have some to share with me, and we wouldn't want to bore Howie. I left it at that.

Some months later, Adrian happened to be waiting on Maxi Mindlin and Pablo Murphy's table. Adrian was always good for gossip picked up from the hotel, and he retailed it with Homeric verve. This had been the night when Murphy sold Mindlin on the idea of *The Oregon Trail*. Maximillian Mindlin, or Maximum Mindlin as he was known, was an independent producer whose pictures were always setting records for cost and supposedly never made a dime; but Maxi continued to operate in high style. The word was that he was bankrolled by the Cleveland mob. In those days of the big studios, only Goldwyn was more prominent as an independent. Pablo Murphy was a director renowned for his outdoor pictures and his cock, reputedly the biggest in Hollywood. As Murphy was about five feet five, he was considered a shoo-in for Ripley's.

The dinner had begun with Mindlin's disapproval of the soup. He sent it back for warming. "Boil the fucker!" Adrian counseled the chef. And Maxi sent his liver-and-onions back three times. When he said well-done, he meant it.

"So I'll eat this crap," was the verdict as Adrian, ever unruffled, at last placed the shriveled organ before him. He took a bite and said, "The trouble is, it still tastes like liver."

Maxi was also fastidious. He wore thin white cotton gloves against germs, and he insisted that the tablecloth be changed between courses. Invisible, Adrian hovered about as Pablo Murphy began his pitch over the baked Alaska. The country was in pathetic shape. People were in despair. The commies were everywhere. Why not capitalize on everybody's misery and desperation by giving them a socko presentation of the sacrifices and bravery and heroism of the pioneers as they crossed the barren wastes and forded rivers and scaled mountains, fending off wolves and tomahawks, enduring blazing sun, bitter cold, disease, and treachery?

"They had wolves?" said Maxi, shoveling in his food. "Around here, we got baboons. I got nothing but monkeys working for me, and one hyena. I'm firing him."

The Covered Wagon had been a smash, Murphy went on. This would be *The Covered Wagon* with sound.

"I will give a tongue to the pioneers," Pablo said. "I will give a tongue to history!"

"I love the concept," Maxi said, "but I hate tongue."

They would do everything outdoors, Pablo continued. There hadn't been a great outdoor sound picture yet. They would have a big cast. Everything big. The biggest. It would cost a lot, but so had the war to save democracy.

"Money I don't worry about," Maxi said. "Money I can always get." Adrian had distinctly remembered this line because it seemed to promise a big tip, an expectation that was to prove false. "I like it, I like it, I love it. So who do we cast?"

For the male lead Murphy had in mind an unknown, a stuntman he had spotted on the Universal lot, the best-looking kid since Fairbanks. The kid could pick up a hat from the ground riding at full gallop, and he had a great walk and a great voice. He was the find of the decade and would come cheap. He was so tough that he would be able to stand up to what was going to be one hell of a picture. They did not need a big star. The picture would sell itself.

"Sign him, sign him," Maxi said. "What about the girl?"

Pablo said he was thinking of somebody refined, genteel, a contrast to the savagery around her.

"So who is this couth refined gentile? How about Annette MacKenzie? She is no fucking star. She is no fucking, either, I can tell you. She is a cunt. I won't have her on my picture. Tell me, who is she going to be, this doll?"

He hadn't come up with the right girl yet, Pablo said. He would have to give it more thought. But she had to be a delicate hothouse-flower type. A gardenia or a camellia. She would have to look like she had never been up to her knees in cow shit, that was the idea.

"So go find her. She's out there."

Adrian, who was replenishing Murphy's gin at this juncture, had immediately thought of me. He knew how frustrated I was at the roles I had been getting. This might or might not be a great one, but it was sure to be a big part in a big picture. With a role like that, I might be able to do more of what else I wanted.

Everything Adrian said was true. (So why wasn't he an agent!) I also liked the idea of a location picture. Weeks away from Hollywood, to say nothing of Mother and Nell, appealed to me. The last time I had called on them, Mother had asked for a boost in her allowance; I had refused, and she had come up with the line, "You have a black heart." It must have come from a movie.

Unfortunately *The Oregon Trail* was not a Fox picture, and I was still under contract. Loan-outs of actors from one studio to another occurred, but somebody had to want you. I asked my new agent to campaign for me.

It helped that Mindlin's secretary was a fan of mine. I called on the mogul at the Beverly Wilshire Hotel, that Italian Renaissance extravaganza that I had always admired but had never entered, at the foot of the bridal path that was Rodeo Drive. Unlike Goldwyn, Mindlin had no studio lot of his own, preferring to rent out space.

I had mostly Adrian's account and gossip to go on. Mindlin's recent wedding to a starlet had been much discussed. He had hired two hundred musicians and had burst into song himself at the altar, serenading his bride with a soulful rendition of "Mary Is a Grand Old Name." I ascended to the penthouse. The outer room was a reception area. Mr. Mindlin had been delighted that my agent had contacted him, the secretary said. He had been screening my pictures all week.

A butler appeared and informed me that Mr. Mindlin would receive me. I had heard about Harry Cohn's office, which had been inspired by a courtesy call on Mussolini. You had to hike sixty feet to reach the great man's desk, where he leered down at you from a dais and told you to kiss his shoes or lift your skirt or get lost. And I had heard about the passageway that led from Cohn's office to the dressing room of whatever actress was enduring his favors. But a butler was something new. The Mindlin touch.

I followed Jeeves into a large sitting room done up in Louis-the-Whatsit style, lots of gold leaf, with a gold grand piano in one corner. The butler motioned me to an enormous couch, where I sank in. In the center of the room, nestled in a heap of fruits, stood a mechanical silver fountain that emitted a comforting low hum and splashed orange juice down a runnel into a drain. The thing had been weaned from alcohol to health, a symbol of the cornucopia that was the Golden State. With flourishes the butler stuck a glass under the flow.

"Juice, madam?"

"Thank you ever so much."

I must have waited a good fifteen minutes. On the wall opposite was a titanic painting of a tart I took to be the latest Mrs. Mindlin.

All at once a door beside the piano opened and there he stood, Maximillian himself, formless, bald, naked. A pink slug, I thought; but when I noticed the dimples, I saw that he was kind of cute.

He did a little bow. I didn't flinch. I had passed the first test.

"That's a nice suit you have," he said. "Very well made. Attractive."

"I wish I could return the compliment," I said.

"That is clever. So you come from the stage. Do you miss it?"

"Not at the moment."

"Tell me something. Do you like music?"

"Very much. I adore music."

"What about Gershwin? You like him?"

"Why, of course. Divine."

"I tried to sign him, but that son of a bitch Goldwyn stole him from me. He's nothing but a goddamned thief. But what do you say we think of better things? Take a listen to this."

He went behind the piano and sat down. I could see the pink top of his head and his toes touching the pedals. He commenced a rendition of *Rhapsody in Blue*. To tell the truth, it was not bad. He added a few grace notes. When he finished, I spontaneously applauded and gave him a couple of bravos.

"My mother wanted me to be a concert pianist," he said. "Do you think I should've stuck to it?"

"Not if you can continue bringing your kind of uplifting entertainment to the multitudes." I was shameless.

Remaining seated at the instrument, he regaled me with the story of his life, from Hell's Kitchen to Hollywood, with forays backward to Warsaw and environs, whence he had fled by walking to Hamburg and slaving on the docks to earn his passage to America. He had started out as a fabric cutter in New York and had financed his first two-reelers there with money borrowed from an aunt. He had been in partnership with Goldwyn for a couple of years, but had left rather than commit murder.

I found all this fascinating and admirable, though lengthy. After reciting the litany of his productions, he started on *The Oregon Trail*. It would be sensational. The screenplay was being rewritten. Some novelist was doing it; Mindlin had torn the first draft to shreds before the writer's eyes, it stank so bad.

"Do you ride a horse?" he asked.

"I am an experienced horsewoman," I lied. "I grew up riding to hounds in Connecticut. My uncle taught me."

"What do they pay you at Fox?" I told him. "I'll double it." That sounded like a bribe. "Would you do me a favor?"

"Why, whatever do you mean, Mr. Mindlin?"

"Tell everybody that Maxi Mindlin is not one of those Hollywood psychopaths. Would you do that? The word on the street is, you're quite a lady. Tell people that Maxi Mindlin's got class."

"I'd be delighted."

"Good. You can go now. We'll contact you. Take a mint on your way out, they're delicious."

29

Nell died while I was in Jackson Hole, Wyoming, on location filming *The Oregon Trail.* An earthquake shook Hollywood one morning while she was at her canning; and, according to the coroner's report, a copy of which Mother thoughtfully sent me, she suffered a coronary arrest. "The old lady never knew what hit her," was the way the coroner rather unprofessionally phrased it.

I received the news in a telegram that reached me as I was perched in my covered wagon whipping the horses over a mountain pass. Pablo Murphy offered to give me a week off— he had comic relief scheduled and would not need me for a few days; but I declined, earning points for dedication and adding "did not even bother to attend her grandmother's funeral" to my ever-lengthening list of sins.

Mother accepted the invitation of a fellow club member, whose daughter had married a studio executive, to live in a big house in Beverly Hills, in return for acting as companion and chauffeur to her senior colleague. I rejoiced for her and continued to send her checks, but between her job and her continuing duties as club president, she was so fully occupied that she did not have time to write me.

They say in the movie business that the ending is inevitable and right when every scene that has gone before fits into a consistent pattern. Thus, the tale of our mutual dependency was reaching a conclusion.

People who know the facts of my relationship with my mother are always asking me if I am bitter. That is usually a way of saying, "You must be eaten up with bitterness." By writing this book, I am inviting a slew of letters from fans (I answer every one by hand, except those from erotomaniacs, of which I receive damned few at this late date, let me tell you) asking the same question. So to stave them off right here, let me say with all the emphasis I can muster that I am not only not in the least bit bitter, I consider myself one of the happiest people on the face of the earth. Tragedy is comedy undernourished. Why should I be bitter when I have such joy?

Working on *The Oregon Trail* made me realize that the frauds and tricks and subterfuges and lies and twists of fate that brought me to Hollywood against my will turned out to be all for the best. I ask you, is there anyone left in the world who believes that the stage is superior to film? *All About Eve* demolished that argument. No, I was a lucky girl to have had such a conniving, greedy mother. I still love the stage, of course; but now that films are preserved, a movie actress's performances live as long as people care to watch. How many stage actresses are remembered at all from the distant past except for their fame? How can we know what their performances were like except by secondhand accounts?

If I was any good, I achieved immortality; if I wasn't any good, then I deserve oblivion along with most of the human race. It's almost like religion, isn't it? If you're good, you get to go to heaven. I won't make heaven; I am insufficiently contrite. But I may last quite a while on videotape!

It's a comforting thought that adds to my happiness.

But the real source of my happiness has been my marvelous experiences, particularly from *The Oregon Trail* on. That film, done with meticulous attention to authentic historical detail, turns out to have been a classic. And I am in it, boiling moose meat and riding like the wind (yes, I did learn how) and powwowing with the Sioux! Who could ask for greater good fortune? The scenes of wagons fording rivers, being lowered down mountain cliffs, struggling up near-vertical slopes; the depictions of frontier clothing and equipment and weapons—all are precise reenactments of a drama that took place 160 years ago, preserved forever—like me!

It was difficult; we were on location for ten months; but I would not trade the experience for anything, certainly not, I regret to have to say, for a part in *Strange Interlude*. And it was *The Oregon Trail* that opened up all those other wonderful roles with which I assume most of you are familiar, or you would not have opened this book.

There was, of course, unpleasantness during the making of *The Oregon Trail*. That highly esteemed, award-winning director Pablo Murphy had the actor playing the villain beaten up and, I believe, maimed for fooling around with Murphy's wife. He never played a villain again, or anything else. Once at the Sequoia location, when we were living in a flea-ridden old circus train, I was about to be raped by a drunken slob of an actor when I was rescued—just as in the movies!—by my leading man, the then-lean and beautiful and stalwart and, sad to say, extremely stupid Tim DeCourcey, with whom I had a vigorous affair for six months.

The company included twenty or thirty prostitutes—real ones, I mean, not just ordinary actresses—a bootlegger, and a gambling tent straight from Reno. There were naturally many violent fights, fortunes lost, diseases spread. Half the men in the company and more of the women than you would suppose were complaining of the clap by the time we reached Jackson Hole. Those sorts of things may lack the uplifting, edifying qualities of high art, but they are not unknown to artists.

We lost horses, oxen, and three men. I had never heard horses actually scream until we forced them to ford a rushing river; I hope I never hear that sound again. A scene dreamed up by Murphy called for a man to ride a wild buffalo and to shoot it when it threw him off. He did—the scene was cut because of the likely public outrage; it looked as authentic as it was.

This was the Hollywood I came to know. Now, it is full of accountants. Then it was teeming with life—raw, slimy, crude, frightening, depressing, dangerous, sexy, sensuous, colorful, wonderful, glorious, happy life! Oh, to have those days back again! I could kiss Maxi Mindlin right on the top of his pink head or what have you for giving me the chance at it! God rest your soul, Mother, you knew not what you did, and it was grand!

Not long after I finished doing *The Oregon Trail* and attending the premiere at the Carthay Circle and suddenly finding that, for a while, everybody wanted me for a picture, I received a package from Frank Hern. Rhoda must have given him my address.

It was a play that he had written about my early life. It wasn't badly done, although I did not recognize myself, my mother, or the circumstances of my youth; I might never have recognized them had Frank not identified them in his letter. The tenement where my character lived was far more grim than Fifty-fourth Street had been. I sat there with my mother, talking to my dolls amid the garbage and rats. But who am I to forbid artistic license? The dialogue was good. I had always known Frank could write.

A band of merry beggars rescues us from the police when the vicious landlord throws us into the street; actors scattered throughout the theater shout "Kill the Oppressors!" and urge the audience to join in.

Of course it seems dated now, and schematic, all of which it was; but it anticipated Clifford Odets, who was much acclaimed before he went to Hollywood. It was called *The Oppressors*. Frank wanted me to play "myself" in it.

He was surprised when I turned him down, as was Rhoda, who could not understand how I could not seize this opportunity to escape from Hollywood. I did have a contract with Fox, with more than a year to run, but they would have given me a few weeks' leave. I simply did not like the play enough, and, far from what Rhoda and Frank must have believed, I was long past being anxious to be on the stage merely for the sake of being there.

Margaret in Hollywood

I would have refused *Liliom,* too, this time, and probably most of the serious dramas written in the thirties. I was not with it. As you may know, I soon did back-to-back pictures for Sammy Maltzman at Columbia, one a Dracula remake and the other a romantic comedy that had a crackerjack script. They were not Shakespeare—but neither is anything else. I enjoyed both of them. It was a new life in a new world.

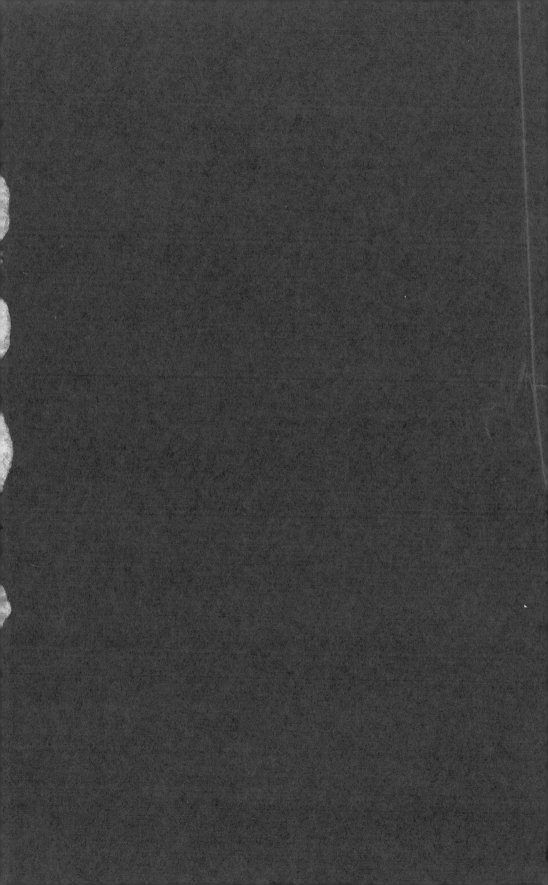